GRAY SALVATION

ALAN McDermott

THOMAS & MERCER

This is a work of fiction. Names, characters, organizations, places, events, and incidents are either products of the author's imagination or are used fictitiously.

Published by Thomas & Mercer, Seattle

www.apub.com

ISBN-13: 9781503933101
ISBN-10: 1503933105

Cover design by bürosüd° München, www.buerosued.de

Printed in the United States of America

For my family

Prologue

15 January 2016

Nikolai tried to spit the blood from his mouth, but the damage they'd done to his lips made it impossible. The best he could do was let it dribble down his chin and onto his chest, where it slowly made its way between his man breasts before coming to rest on the top of his distended beer belly.

The last thing he remembered was walking to the bar to meet his handler when the lights went out, and he'd woken to find himself being pummelled by giant fists. The initial onslaught had lasted only a few minutes before he was left alone, not a single word having been spoken.

They'd obviously learned about his new allegiance, but how they could have done so eluded him. He wasn't stupid enough to have mentioned it to anyone, and he hadn't seen any sign in recent days to suggest he'd been followed.

He heard faint voices coming from outside the door and knew his captors would be back soon. His heavily bruised eyes darted around the dimly lit room, looking for a way to escape, but all he saw was solid brickwork and the steel door. No windows, no attic access, not even an air duct to crawl through. Even if he'd spotted a way out, the handcuffs and chains securing him to the chair would have made it irrelevant.

Nikolai closed his eyes and prayed that it was all a dream, that he wasn't being tortured but instead back in Soho enjoying the companionship of one of the ladies in his boss's stable – the young Lithuanian with the long, dark hair and breasts that defied gravity . . .

The heavy bolt on the door squealed as it was pulled aside, and the Beriya brothers once again entered the tiny room.

Aslan and Beslan, twins from Grozny. He'd known them for some time but never imagined that he would be on the receiving end of their brutality.

The brothers stood aside and made room for a third visitor, who, while not a small man, was dwarfed by the Beriyas.

Alexi Bessonov walked into the room and looked Nikolai in the eye.

'Nikki, Nikki, Nikki. Whatever am I to do with you?'

'I swear, I don't know what any of this is about!'

Denial was his natural reaction in a situation that didn't warrant honesty.

Bessonov rubbed his closely shaven head, the stubble rasping audibly. 'Please, don't insult me.' He took a handkerchief from his coat pocket and wiped a foldaway chair before sitting on it, not wanting to get a stain on his expensive Savile Row suit.

'How long have we known each other?'

'Twenty years,' Nikolai said.

Bessonov's head bobbed. 'Twenty long years. In that time, I'd say I've been more than generous.'

'I know.' Nikolai began weeping. 'And I'm truly grateful. I just don't understand what you think I've done wrong.'

Bessonov remained passive, checking his fingernails for signs of dirt, and Nikolai couldn't tell if his boss was bored, happy or bordering on fury. Bessonov never gave anything away, and few people had ever seen him lose his temper, which made him entirely unpredictable.

'I wish we didn't have to play these games, but if you insist on dragging this out . . .'

Bessonov gestured with his hand and the two men left the room. They returned a couple of minutes later, dragging a body with them. They dropped the corpse on the floor and Aslan turned it over so that the face was visible.

Nikolai instantly recognised the man, despite the terrible injuries he'd suffered.

'You know him?'

Nikolai swallowed a mouthful of blood and saliva, then shook his head.

'Interesting, because this man said he knew you. With a little encouragement from Aslan and Beslan, he even told us about your recent meetings.'

Staring at the body on the floor, at the man who'd made him betray his boss in exchange for the paltry sum of five thousand pounds, Nikolai knew his time on the planet was close to an end. It was only a matter of how he would spend his last few hours.

'Alexi, I'm sorry—'

Bessonov simply shook his head, a look of genuine disappointment on his thin, Slavic face. 'Tell me what you shared with him and I'll make this quick.'

Nikolai broke down completely. 'I beg of you, please—'

Bessonov rose and straightened out his suit. 'Have it your way.' He turned to Aslan. 'Take your time, and don't waste a bullet on him.'

The screams for mercy went unheard as Bessonov left the room and closed the door, leaving Nikolai with only the grinning Beriya twins for company in his final, agonising hours.

Chapter 1

18 January 2016

Andrew Harvey was shaken from a dream by his alarm clock, and he quickly silenced it before it disturbed his girlfriend's slumber. Sarah Thompson mumbled something in her dream, and he gently brushed the long blonde hair from her face and gave her a tender kiss before rising to complete his morning ritual.

He stood in front of the bathroom mirror and took in his reflection. For someone in his mid-forties, he thought he looked surprisingly good, and he attributed the improvement to Sarah. Since she'd moved in with him twelve months earlier, he'd taken on a new lease of life. It had felt strange at first, sharing a house with someone else after years living the bachelor life, but his single days now seemed a distant memory.

He applied shaving foam and scraped away two days' worth of stubble, then hit the shower, letting the hot water flow over his body. As he washed his stomach he sensed he'd lost an inch from what was an already trim waist; he put that down to the nightly exercise they'd been enjoying.

He finished his shower and combed his short, dark hair into a rough side parting. By the time he made it back to the bedroom he found the bed empty and the smell of coffee drifting up the stairs.

He followed his nose down to the kitchen, where he found Sarah at the sink looking stunning in nothing more than a white towelling robe and a smile. He kissed her on the cheek and sat down to a plate of bacon and eggs with French toast.

'Can't think of a better way to start a Monday morning,' he said as Sarah took a seat opposite him.

Her breakfast consisted of bran flakes with banana, accompanied by fresh orange juice. 'Enjoy it while it lasts,' she said. 'Once we hit the office, it's back to reality.'

Even the thought of a twelve-hour stint at Thames House couldn't change his mood. The Brigandicuum surveillance system, which had only ever been online for a few short days, had caused a political storm that resulted in the prime minister stepping down and the home secretary being jailed, pending trial. The system had been taken offline, much to the consternation of the Americans, who'd invested several years and billions of dollars getting it up and running, but the data it had collected during that period was still being analysed. So far, it had drawn their attention to over two thousand possible terror suspects, with more being added to the pile daily.

Brigandicuum had been the intelligence community's greatest asset, able to alert the security services whenever anyone typed a predefined word or phrase into their device. It had also been capable of recognising voice and image data, all of which triggered downloads of the information from the suspect's device.

The material gathered during its brief existence represented more than three hundred million terabytes of data, and sifting through it to sort the innocent from the potentially deadly was a time-consuming challenge. With Brigandicuum offline, analysts could no longer download the entire contents of a suspect device to see the context in which the keyword had been written. Now they had to decide from a few lines of text whether its author was a potential terrorist planning an attack, a journalist in the process of creating their next story or simply a student working on their thesis.

Despite the large number of false alarms he'd come across, Harvey actually looked forward to getting to work in the mornings and sifting through the mounting pile in his inbox.

'Sorry if I woke you this morning,' he said. 'I was going to give you a shout at seven.'

'I had to get up anyway.' She glanced at her watch. 'My interview isn't until ten, but I need to get in early and check for updates on my latest case.'

Sarah's request to be transferred from her current role at MI6 to join him at MI5 would be discussed with the heads of department this morning, and he hoped it would be approved. His own boss, Veronica Ellis, would be involved in the decision-making process, so he knew Sarah would have at least one friendly face on the panel.

Harvey dropped Sarah off at Vauxhall Bridge and drove across the river to the car park underneath Thames House. He got into his office at a quarter to nine and found Hamad Farsi already deep in conversation on the phone.

'Ellis wants to see you,' Farsi mouthed, pointing towards the boss's office.

Harvey dumped his briefcase on his desk and knocked on Ellis's door. He could see through the tinted glass that she was on the phone, but she waved him in and motioned to the chair facing her desk.

'Okay,' she said into her phone. 'I'll be down in the next few minutes.' She put the telephone down and looked at Harvey. 'Do you know Jason Willard?'

'Works the Russia desk,' Harvey said.

'He used to. The police pulled his body from the Thames minutes ago. I want you on the scene.'

'Of course,' Harvey said, shocked at the news. It wasn't often that the security services lost one of their own, especially on home soil. 'Do we know what he was working on?'

'Willard's last log entry said he was going to meet an informant on Friday afternoon, but it looks like someone had other ideas.' Ellis told him where the discovery of the body had taken place, and Harvey took that as his cue to leave.

He stopped briefly at Farsi's desk to explain that he wouldn't be around for a couple of hours, then headed out of the building and across the road to the embankment. He'd considered taking the car, but knew it would be quicker to walk than battle his way through the rush-hour traffic.

Twenty minutes later, he saw the ambulance and police cars parked at the side of the road, and when he peered over the wall he saw four men in an inflatable, two of whom were dressed in scuba gear. The small craft bobbed in the wake of a water taxi that chugged by, a few of the passengers on board watching the unfolding drama. Given the time of year, Harvey didn't envy the divers' job of spending hours in the freezing Thames.

Harvey sought out the senior officer and introduced himself. 'What do we have?'

'Two males, and the divers are searching for others.'

'Two?' Harvey asked. 'I was only told about one.'

'We only found the second one a few minutes ago. It looks like they were both weighed down, but the first one slipped his ropes.'

'Any idea how long they've been in the water?'

Harvey knew it must have been some time after Willard had last made an entry in his activity log on Friday morning, but if he could narrow it down from three days to within a couple of hours it would make tracing the killers easier.

'Best I can offer at the moment is a couple of days,' the policeman said. 'We'll know more after the autopsy.'

'What about a cause of death?'

'Both had severe facial injuries, but we don't yet know if they were dead before they went into the water.'

The officer took Harvey to see the bodies, and when he pulled back the first sheet, Harvey saw why cause of death was hard to establish. Willard's face looked like a giant blueberry, swollen and covered with bruising. The time spent in the water hadn't been kind to him either.

The second cadaver, which Harvey assumed was that of the informant Willard had been planning to meet, looked much the same, but it was also missing its ears.

'Any ID on this one?'

'Nothing in his pockets,' the policeman said. 'We're going to have to wait for a DNA match.'

'Wouldn't fingerprints be quicker?'

The policeman pulled the sheet aside to show the dead man's hands, and Harvey saw why that wasn't an option. Every digit had been removed, and the surgery didn't look too sophisticated. It looked as if each finger had been pulled off at the knuckle, rather than sliced with a sharp instrument.

Harvey used his phone to photograph the unidentified corpse, then forwarded the pictures to the office with a message asking Hamad Farsi to make a start on the identification process. He thanked the cop and began the walk back to the office. There wasn't much more to gain from being at the scene, and he was keen to find out exactly what Willard had been up to on Friday. On the way, he stopped at a deli and picked up a sandwich for his lunch, knowing it was unlikely he'd be able to get out later.

When he arrived back at Thames House, he updated Veronica Ellis on developments.

'Whoever did this was clearly trying to extract information,' he said. 'At least from the second man. They made a real mess of his body.'

Veronica Ellis pushed a few errant strands of platinum hair behind her ear and turned her computer screen so that Harvey could see the image she'd been looking at.

'Is that him?'

'It could be,' Harvey said. He dug out his phone and compared the photo on Ellis's monitor with the one he'd taken. 'Yes, I'd say that was him. At least the physique's the same. We'll obviously need confirmation, though.'

'For now, we go on that assumption. His name is Nikolai Sereyev, and he was a mid-level player in Alexi Bessonov's organisation.'

'I've heard of Bessonov,' Harvey said. 'Nasty piece of work.'

'And then some. I've just been looking through his file, and it makes scary reading.'

'Any particular reason he's still walking the streets?' Harvey asked.

Ellis stood and straightened her pencil skirt. 'You'll see the ins and outs for yourself when I send you the case details,' she said. 'For now, just know that he's got friends in high places and he's very careful about how he conducts his activities.'

'You want me to work this?' Harvey asked.

'The Russia desk was already under-resourced, but with Willard gone, they'll need your help. He was their only experienced field operative.'

'No problem. I'm guessing this takes priority over everything else I'm working on.'

Ellis nodded. 'The police have been told to keep Jason's name out of the papers, but you know how these things tend to leak after a while. I'd like to have it wrapped up before that happens.'

Harvey promised to get on it, and by the time he returned to his desk, the case notes for Nikolai Sereyev were waiting for him. Before he could make a start, though, he knew he'd have to hand over his current assignment to his colleague.

He looked over his monitor at Farsi and gave him the bad news, apologising for adding to his workload. 'I wish I could just leave it until I wrap this up, but it relates to a bomb threat.'

'I'm intrigued.'

'Don't be. The police have already been round to visit him and found nothing incriminating. At the moment we're just monitoring his activities, but he appears to be clean.'

The smile disappeared from Farsi's face. 'Sounds like more wasted hours. When are the analysts going to give us something to get our teeth into?'

Harvey tut-tutted his friend. 'Be careful what you wish for.' He walked around and put the Notley file on Farsi's desk. 'These are the most recent notes from the Met. They'll need to be added to his record.'

Farsi looked at the name and case number on the file and navigated to the electronic version. The face that appeared was unremarkable. Brown hair combed backwards, spectacles, green eyes, no scars. He read through the initial data that had been downloaded by Brigandicuum and the subsequent action taken.

'It says the police found nothing on his computer. Are they sure they got the right one?'

'They double-checked that,' Harvey said. 'Brigandicuum had downloaded the network card's global unique identifier, and the police's technical forensics team confirmed that they had the right machine. They just couldn't find the data that was supposed to have been on it.'

'A new hard drive?' Farsi suggested.

'It could be,' Harvey admitted, 'or perhaps he used a program to destroy any incriminating data before his computer was seized. I ran it past Gerald and he said both were possible explanations.'

When it came to anything electronic, there wasn't much that MI5's resident technician Gerald Small didn't know.

'What did a background check reveal? Anything to suggest a motive?'

'Nothing,' Harvey said. 'Notley looks to be squeaky clean, but we can't take any chances given the supposed threat.'

'So what was your next step going to be?' Farsi asked.

'We've got taps on his phone and all data streamed through his Internet service provider is being channelled to us. So far there's been nothing unusual. All we can do now is assign a resource to him and see where he goes.'

'I'll get on it,' Farsi promised.

Harvey returned to his desk and found an internal message from Ellis. It contained a link to the file Willard had been working on, and he opened it to see the now familiar face of Nikolai Sereyev.

Harvey raised his arms and stretched, then leaned over his keyboard.

'Let's see what you've been up to.'

Chapter 2

18 January 2016

Harvey was adding to his growing list of notes when his mobile phone tore him away from Nikolai Sereyev's file. He checked the caller ID and smiled as he answered.

'Hi, honey. How did it go?'

'Looks like I'll be moving office,' Sarah said.

'Excellent! Do you know when?'

'I haven't got a clear date. Martin wants me to hand over all of my assignments first, so it won't be before the end of February. He isn't happy about it, though.'

'His loss is my gain.' Harvey leaned back in his chair. 'Thankfully he saw sense.'

'Only after I threatened to resign if he blocked the move,' she said.

An email from the Russia desk interrupted him. 'You'll have to tell me about it when I get back to the flat,' he said. 'I've got to pop down and see someone about a new case I've been assigned to. If you can throw something together, I'll get a bottle of wine on the way home.'

The evening's plans made, he said his goodbyes and walked downstairs to see Gayle Cooper, head of the Russia section.

'I'm so sorry to hear about Jason,' Harvey said as he walked into Cooper's office. He could tell she'd been crying, and she suddenly looked a lot older than her forty years.

'It's knocked us for six,' Cooper admitted. 'Veronica says you're going to be leading this up, so I wanted to give you everything we have on Bessonov.'

Cooper had a laptop mirrored on a wall-mounted TV, where the Russian mobster's face already filled the screen. She clearly wasn't in the mood for conversation, so Harvey let her launch into the presentation.

'Alexi Bessonov, born in Moscow on 30 May 1962. His mother was a seamstress, his father a machine operator in a munitions factory. He became delinquent at thirteen and was arrested four times before dropping out of school at fifteen. He took up with a local black marketeer, where he earned a reputation as an enforcer. Bessonov reportedly killed his first man at age sixteen, and a dozen other deaths in Russia have been attributed to him.

'At twenty he was sent to London to help out in a power struggle between two Russian gangs. Thirteen people died in less than a week, including the head of the rival mob, and Bessonov became one of the personal bodyguards of the victor, Yuri Adaksin. It was a position he held for eight years until Adaksin's death in 1990.'

'How did his boss die?' Harvey interrupted, and the look he got from Cooper made him wish he hadn't.

'A car accident,' she said evenly. 'His SUV was hit by a rubbish truck and he died at the scene. Bessonov suffered a broken arm in the incident.'

Harvey was reluctant to interrupt her again, but wanted to get an idea of the circumstances.

'What about the truck driver?'

'Fled the scene,' Cooper said, 'and the truck turned out to be stolen.'

'A rival gang?'

'So it seems. It was never established who ordered the hit, but Adaksin's death created a vacuum, and several smaller gangs made plays to grab power. None were successful, and it soon turned into all-out war. Adaksin's lieutenants were taken out one by one, until Bessonov was fit enough to rejoin the fight. Reports suggest he personally took out two rival bosses before the others got the message, though there was never enough evidence to secure a conviction.'

'So Bessonov took over running of the firm at that point?'

Cooper switched images on the screen to show a much younger version of the mobster standing outside a diner. 'He's been the *Pakhan* – or Godfather – for the last twenty-six years, during which time the group has diversified into prostitution and human trafficking. That's on top of their drugs and protection businesses. The money is laundered through a series of legitimate companies, including that restaurant. It has six tables and we've never seen more than two dozen people walk through the door, but last year's accounts showed a profit of over a million on three million turnover.'

'That's some expensive borscht,' Harvey noted. 'Is there any particular reason why we haven't been able to take him down?'

Cooper moved on to the next image, a man in his sixties with heavy jowls and thinning grey hair. 'This is Grigory Polushin, senior counsellor at the Russian embassy and the ambassador's number two. He visits the restaurant twice a week, and I believe it is his political influence that keeps Bessonov out of our reach. We haven't been able to ascertain what happens at these meetings, but the assumption is that Polushin carries away significant amounts of cash. Often he's been seen leaving with a large holdall. We suspect that's how Bessonov's illegal gains are being shipped back to Moscow through diplomatic channels. The police have pulled Bessonov in twice, but both times he had alibis provided by high-ranking Russian officials. We believe Polushin arranged them for him, and it's difficult for the CPS to push ahead with a prosecution without calling them liars.'

It was a familiar story to Harvey: known criminals operating with impunity in order to prevent political shitstorms. It wasn't just the Russians, either. Several Chinese gangs had close ties with senior diplomats, and while those who lived in their community knew what was going on, the Triad bosses never seemed to be held accountable.

This wasn't about an illegal brothel or gambling den, though. Bessonov had taken out an MI5 operative.

'You say you don't know what goes on at their regular meetings,' he said. 'Have you tried bugging the place?'

'Impossible,' Cooper said. 'It's open and staffed twenty-four hours a day, so there's no opportunity to break in and plant anything. We once tried sending a transmitter in with a newspaper delivery, sewing it into the spine of a magazine, but they sweep the place before each meeting and our device was found before it could do any good.'

'I suppose his home is out of the question, too.'

'All three of them,' Cooper confirmed. 'The closest we could get to Bessonov was through Nikolai Sereyev . . .'

Her words tailed off, the memory of Willard's death filling the empty space.

'I read Willard's notes,' Harvey said, after a respectful pause. 'He mentioned that Sereyev knew of something big on the horizon. Did he ever elaborate?'

'I don't know anything beyond what you've read,' Cooper said, 'though the timing worries me.'

Harvey perked up. 'What do you mean?'

'I take it you've heard of the recent troubles in Tagrilistan,' she said, soliciting a nod from Harvey.

The sanctions imposed on Russia following their annexing of Crimea had hit the country's economy hard, and its reliance on energy exports added to their woes with the slump in oil prices. The rouble had lost more than sixty per cent of its value against the dollar in one year, and foreign investment had all but dried up.

Far from learning their lesson, though, the Russians had turned their attention to Tagrilistan, one of many former Soviet republics bordering Russia to the south. As with Ukraine, a pro-Russian government had once led Tagrilistan, but their recent defeat in the elections had caused serious unrest. Russia seized the opportunity to stoke up further resentment and had sent in troops and equipment, though they denied having anything to do with the civil war ravaging the country. Those sent to fight wore no insignia and carried no identification, and the weapons they used were available in many countries in the region, though no-one was under any illusion as to their real origin.

'I was as surprised as anyone when Demidov sent his troops there,' he said. 'It didn't work out too well in Ukraine.'

'It's all about securing his own future,' Cooper said. 'With Ukraine, he was still reeling from accusations of vote rigging in the 2012 elections, and he saw it as the perfect chance to unite the nation and increase his approval rating. It worked for a while, but once their economy took a nosedive, so did his popularity. Focusing on a new enemy in Tagrilistan allowed him to bounce back a little, but he doesn't seem to have a clear strategy, and that makes him unpredictable.'

'So what does this have to do with the big thing that Sereyev told Willard was on the horizon?'

'Viktor Milenko is Tagrilistan's new president, and he'll be visiting London at the end of next week,' Cooper said. 'He's looking to sign a trade deal with us and the rest of Europe, and the Russians aren't happy about it. Tagrilistan is sitting on a large oil deposit, and Milenko is offering it to us at five dollars a barrel below Moscow prices. If this deal goes ahead, it will push Russia further into recession.'

'You think they'll try to hit Milenko while he's over here?'

'In the absence of any other information, I have to assume the worst. I'm preparing a report for Veronica detailing my concerns, but this is one time I'd be glad to be mistaken.'

Harvey agreed. If Milenko were assassinated in London, it would send out the message that dealing with Britain came at a hefty price.

'If you could copy me into that report, I'd appreciate it,' he said. 'In the meantime, I'll try to find out what Bessonov is really up to.'

Chapter 3

18 January 2016

Stanislav Yerzov pulled up at the front of the Novotel nestled in the centre of the Tagrilistani capital and handed the valet the keys to his two-year-old Toyota RAV4 before heading inside the hotel. Normally he would have had a driver take him everywhere in his armour-plated BMW, as befit Tagrilistan's vice president, but this wasn't a typical social meeting.

He made straight for the restaurant and walked past several foreign businessmen before taking a seat at the table he'd reserved. His two dinner guests arrived just as he gave the waiter his order from the wine list, and he greeted them nervously.

'I'm not happy at the thought of being seen with you,' he whispered. 'Is it really necessary?'

'This isn't something we could have done over the phone,' the first Russian said. He was almost as large as Yerzov, but carried muscle rather than flab. His companion was a complete contrast, his grey suit almost falling off his short, wiry frame. Both were in their mid-forties, with the larger one, Sergei, doing all the talking.

'What is so important that it risks revealing our relationship?'

'We had an incident in London,' Sergei said. 'It seems the British are taking an unhealthy interest in our people over there.'

'What do you mean?' Yerzov wiped his brow with a napkin. He'd been apprehensive about the meeting with the Russians, but now he was close to full-blown panic.

The waiter returned and asked for their order. Sergei and his companion waved him away, but Yerzov requested the salmon.

'The security services tried to infiltrate our organisation, but we dealt with it,' Sergei said, once they were alone again. 'We interrogated the mole for some time, but it seems he didn't have a chance to pass on any damaging information. The question is, who pointed MI5 in our direction?'

Yerzov looked at both of the men in turn, their blank faces giving nothing away. It took him a full minute to realise what they were suggesting.

'You . . . you think I had something to do with it?'

'Not at all,' Sergei assured him, trying to smile but only managing to look menacing. 'You have too much to lose, we both know that. Did you mention our plan to anyone else?'

'Not even my wife, I swear.'

'Good,' Sergei said, seemingly satisfied. He pulled a manila envelope from inside his jacket and handed it to Yerzov, who opened it and read the one-page message.

'That's the press release we want you to put out once his assassination reaches the news wires. You will follow up shortly afterwards with the announcement that you think Britain was complicit in his death, that they cannot be trusted and that you will therefore be forging ties with Moscow instead.'

'Understood,' Yerzov told him, though his only concern was the two million dollars that would hit his Cayman bank account once his deal with the Russians was ratified. He was born a Muscovite and had moved with his parents to Tagrilistan when he was seven years of age. But it was simple security that motivated him, not some misguided notion of patriotism.

'That's good,' Sergei said. 'We don't want you changing allegiance at the last moment.'

The threat hung in the air, but Yerzov needed no warning. He was under no illusions as to his future if he didn't deliver, and a long life with plenty of cash was far preferable to no life at all.

'Are plans in place to pull the troops back to the border?' Yerzov knew that Moscow wasn't happy with the idea of being seen to capitulate, but he could hardly enter into trade negotiations while Russian soldiers held a large swath of what would soon be his country. Battles had been fought in several cities near the border, with a death toll of almost five hundred in the last three months alone.

'A phased withdrawal has already been implemented,' Sergei said. 'There will be no troops in Tagrilistan by Wednesday, and the local Russian population have been ordered to abandon their posts on the twenty-ninth.'

The day Milenko was due to relinquish his position, though he didn't yet know it.

The waiter arrived with Yerzov's meal, and Sergei took it as his cue to leave.

'We'll be back in a couple of weeks when we escort the president to the talks,' Sergei said as he rose. 'Make sure everything's ready for his visit.'

Andrew Harvey stuck his head into Gerald Small's office and saw the technician tinkering with a toy helicopter.

'Busy as always, I see.'

Small smiled and held the chopper out for Harvey to take. 'This is my latest surveillance drone.'

'It looks like the one I bought my nephew for Christmas,' Harvey said, giving it a once-over. The toy was six inches long and weighed only a couple of ounces. 'It feels a bit heavier than his, though. What have you done to it?'

Small took the craft back and turned it over. 'This is a directional microphone,' he said. 'The bird can hover at a hundred feet, and this baby will pick up an ant farting on the ground.'

'Really? That good?'

'Well, maybe not an ant,' Small conceded, 'but it could certainly pick up a conversation as if it were happening a few feet away.'

'It might be just what I need,' Harvey said, and explained the problem he faced in getting a recording device into Bessonov's restaurant.

'That wouldn't do you any good,' Small said. 'It relies on line of sight and isn't that effective through walls. I have something here that might be useful, though.'

Small delved into a drawer and brought out a transparent circle of film.

'We want to hear what Bessonov says, not help him to quit smoking.'

'Look closer,' Small said.

Harvey held the disc up to the light and saw that far from being just plastic, it had dozens of tiny filaments running through it, each thinner than a human hair.

'It's one of the latest passive recording devices,' Small said. He held out his hand and showed Harvey another circle, this one a little thicker and backed with paper.

'And that's just the battery. This is the same thing paired with the transmitter. Once you peel off the backing, it will stick to any surface and is almost impossible to remove without the accompanying solvent. In your case, we could design it to look like a table manufacturer's logo. You could stick it under a table in Bessonov's restaurant, and it would stand up to the closest scrutiny.'

'They sweep for bugs every day,' Harvey reminded him.

'Not a problem. This thing stores the information it records and only transmits to us when it senses no electrical signal nearby. Even if someone has a scanning device right next to it when the conversation starts, it won't be detected.'

It seemed the ideal way to find out what Bessonov was up to, but as with all things technical, there had to be a flaw.

'So what's the down side?'

'In order to pick up its transmission, you need to be quite close. Within fifty yards, to be exact.'

That meant parking virtually outside the shop, which wasn't something Harvey was comfortable with.

'Can't you boost the signal somehow?'

'Not mine to do.' Small shrugged. 'I got this from an American friend. It's ten years ahead of anything we've got, and if it came to modifications I wouldn't know where to begin.'

'In that case, does someone have to be on the other end, or can we just set up a receiver somewhere and pick it up later?'

'Sure.' Small picked up a metal briefcase and placed it on the desk. 'This is all you'll need.' He opened it and flicked a couple of switches to demonstrate how it should be operated.

'Could I leave that in the boot of my car and come back for it after the meeting?'

'Yes, but the battery life is something like five hours, so don't leave it too long.'

Harvey thanked Small and asked him to make sure the receiver was fully charged, then headed back to his desk and checked Bessonov's file to see when Polushin usually visited the restaurant. According to the surveillance logs, they met every Tuesday and Friday, always around two in the afternoon.

That gave him twenty-four hours to come up with a way to plant the bug and learn what secret was big enough to kill for.

Chapter 4

19 January 2016

Hamad Farsi pulled over opposite the Petrushkin restaurant at three in the morning and killed the engine. Lights still shone through the windows of the eatery, and a couple of burly men stood chatting outside, one of them smoking a cigarette.

He'd driven past the restaurant four times in the previous two hours, looking for a parking space within range of the front door, and finally he was able to drop the car off in a spot that was marked as residents' parking from eight in the morning until six in the evening. He knew some officious traffic warden would be issuing him with a parking ticket just after breakfast, but it wasn't his problem. The company would pick up the tab on that one. His only concern was that the car might be towed before Harvey could get there to switch cars at lunchtime.

He locked the Ford and walked east, never glancing in the direction of the two men guarding the front of the Petrushkin. When he reached the end of the road, he turned north and found Harvey waiting in his own car.

'Finally found somewhere, then?'

'Yeah,' Farsi said. 'It's a nightmare parking in this area.'

Twenty minutes later, Harvey dropped Farsi off at his flat. 'Sleep fast, my friend,' he called out the car window as Farsi walked up the steps. 'I'll see you bright and early.'

'I wish someone would invent a microwave bed,' Farsi retorted. 'Then I could get eight hours' sleep in thirty minutes.'

Andrew Harvey was looking through the preliminary coroner's report when Farsi rolled in ten minutes late.

'You look like crap.'

'Thanks,' Farsi said, giving in to a yawn. 'I managed about two hours last night. It'd better be worth it.'

'Consider yourself lucky you aren't the one going in,' Harvey said. 'These aren't the kind of people you want to meet alone in a dark alley.'

He told Farsi to take a look at his screen, where the details of Sereyev's death were laid bare.

'They cut off his ears and tongue *and* gouged out his eyes?' he noted. 'Nice people.'

'I think it's a reference to the three wise monkeys: see no evil, hear no evil, speak no evil.'

'Or one mad Russian,' Farsi said. '"Cross me and I'll righteously fuck you up."'

'Either way, let's be on our toes today.'

Veronica Ellis appeared at the door to her office and gestured for the pair to join her, and when they entered the room she told them to close the door.

'You've seen the report Gayle sent to me,' she said to Harvey.

'Yeah.' Cooper had done as he'd asked and copied him in.

'I just got off the phone with the commander of SO1, and I get the feeling he isn't taking this seriously.'

SO1, the Specialist Protection Branch from the Specialist Operations directorate of London's Metropolitan Police Service, was tasked with protecting the prime minister as well as foreign dignitaries. They were in charge of the security operation for Viktor Milenko's upcoming visit, and they received dozens of VIP-related threat alerts every day. The fact that this warning had come from MI5 should have moved it to the top of the list, but apparently that wasn't the case.

'What did he say?' Harvey asked.

'He wants definitive proof before he assigns any resources to it.'

'An MI5 agent and his Russian snitch in the morgue so close to Milenko's visit isn't good enough for him?'

'Not even close. I passed him Cooper's report, and he said it was too thin. He said that if we can come back with dates, names and locations, he'll look into it further.'

It was frustrating, Harvey knew, but understandable. If the PM had been under threat, SO1 would have hopped to it. But every whack job and his brother made threats against the PM each day, straining even the large security force's resources. It simply wasn't feasible to assign already scarce personnel to the coming visit of the president of a petty principality like Tagrilistan. Not without hard proof of a threat.

'I'll get the team to work up possible attack scenarios. In the meantime, let's hope we can plant the device and get Polushin and Bessonov to give us something to work with.'

'You look like your grandfather,' Farsi said as Harvey climbed into the car.

'As long as it fools Bessonov's thugs, that's fine with me.' Harvey was wearing a tweed jacket and fedora hat; a pair of horn-rimmed glasses completed the disguise. It wouldn't stand up to close inspection, but he only needed it to walk to the car Farsi had parked earlier that morning and drive it away.

Farsi drove to the street adjacent to the Petrushkin and dropped Harvey off at the side of the road.

'Give me three minutes, then bring the car round,' Harvey said as he climbed out. He opened the boot and switched on the receiver, then slammed it shut and banged once on the roof of the car.

He walked round the corner and saw the restaurant on the opposite side of the road. A lone man stood outside, trying to look casual as he studied his mobile phone, but the telltale signs were clear. The Russian glanced up every few seconds, taking in the passing traffic and footfall that trudged past the door. Harvey hoped that nothing about his disguise or behaviour would give the lookout cause to take an interest in him.

Harvey walked to the car and, as expected, found a parking ticket stuck underneath the windscreen wiper. He snatched it up with an angry gesture and stuffed it into his pocket, then opened the car, climbing in gingerly as if his joints were protesting each movement. He put on his seatbelt and checked the side mirror, waiting for Farsi's approach. Thankfully, traffic was light at eleven in the morning, and he saw the car pull out of the side road and approach him. He let it get closer, then indicated to pull out. As planned, Farsi flashed his headlights to let Harvey make the manoeuvre, then pulled into the slot that had just been vacated.

Harvey drove around the corner and parked on double yellow lines, then discarded his disguise and donned a raincoat just as his colleague joined him.

'You ready for this?' Farsi asked.

'Ready as I'll ever be,' Harvey replied, though the tension in his voice betrayed his true feelings. He was about to venture into the lion's den, and after many hours looking at Bessonov's file – not to mention the images of the recently deceased – he was under no illusions as to what to expect if things turned nasty.

Harvey took a miniature bottle of whiskey from his pocket and rinsed his mouth with it, then rubbed a few drops on his neck and coat until he was satisfied that he smelled like he'd spent some time in a pub.

'Wish me luck,' he said, and climbed out of the car and into the rain shower that had started minutes earlier.

He strolled clumsily round the corner and crossed the road, looking in the shop windows he passed. When he reached the Petrushkin, he stopped and looked at the menu in the window. He quickly realised why few real diners ever ventured inside. The cheapest starter cost more than fifteen pounds, and main meals began at forty-five. He guessed that was how Bessonov managed to account for such a high turnover for the company. He would ring up fake orders each day and put his own money in the till, enabling him to launder his ill-gotten gains through the business. It meant he paid only twenty per cent corporation tax, a small hit to take under the circumstances.

Harvey had the transmitter cupped in his hand, the backing already removed to make it easier to attach it. His peripheral vision told him that the doorman had lost interest in him, probably assuming he was going to be put off by the prices, and he took the opportunity to dart inside. There were two dozen tables arranged along both walls, enough to seat more than fifty diners, though none was occupied. A solid silver samovar housed in a glass case dominated one wall, and reproduction Fabergé eggs dotted the room. Cooper's notes told him that Bessonov always sat at the round table near the kitchen, so Harvey made his way to it before anyone could stop him.

He sat down heavily at the empty table and managed to get the sticker attached to its underside before the waiter had time to come round from behind the counter and confront him.

‘Not there!’ the man shouted.

Harvey raised his hands in the air, as if surrendering. ‘Whoa, chief! Calm down, will ya?’

‘You cannot sit there,’ the waiter repeated, urging him to get to his feet.

‘Why the fuck not?’ Harvey slurred. ‘It’s a free country, ain’t it?’

The commotion had brought other staff into the dining room, and a giant of a man grabbed Harvey by the collar and pulled him effortlessly out of the booth and thrust him towards the door.

Harvey stumbled a few paces, then turned, planning to launch a final tirade before leaving, but the sight of the huge aggressor marching towards him gave him a change of heart. He scampered to the door and ran outside, then dashed across the road and disappeared around the corner.

His pulse was still pounding in his ears when he reached Farsi’s car and climbed in.

‘Let’s get the hell out of here.’

Chapter 5

19 January 2016

Alexi Bessonov arrived at the Petrushkin just after midday and went straight to his table, not needing to inform the waiter of his order. He knew the espresso would be brought to him within a minute, and he took off his coat and hung it on the hook on the wall.

'What's this?' he asked, and three members of staff immediately went to see what he was referring to. A few drops of water were clearly visible on the leather seat, and a waiter quickly whipped out a cloth to dry it off.

'How did they get there?' Bessonov asked, his voice calm as always, masking his true emotional state.

'Some drunk came in and sat in your chair before we could stop him.'

Bessonov waited until the waiter had dried the seat, then sat and felt under the table for anything out of the ordinary. When he found nothing, he got down on his knees and gave the underside a visual inspection.

All he could see was a sticker proclaiming the table fire resistant; he rubbed his hand over it before standing again.

'Tell Aslan to sweep the entire room,' he ordered as he got to his feet.

The Chechen arrived minutes later with his electronic wand and scanned the booth thoroughly, but no telltale beeps were emitted from his device. He moved to the door and in the next twenty minutes covered the entire room before declaring it clear of listening devices.

Satisfied, Bessonov relaxed and ordered the chef to whip up some caviar and blini, followed by *kalduny*, dumplings of unleavened dough filled with lobster. Polushin never ate during his visits, preferring a liquid lunch. But Bessonov didn't like to drink on an empty stomach.

The waiter was clearing away his plates when Polushin walked in the door, his bodyguard shaking hands with Bessonov's men before taking a seat near the front of the restaurant.

'Grigory, welcome.'

Polushin took a seat and placed his attaché case on the table. Bessonov opened it and placed two bulging envelopes inside before locking it. With that part of the meeting out of the way, Bessonov snapped his fingers and the waiter appeared with a bottle of Stolichnaya Elit and a couple of shot glasses. He carefully poured two measures of the £2,000-a-bottle spirit.

'*Za vas!*' Polushin said as he raised his glass.

'To you,' Bessonov echoed.

They drained the liquid, and Bessonov poured two more generous shots.

'I understand you had a bit of a problem over the weekend,' Polushin said.

Bessonov shrugged. 'Nothing I couldn't handle.'

'So I heard. But I don't like the idea of the British security services sniffing around. I need assurances that nothing is going to get in the way of our plans.'

'It was nothing, really. MI5 have been trying to infiltrate my organisation for some time, and they thought Nikki would be a good way in. The poor soul liked his vices too much.' Another shrug. 'Evidently, he couldn't afford to indulge them on the salary I paid. They saw the opportunity and offered him the money he wanted, and I dealt with the problem.'

'Couldn't you have dealt with it in a different way?' Polushin asked.

'You have nothing to fear,' Bessonov assured him. 'The team tasked with carrying out the operation is ready. Everything is in place, so there is no need for further communication between us until it is all over.'

'And where is this team?'

'I am housing them in a furniture factory,' Bessonov said. 'It is just one subsidiary of one of many holding companies I control. It would take them a year just to discover that I have an interest in it, by which time it will all be over and they'll be back in Moscow.'

Spetsnaz veterans had been flown in a month earlier on staggered flights from Sheremetyevo International Airport, each man a hardened warrior with plenty of combat experience. Polushin had arranged travel documents and work permits, allowing them to pose as workers should anyone from the immigration service decide to pay a surprise visit. The only tricky part had been securing the weapons they would need to carry out their assignment, but when price wasn't a concern, anything became possible.

'Very well,' Polushin conceded, as he downed his third glass of vodka. 'I will pass that on to Moscow. Thank you, as always, for the warm hospitality.'

Both men rose and embraced, then Polushin headed for the door.

Bessonov watched him leave, with a hundred grand in cash – minus Polushin's cut – heading for his Swiss account after a brief stopover in Russia.

'Polushin just left,' Harvey said over the comms unit.

He was sitting in a café a hundred yards from the Petrushkin, nursing a latte and once again wearing the tweed jacket and hat.

'I'll be there in five,' Farsi replied.

Harvey watched his colleague saunter into view and make for the parked car; once Farsi had driven away, Harvey walked out of the café and to his own vehicle.

Hopefully, the conversation they recorded would not only contain incriminating evidence that could lead to Willard's killers being caught but also give them the proof they needed to get SO1 to take them seriously. They wouldn't know until Gayle Cooper translated it into English.

When he arrived at the underground parking lot, he saw that Farsi had beaten him to Thames House. He took the elevator up to his floor and found a cup of hot decaf waiting for him.

'Where's the receiver?' he asked.

'Gerald already extracted the recording and put it in the database,' Farsi said. 'I called Gayle and said we'd be down in a few minutes.'

Harvey grabbed his mug and the pair took the stairs down to the Russia desk, where Cooper sat with headphones over her ears as she typed up the conversation. She noticed them entering the room and held up a finger, then continued with the translation.

Harvey stood behind her and watched the words appear on the screen. It took another four minutes before Cooper was done, and she printed out three copies.

'Bessonov specifically mentions us and Sereyev,' Cooper pointed out. 'I think that's enough to bring him in.'

Harvey continued reading, and once he reached the end he took a seat and started over.

'I don't think so,' he eventually said. 'Sure, he mentions a Nikki, but that could be one of a million people, not necessarily Nikolai Sereyev. It also says he dealt with the MI5 issue, but doesn't elaborate.'

'What about this?' Cooper asked, pointing to a line on Harvey's printout.

GP: So I heard, but I don't like the idea of the British security services sniffing around. I need assurances that nothing is going to get in the way of our plans.

'Those plans could be anything,' Harvey said. 'They could claim to be organising a birthday party or a weekend in Paris. All we have is Bessonov saying MI5 were investigating him, which is true. He said he dealt with the matter, which could mean he gave Sereyev a warning or sacked him.'

'But—'

'Here's how it would play out,' Harvey said, holding up his hand. 'Bessonov calls his lawyer, who says that yes, his client admits to knowing that MI5 were trying to infiltrate his organisation, which, by the way, is totally legitimate and pays its taxes every year. When he said he'd dealt with the problem, he meant he'd given Sereyev a pay rise and bonus, but he disappeared shortly afterwards. The plans he was referring to related to a birthday surprise they were organising, and it wouldn't have been good if Bessonov had been pulled in for questioning and had to miss it.'

'But what about the team they mentioned?' Cooper persisted.

'It could be a team of strippers for the birthday bash they're organising,' Harvey said, 'and they don't want MI5 pulling them in and thinking they were prostitutes being trafficked into the country, which is an accusation that has been levelled at Bessonov more than once.'

Cooper sat heavily in her chair, deflated.

'I'm sorry, Gayle,' Harvey said, as he stood and headed for the door. 'I want to bring Bessonov in just as much as you do, but we're going to need more proof than this. It might be enough to get SO1 off their backsides, though, so email Veronica a copy and she can have a word with them. Hamad and I will try to find Bessonov's furniture factory, and if we do, we'll be able to see what he's hiding.'

Andrew Harvey munched on a sandwich as his frustration with the search grew. It was already after six in the evening and the office was emptying fast, but he was still no closer to finding any furniture business in Bessonov's little empire.

He had been through the maze of limited companies and subsidiaries in the Russian's file, but none of their names even remotely matched what he was looking for.

Could Bessonov have started a company in a different name? Unlikely, given the checks that would be made by HMRC and other government departments.

It is just one subsidiary of one of many holding companies I control.

The word 'control' leapt out at him, and he cursed himself for not spotting it sooner. Bessonov didn't have to *own* the company, only have a sizeable stake in it.

He logged into the Companies House database and looked for all companies that Bessonov had shares in. When the results came back, he was hugely disappointed. Apart from Petrov Holdings Limited, the Petrushkin and another restaurant north of the river, there was nothing.

Dejected, he went back to the original list and began going through the names once again. This time, he paused when he got to Riviera Investments Limited. The name suggested a property company in the south of France, but when he opened the file he found it dealt with ordinary shares. He quickly typed Riviera Investments into Companies House and sat back, a huge smile on his face.

'I think I've found it,' he said, beckoning Farsi round to his side of the desk to look at the screen.

The Olde Oak Furniture Company logo was in the top corner, with an address in Wandsworth shown underneath.

'How sure are you?' Farsi asked.

'About ninety per cent. It isn't actually owned by Bessonov, but one of his subsidiary investment companies has a forty-nine per cent share in it.'

'Let's pass it on to Ellis and see what she wants to do with it.'

Harvey was already up and walking to her office. He knocked on the door and saw his boss typing away on her computer, still looking fresh after a twelve-hour shift.

'We have something we'd like to work up,' Harvey said, and told her what he'd found.

'What do you propose?'

'A simple drive-by – just me and Hamad.'

'I'd prefer it if you had backup,' Ellis said. 'If this really is what we think, things could turn nasty in a heartbeat.'

'That's why it's best if just the two of us go,' Harvey insisted. 'The fewer people on the scene, the more likely it is we remain undetected.'

Ellis considered his pitch and seemed to come to a decision.

'Okay, so what do you need from me?'

'Night-vision glasses and comms.'

Ellis wrote out a requisition form and handed it over.

'This says we can draw firearms,' Harvey said.

'Bessonov's already shown us what he does to those who interfere in his operations,' Ellis said. 'I'd rather you had them and not need them, if you know what I mean.'

'We'd better grab these before the stores close,' Farsi said. 'What time do you want to head out?'

'Let's leave it until after midnight,' Harvey told him. 'That'll give us plenty of time to scope out the area on satellite imagery and decide where to lay up.'

They made to leave, but Ellis called them back.

'I'm hearing from the MOD that Russia is pulling its troops back from the Tagrilistani border. That was totally unexpected, given Moscow's stance over the last few months. Whether that has anything to do with events over here isn't clear. Military intelligence seems to think the withdrawal is Russia's way of extending the olive branch in the hope of starting their own trade talks.'

'Seems a little too late for that,' Harvey said.

'That's my feeling, too, but if Tagrilistan signs a deal with Britain, that horse will have bolted forever. President Demidov can't afford another pro-European country on his border.'

'Pulling his men back won't do him any good,' Farsi said. 'Tagrilistan's president is openly anti-Russia. There's no way he'd turn his back on Europe and sign a pact with Demidov.'

'Whatever the motive, it looks like Russia is finally playing ball. We can only hope it leads to a full retreat and an end to the troubles in Tagrilistan.'

Harvey hoped Ellis was right. The sanctions imposed by Europe had been disastrous for Russia's economy, but Demidov's tit-for-tat decision to ban imports from neighbouring countries had had its own impact. European meat and milk producers, along with fruit and vegetable suppliers, were seeing large consignments of their perishable products being left to rot as the market contracted, costing millions in lost revenue and the closure of many businesses. The chances of a global recovery were slim while the Russian bear continued along its current path.

‘What about the assassination attempt?’ Ellis asked. ‘What do you see as the most likely method?’

‘Given the location of the meeting, we’ve ruled out a sniper. There simply isn’t a decent vantage point along Whitehall. Besides which, Bessonov mentioned a team. I think it most likely they’ll try to hit him en route to Downing Street.’

‘Those cars are heavily armoured,’ Ellis pointed out. ‘It would take an enormous amount of firepower to get to Milenko.’

Harvey shrugged. ‘Barring an aerial assault, that’s all we could come up with.’

‘I’ll pass that on to SO1,’ Ellis said. ‘I gave them a transcript of the conversation between Bessonov and Polushin and I’m waiting for them to get back to me. Hopefully we’ll be able to bring them all in before they have a chance to strike.’

Chapter 6

20 January 2016

A distant police siren was the only sound the night gave up as Harvey and Farsi sat in the car two hundred yards from the Olde Oak factory. They'd been waiting for more than an hour, hoping to see signs of life within the sprawling building, but the only three windows they could see had remained dark.

Harvey's thoughts turned to Sarah, who would be tucked up in bed by now, and while he was determined to bring Bessonov down, part of him wished he could blow off the mission and join her.

'We need to get in closer,' he said, returning to the job at hand. 'If anyone's in there, they'll be asleep by now.'

It was almost two in the morning and the area was deserted, apart from a couple of big rigs parked in the loading bay and a few cars lining the street.

Harvey checked his Glock to ensure he had a round in the chamber, then climbed out of the car and quietly closed the door. The wind whipped at his jacket as he made his way towards the building, the third of seven on the mile-long road. He kept to the shadows but walked nonchalantly, hoping to give the impression of someone on their way home after a night shift. Stooping and running would look suspicious to any eyes out there, whereas someone on a casual stroll wouldn't raise any alarms.

He reached the corner of the building adjacent to the furniture factory without incident. There, he took his jacket off and turned it inside out so that the beige suede gave way to black leather. He then pulled his balaclava from his pocket and put it over his head. Next came the night-vision glasses, through the eyepieces of which the world shone a hazy green.

Harvey began looking for signs of CCTV cameras and found two covering the front and side of the building. The lights in the top corner of each unit told him that they would be recording his approach. He thought it unlikely anyone would be manning the cameras, and his headgear meant anyone reviewing the tapes would have a hard time identifying him.

Harvey stuck his head round the corner and was able to see down the side of the building, which stretched into the darkness. Still no lights visible. He flicked the setting on the glasses to infrared but detected no telltale heat signatures radiating from inside the warehouse.

Not for the first time that evening, he wondered if he'd identified the correct business.

There was little point in worrying about that now, though. After another quick scan of the area, he broke cover and jogged across the open ground to the wall of the factory. No alarms pierced the night, and no spotlights caught him in their luminous gaze.

He tiptoed down the side of the building, heading towards the rear, where hopefully he would find a way inside. The only windows were two storeys above him – out of the question, given the gear that Farsi and he had brought.

Seventy yards later, he reached the rear of the factory and stuck his head around the corner. Two SUVs were parked near the reception area, and when Harvey switched back to infrared he saw that the engine cavities were cold. That meant they hadn't been used in a while, but their very presence suggested someone was in the building.

Warier now, he scanned the area for more cameras and saw only one, pointing towards the vehicles. This side of the building had a set of ground-level windows. He toggled his glasses back to night vision and moved towards the rear door, which looked fairly new and impregnable. The older-looking windows offered a more realistic proposal. He was feeling around the frame for signs of an alarm system when cold steel pressed against the base of his skull.

'What the—'

'Don't move,' a heavily accented voice said as the glasses were pulled from his head.

Harvey hadn't heard a sound, yet he was now held by two men – and one of them was frisking him none too gently. The Glock was confiscated next, along with the comms unit, and plastic ties secured his wrists before he was pulled away from the window and thrust towards one of the SUVs. Rough hands pushed him through its open rear door.

An order was given in Russian, and the doors to the reception opened. Eight men walked out, each carrying a dark holdall, and began piling into the vehicles. Harvey was struggling to think of a way out of a situation that had, within seconds, gone from routine surveillance to life-threatening. Unless he managed to alert Farsi, he would be whisked out of the area in minutes, and no-one would have a clue where to begin looking.

That these were Bessonov's men was now beyond doubt, and their bearing told him they were soldiers – former or current, it didn't really matter. That they allowed him to see their faces was another bad sign. It meant they didn't plan to let him go, and all Harvey could picture in the next few hours was a version of the torture Willard had endured in his final hours.

The vehicles set off, and Harvey desperately tried to think of a way to let Farsi know what was going on. Had he been picked up, too? Did the Russians even know he was in the area?

The answer soon became apparent as Farsi ran into the road and held his Glock in a two-handed grip, pointing at the windscreen of the lead SUV. Harvey could see him shouting something, but couldn't hear what his friend was saying above the roar of the engine. One thing he did know was that getting his head down was the best thing he could do in the circumstances.

He ducked behind the driver's seat as soon as he saw the muzzle flash from Farsi's weapon, but instead of the sound of shattering glass, he heard the slug thud against the window and bounce off. Three more thuds followed before the driver swerved and the whole car shook as it made contact with something.

Harvey instinctively knew that something was Hamad Farsi, and he sat up and looked out of the rear window to see his close friend lying at the side of the road, his body in an unnatural position.

The SUV turned a corner and powered out of the industrial park, joining the dual carriageway as it headed away from the centre of London.

A sharp Russian command came from beside him, followed by a bag drawn over his head.

Harvey knew what lay ahead wasn't going to be pleasant, but he couldn't bring himself to care. His mind had been branded with the lasting image of his dear friend, almost certainly dead at the roadside.

Chapter 7

20 January 2016

'Cup!'

'Thank you, sweetheart,' Gray said, taking the heavy coffee mug from Melissa's tiny hands and putting it in the cupboard.

His daughter immediately dived back into the box, this time pulling out her favourite dinner plate.

'Thanks, darling, but I think it's best if you leave this lot to me.'

He picked her up and carried her through to the living room, once again marvelling at the sheer size of it. This room alone was almost as large as the entire ground floor of his home back in England, and his decision to relocate stateside looked to have been a good one so far. He'd been able to put down a hefty deposit on the property and, once the sale of his home in the London suburbs was completed, he planned to pay off the balance. Being debt-free was important to him, and it was a philosophy he wanted to instil in Melissa once she was old enough to understand. As she was just two and a half years old, he had plenty of time to prepare for those conversations.

Gray set her down on the hardwood floor and pulled a box of soft toys over to her, slicing the tape with his penknife.

'How about you help me unpack these, eh?'

Melissa stood and pulled open the flaps.

'Whiskers!' she screamed as she sprang her black-and-white stuffed cat from its cardboard prison. Other toys soon followed, until the floor was littered with just about every toy animal conceivable.

'I'll leave you to it,' Gray said, and his daughter didn't seem in the mood to argue.

He returned to the kitchen and started loading the rest of his possessions into the cupboards. He'd only packed the essentials, enough to keep them going for a couple of weeks. He reminded himself to visit the local shops – *stores*, he corrected himself – and stock up on everything they would need for their fresh start.

Gray was thankful that his daughter was still young enough that she wouldn't be affected by the upheaval. An older girl might complain about having to make do with sleeping bags and camp beds, part of the consignment he'd had shipped over from England prior to leaving to start their new life in northern Florida.

He'd already been to Walmart to stock up on food, cleaning products and other daily necessities, and up next was a trip to furnish the house, to the *mall*, Gray thought wryly. He still needed to kit out the bedrooms, living room, dining room and kitchen, and as he wasn't particularly fussy when it came to styling, it shouldn't take him too long.

A couple of years ago, Vick would have taken great delight at the prospect of furnishing an entire home. He could imagine her going from store to store looking for the perfect rug to match the curtains, and a sofa that went well with the polished wooden floors . . .

Thinking about his late wife created a hollow sensation in his chest. A part of him had been ripped out and tossed into the fire that had stolen his wife and nearly his daughter. He barely spent a day without thinking about her, and often he found himself unable to shake the image of the flames leaping around her, as she lay helpless.

He shook his head, trying to clear away the image. He had to move on, to take care of Melissa, something he wouldn't be able to do if he let such thoughts consume him.

He picked up the local directory and flicked to the daycare section, trying to take his mind off the past. Melissa would need to start integrating with other children her age, and then there was schooling to sort out, which meant he would be busy for the next couple of weeks at least.

The doorbell rang, a strange sound he was hearing for the first time. He walked into the hallway and saw Melissa looking up at him, also puzzled by the odd tone.

Gray opened the door and saw a couple standing on the porch, smiling, with arms around each other as they held out a basket between them. They both looked to be in their late fifties.

'Howdy, neighbour!' the woman said. 'I'm Sue Wilburn, and this is my husband, Frank. We live next door and just wanted to welcome you to the neighbourhood.'

Gray was momentarily taken aback. This wasn't something he was used to, and had certainly never happened to him back in England.

'I— Er . . . thanks.'

Melissa wandered up beside him and clung to his right leg.

'Oh, isn't she adorable! What's your name, honey?'

'This is Melissa,' Gray said, lifting her up. 'I'm Tim. Tim Grayson.'

An awkward silence ensued, until Gray found his manners. 'Won't you come in?'

He stood aside and let the couple walk into the hallway.

'So where'd ya move from, Tim?'

'England,' Gray said. 'We had a little place just outside London.'

'Oh, I love London,' Sue said, her high-pitched voice already beginning to get on Gray's nerves. 'Wasn't it terrible what happened last year? My God! It must have been awful with all those bombs going off. Were you and Melissa affected at all?'

'No,' Gray said, 'we were visiting family abroad when it happened.'

It was a lie he'd been working on for some time, along with the pseudonym. The whole point of leaving Britain was to get away from Tom Gray's past and build a safe future for Melissa. He'd decided against a new forename for his daughter because changing it now would have been too confusing for her.

He didn't like lying to his new neighbours, but it was easier than explaining that he had once been Britain's most notorious criminal, presumed dead for more than a year before returning to the limelight and exposing the UK government's wet-ops team that had tried to kill him and his friends. It wouldn't be easy to get across the fact that, though he'd subsequently killed half a dozen men, he was really an okay guy who simply wanted to make a fresh start in the good old US of A.

The move abroad had taken a lot longer than he'd planned. Nine months longer, to be exact. The bombings Sue mentioned hadn't been confined to London. The entire country had been hit, with blasts reported in every major town and city. More than ten thousand people had lost their lives, and the effect on the economy was still being felt. Gray had hoped for a quick sale on his house once the dust settled, but the bottom had dropped out of the property market weeks after the attackers were rounded up. He'd put his home on the market at below the suggested price in order to get a quick sale, but interest had been minimal. Even dropping it to eighty per cent of its true value hadn't been an instant success, but eventually a property tycoon had come along and snapped up the bargain.

'What do you do for a living, Tim?' Frank asked.

'I'm an engineer,' Gray said, being as vague as possible. 'Can I get you guys a drink? Coffee?'

Frank and Sue followed him through to the kitchen, where he tried to put Melissa down, with little success.

'She's still at that clingy age,' he apologised, trying to prise her arms from around his neck. Eventually he gave up, and Sue jumped in to do the honours. She took a bag of roasted beans from the hamper and had a jug of strong coffee ready minutes later.

'What about you guys?' Gray asked. 'What do you do?'

Frank explained that they were both retired, and their two children had long since grown up and flown the coop. 'We lived in Maryland all our lives, but decided to spend our twilight years somewhere warmer.'

Frank had been in insurance, it turned out, while his wife had been a schoolteacher.

'If Melissa needs any home schooling, or you just want to get away by yourself for a few hours, you know where to find me,' Sue said with a smile.

Gray thanked her for the offer and pressed her about the local schools. Sue took great delight in explaining the American education system, and half an hour later he had the names of three local preschools that would take Melissa when she hit three years of age.

Melissa began to fidget, and Gray explained that he needed to get her down for her nap. Thankfully, his visitors took the hint. They made him promise to pop round whenever he or Melissa needed anything.

Once they were gone, Gray took his daughter up to her room and set her down on the camp bed, covering her with one half of the open sleeping bag, and he sang her a lullaby until her eyes closed and she fell asleep.

Back downstairs, he went through the hamper and found tinned ham, jams and a bottle of red wine, as well as a loaf of bread that was still warm and a bag of sweets that he pegged as Melissa's.

The first hurdle was now out of the way. He'd met his new neighbours, nobody had died, and although Sue's voice grated on him and Frank seemed duller than dishwater, he felt confident that he and his daughter would enjoy their new lives in Florida.

Chapter 8

20 January 2016

Veronica Ellis hurried along the hospital corridor, following the signs that directed her to the major trauma unit. Once she reached the nurse's station she asked for Hamad Farsi and was directed to a private room, where she found two uniformed officers chatting outside the door.

She flashed her ID and asked if anyone else had tried to see the patient.

'No-one except hospital staff, ma'am.'

'Okay, keep it that way.' She opened the door, then turned back to them. 'His parents will be coming down from Oldham today. Write down your phone number and I'll send you their pictures. Apart from them, no-one gets in. Understood?'

Both men nodded, and Ellis entered the room.

Farsi's was the only bed in the room, and other than a side table and one chair, the rest of the space was taken up with medical equipment. A nurse was in the middle of taking his blood pressure and looked up when Ellis entered.

'How's he doing?'

'He's doing well,' the nurse replied. 'It was touch-and-go when he first came in, but we managed to stabilise him.'

Ellis stood by the side of the bed and looked down at Farsi, who looked anything but well. A bandage covered his skull and a plaster cast covered one side of his body from the waist down.

'What happened to him?' Ellis asked. 'I mean, what damage has he sustained?'

Her voice cracked just a little as she gazed upon the unconscious figure on the bed. Tubes emerged from Farsi's arm, and his face looked terribly swollen, as did his chest.

'He broke his pelvis in three places and fractured his skull. There was severe internal bleeding, but the surgeons brought it under control.'

'How long before I can talk to him?' Ellis asked.

'Not for some time, I'm afraid. He's heavily sedated, and further surgery is scheduled for three this afternoon.'

It wasn't what Ellis wanted to hear. When the call first came through that Farsi had been found by a factory worker at five that morning, her first action had been to call Harvey's mobile, but it went straight to voicemail. She'd then ordered the phone's location to be triangulated, but it wasn't showing up on the system. Finally, she'd sent a team in to check out the factory, but they found nothing untoward.

With her section lead missing and his number two lying unconscious in a hospital bed, all she could think of was Bessonov. The Russian mobster had to be behind this, and that meant Harvey was in terrible danger, if not dead already. Bessonov had already shown how he treated MI5 agents, and the pictures taken of the late Jason Willard jumped into her head.

Ellis thanked the nurse and gave her a business card, asking to be informed as soon as Farsi's condition changed. She left the hospital and climbed into her Jaguar, anger causing her to shake as she struggled to fit the key into the ignition.

She pulled out of the car park and into traffic, horns blaring as she cut off two cars in her rush to get back to Thames House.

She made it in record time, and as she walked to her office she told three members of Harvey's team to meet her in the conference room in two minutes.

She reached her desk and pulled up Bessonov's file. After taking a deep breath, she dialled his mobile number.

'*Da.*'

'Alexi Bessonov?'

'Yes.'

'This is Veronica Ellis calling from Thames House. I'm sure you know what we do here.'

'I do indeed, Miss Ellis. What can I do for you today?'

The English was slightly accented and his voice was calm, assured, though that wasn't unexpected. Anyone who'd run an illegal empire for so long was unlikely to be flustered by a phone call from the security services.

'Two of my men were near the Olde Oak furniture factory early this morning. One of them was involved in a hit-and-run, and the other is missing.'

'How unfortunate,' Bessonov said. 'Have you tried contacting the police?'

'Don't play games with me. I know you're involved. I just called to warn you that if the missing operative is harmed in any way, I will come for you personally.'

'I'm afraid I don't know what you're talking about, Miss Ellis, but I assure you I will be passing a recording of this conversation to your superiors.'

The phone went dead in her hands, and she sat back in her chair, cursing herself for being so hotheaded. It had been a desperate attempt to ensure no harm came to Harvey, but it looked to have backfired big time. If Bessonov carried through with his threat, she would be warned off him, giving the criminal carte blanche to carry out his plan, whatever it might be.

She rose and walked quickly into the conference room, where her team were already gathered, their laptops open and ready to take notes. If she acted quickly, she could still get her message across to Bessonov before her hands were tied.

'How is Hamad?' Elaine Solomon asked. With Harvey missing, she was the most experienced remaining operative on the team, and Ellis had given her temporary section lead until Harvey was safe and well.

'He'll live, thank God, but he'll be out of action for a while. Our focus now is on finding Andrew. How did you get on with the CCTV cameras?'

'Nothing from Olde Oak, but the neighbouring unit recorded two SUVs leaving the scene, including the moment they took out Hamad. He got off five shots before the lead car swerved to hit him. I watched it twice and can't believe he's still with us.'

'Can you ID the vehicles?'

'Too dark and grainy,' Solomon said. 'I've asked Gerald to work his magic on it, but he isn't hopeful. It's an old system re-recording on VHS tapes.'

'I'm in sore need of an update,' said Eddie Howes, adjusting his glasses as he took a sip of his energy drink. 'Can we start with who's behind this?'

'Alexi Bessonov,' Ellis said, as she moved to the head of the mahogany conference table.

'Do we have enough evidence to bring him in?' Gareth Bailey asked. He'd been with the team less than two months, and the training manual was still fresh in his mind.

'What we have is circumstantial,' Ellis said, before giving the team a condensed version of events over the last forty-eight hours. They'd all heard about the discovery of Willard's body, but not the surveillance mission carried out at the restaurant the day before.

'It sounds like we have enough for a search warrant,' Bailey persisted.

'Perhaps,' Ellis agreed, 'but his team clearly left the building. You saw the video. It seems highly unlikely that he'll have left any incriminating evidence or personnel behind.'

'What about elsewhere?' asked Bailey.

'Indeed,' said Ellis, 'but where do we begin? Bessonov owns or controls over seventy businesses in London alone. Would he choose to leave useful evidence at any of them? And if he has Andrew, do you really think he'll keep him at a location that's clearly under his ownership?'

'We could search them all,' Howes suggested.

'Nice idea, but I have the feeling time isn't on our side.'

'I assume we have access to his phone records,' Solomon said.

'We do,' Ellis confirmed, 'but he uses it purely for his legitimate businesses. We've been listening in for over two years and haven't heard anything incriminating.'

'We could dig up the floor plans for each of his businesses and see which of them has a basement,' Bailey suggested. 'If you're going to hold someone prisoner and interrogate them, underground would be the logical choice.'

Ellis thought he watched too much television, but it was at least a start. 'Okay, you run with that. Elaine, get me a list of all Russian and Tagrilistani nationals who have entered the country in the last thirty days and cross-reference them through HMRC against Bessonov and his companies, particularly Olde Oak Furniture Limited. Use that same list to find matches in the Interpol database. Eddie, follow the CCTV trail. They must have been picked up by other cameras in the area, so find out where they went. Bessonov will want to distance himself from Andrew if he has something big coming up, so his out-of-town team are the ones we'll concentrate on.'

Ellis sent them on their way, and once she was alone, she sat and closed her eyes, saying a silent prayer for her fallen colleagues.

Alexi Bessonov ended the call and checked the Total Call Recorder app to make sure it had captured the conversation. Satisfied, he dialled Grigory Polushin's number and told the diplomat that they had to meet, urgently. As usual, Polushin didn't ask why. He simply said he'd come to the restaurant within the hour and hung up.

Bessonov opened a new browser on his phone and typed the name Veronica Ellis into the search engine. The results confirmed her position within MI5, and he wondered how the security services could have possibly known about his men at the factory. His people knew better than to open their mouths; the recent death of Nikki Sereyev had been a timely reminder to all that betraying Alexi Bessonov came at a high price.

He thought long and hard about whom he'd spoken to regarding the Spetsnaz team, but all he could recall was the conversation with Polushin the previous day, and the senior counsellor was unlikely to be talking to the enemy.

He knew the restaurant couldn't have been bugged, but he couldn't help thinking back to the previous day, when a drunk had sat in his seat. Bessonov stood from the table, then got down on his knees and looked under it once more, seeing nothing apart from the manufacturer's sticker. He tried peeling it off, but it was stuck too firmly. After a few attempts, he gave up. Nothing that thin could be a transmitter, but to be on the safe side, he told the restaurant manager to arrange for the entire booth to be replaced.

'I want new seats, table, flooring. In fact, everything in this area. Understood?'

The manager nodded.

'Good. And make sure you use *our* people. No outsiders.'

Another nod, and the manager got on the phone to make arrangements, just as Polushin walked through the door and made his way to the booth. Bessonov signalled for a bottle of vodka, even though this would be a fleeting visit. He put a finger to his lips, bidding Polushin to remain silent, then poured two shots.

'It looks a nice day for a drive,' Bessonov said. 'Come, let's see a little of the city.'

Polushin downed the clear liquid and followed him out of the restaurant, telling his driver to remain where he was. Outside, he saw Bessonov's armour-plated Lincoln Navigator, the engine idling. They climbed in the back seat, and Bessonov's driver pulled into traffic.

'This is all very cloak-and-dagger,' Polushin said. 'I trust nothing is wrong.'

'Merely precautions,' Bessonov said. 'I'd like you to listen to this.'

He played the brief conversation he'd had with the head of MI5.

'Who is this missing operative she refers to?' Polushin asked.

'I don't know his name yet, but I'm working on it.'

'So you do have him?'

'My team does,' Bessonov said. 'He was snooping around the factory where they were staying and they spotted him on CCTV. They knew the hideout was compromised, so they seized him and left. They called our intermediary and explained the situation and I told them to take him to a farm in Oxfordshire. They're awaiting further instructions.'

Polushin was clearly unhappy with the developments. 'How does this affect the plan? If you were to fail in your mission . . .'

So it's now my *mission*, Bessonov thought. *The first sign of trouble, and Moscow's already covering their arses.*

'It makes no difference at all,' he assured Polushin. 'In fact, it is a blessing in disguise. The team have already scoped out Milenko's route and think it will be hard to get close to him, but a single sniper might be able to pull it off. It'll take a specialist, though.'

Polushin raised his eyebrows in enquiry.

'I have someone special in mind.' Bessonov wrote a name and contact number on a piece of paper and handed it to Polushin. 'I want you to pay for this man's services.'

Polushin nodded and pocketed the sheet. 'That still leaves this Ellis woman crawling all over you.'

'It does indeed,' Bessonov said, 'but I have a plan that will take the heat off me and cause severe embarrassment to the British government. I'm going to need your help.'

'What do you need?'

'Some medical equipment and access to the diplomatic bag.'

Chapter 9

20 January 2016

When the bag was finally pulled from his head, Andrew Harvey blinked as sunlight assaulted his retinas.

He reckoned the journey had lasted two hours, not counting the stop they'd made to move him from the back seat to the trunk of the vehicle. After arriving at their destination, he'd been dragged from the trunk and forced to walk over slick ground to a building. The smells reminded him of a school trip many years earlier, but apart from identifying the location as a farm, he had no idea where it might be. Two hours by car from the factory meant he could be anywhere from Yeovil to Northampton, or even Norfolk.

On entering the building, he'd instantly known he was in a kitchen, the familiar smell of fried bacon reminding him that it had been almost half a day since he'd last eaten. It soon became apparent that they hadn't invited him here for breakfast. Two muscular arms forced him into a chair and bound his arms behind him. His legs were also tied to the chair, and the waiting had begun.

In the hours that had passed before the bag was removed, Harvey had spent most of that time thinking of three people. Hamad had been a good friend for more than five years, and they'd been through more than a few scrapes together. Most of them had involved Tom Gray, a man he wished could be with him right now. Gray was a loose cannon at times, but he was the one man you'd want around when the shit started flying. It hurt to think he'd never see Hamad again. Or Gray, for that matter.

More prominent in his thoughts, though, was Sarah.

After living alone for much of his adult life, he'd finally found someone he cared enough about to say goodbye to bachelorhood and settle down in a proper relationship. He'd had flings over the years, and one woman had managed to stick to him for a few months before his unsociable work hours had driven them apart, but none of them was like Sarah. The stunning body was one thing but more importantly, she was his intellectual equal. They shared the same tastes in music and television shows – not that they'd spent much time listening or watching. As a single man, he'd cooked for himself on his days off, but most evenings he'd settled for sandwiches, takeaways or microwave meals. In the past year, his passion for cuisine had been reignited as he fought Sarah for title of best cook in the household. On most weekends they'd entertain guests, usually Hamad or Sarah's friends, but he looked forward to the time in which they relaxed together with a bottle of red wine, laughing at the way MI5 was portrayed in TV dramas.

Now, as his eyes adjusted to the bright morning light, one of his captors turned his chair around so that Harvey faced a wooden table. Opposite him sat a man with a thin face dominated by a bulbous nose, his head sporting a crew cut. A slight scar ran from the side of his right eye to his upper lip; Harvey couldn't see an ounce of fat on him. Five more men sat around the room, all dressed in jeans and short-sleeved T-shirts. Each of them had the same haircut, confirming his assumption that they were a military unit.

While memories of Sarah had seen him through the previous hours, Harvey now felt something he hadn't experienced in a long time.

Fear.

Was this where they'd brought Willard for his final few hours? *Probably not*, Harvey thought, *given the man's final resting place.*

'Name,' Scarface said, sounding bored. He sliced a piece of cured sausage and popped it into his mouth.

'Andrew Harvey.' There was nothing to lose giving them that information, but he knew the questions would soon get tougher.

'Who you work for, Andrew Harvey?'

'No-one.'

'Then what you do at factory?'

'I was going to rob the place,' Harvey said.

'Rob?'

'Break in. Steal things.'

Scarface looked at one of his men and nodded. A fist came from nowhere and caught Harvey high on the right cheekbone. His head snapped sideways, and he let it stay there for a moment before gingerly shaking it to check for damage. He'd never been hit so hard in his life, and he was surprised that nothing felt broken.

'With these?' Scarface said, holding up the night-vision glasses and government-issue communication unit. 'Try again.'

Harvey eyed the man to his right, who was cracking almonds with a pair of pliers. A grin appeared on the man's face as he tossed a nut into his mouth, and he held up the tool so that Harvey could get a good look at it.

The message was loud and clear, a taste of what he could look forward to in the coming hours, perhaps even days. The interrogation training he'd been through many years ago had been rudimentary at best, and hadn't prepared him in any way for what he was facing. The idea had been to hold out, as long as possible until help came. But despite having a high pain threshold, he knew that he wouldn't last long.

The anticipation of the torture is usually worse than the actual pain, his instructor had said. Judging by the stern looks on the faces of his captors, Harvey seriously doubted that.

The way he saw it, he had two options. The first was to tell them which organisation he worked for. If he could convince them that their journey had been tracked all the way, they might decide to move on, and the longer he could keep them on the road the greater the chance of his colleagues locating him through the country's mass surveillance network.

The downside was that he had no idea what information they wanted from him. If he revealed the nature of his job, they might decide to kill him immediately, or torture him until they knew everything MI5 did about their mission.

Option two was to tell them nothing in the hope that Ellis had actually managed to follow the trail. The question was, how long could he hold out for? Minutes? Hours? Days?

They would eventually get the information out of him, but would the delay in talking give Ellis enough time to follow the trail?

He doubted it. If she hadn't managed to find him leaving the business park on CCTV by now, she never would.

'I work for the government,' he said at last.

The decision to talk was ultimately an easy one. It wasn't as if he was protecting anyone. No-one would die if he gave them what they wanted, and a swift end was far preferable to endless hours of agony. Ellis would assign others to the case, and Bessonov would be stopped before he could carry out his plan. Telling them what he knew might even make them reconsider and cancel their operation. A win-win for everyone.

Apart from himself.

Scarface sliced another chunk off the sausage and stabbed it with his knife. 'What government? MI5? MI6?'

'Five,' Harvey said, 'and we know exactly what you're up to. We know you plan to kill Viktor Milenko during his visit. My boss needed proof, and when you killed my friend and kidnapped me, you gave it to her. Security will be screwed down so tight, you won't be able to get within a mile of him.'

Scarface grinned, genuine amusement in his eyes. 'Vasily, show him your new toy.'

One of the men went into another room and returned with a black leather case. He opened it and within seconds had assembled the component parts into an impressive-looking weapon.

'Accuracy International AS50,' Scarface said. 'Designed and built for US Special Operations Command. In two seconds it fires five .50-calibre rounds at a range of two thousand yards. Already this month we have had your prime minister in the sights twice. We could have killed him any time we like.'

The revelation confirmed Harvey's fear that he wouldn't be walking away from this situation with his life intact. Not only had they revealed their faces but they'd also shown him their weapon of choice.

'My people will come looking for me,' he said. 'They'll find me eventually.'

'*Da*, in small pieces!' Scarface laughed, and a couple of the others joined in.

Vasily spoke in Russian, and Scarface translated.

'He says your head would make a good target to check his weapon . . . How you say? Zero the sights.'

While he was relieved at the thought of a quick death, the prospect of being taken out by one of the thumb-sized rounds wasn't something he was looking forward to. The overall length, including the casing, was just short of six inches, and the bullet itself had a diameter of thirteen millimetres. He'd seen footage of the devastation caused by these weapons; a headshot meant that his would not be an open-casket funeral.

Scarface replied to Vasily, then turned to Harvey.

'First we eat, then target practice.'

'Anything from CCTV?' Ellis asked as she appeared next to Eddie Howes.

'We managed to get the licence plates from a street camera. We've tracked them west, but they entered an area that has no coverage. We're going through every possible road out of the area, but no luck so far.'

'Did you send out the alert to all forces?'

'Two hours ago. No sightings yet.'

'Keep on it,' Ellis said, and moved on to Elaine Solomon's desk. On the monitor Ellis saw a couple of names under a progress bar that showed the search was only twenty-four per cent complete.

'Who are these two guys?' she asked.

'They work for one of Bessonov's companies,' Solomon said, 'but they aren't the people we're looking for. One of them works in a butcher's, the other for a car wash. Both have just returned from holidays in Russia, and neither fits the profile.'

Watching the screen wasn't going to make the search run any faster, so Ellis headed for her office. She had only gone a few steps when Sarah Thompson burst into the room, making a beeline for her.

'When were you going to tell me about Andrew?' she fumed.

All heads quickly turned her way, and Ellis took Thompson by the arm, leading her into her glass office and closing the door.

'I tried calling you a couple of times,' Ellis said, 'and since then I've been preoccupied with trying to find him and making sure we get him back safe.'

Thompson stood with her hands on her hips, then her stance melted. 'I was in meetings all day,' she eventually said. 'I wasn't surprised when he didn't come home this morning, but it wasn't good to hear about it in the canteen over at Six. What progress have you made so far?'

'Nothing yet,' Ellis admitted, 'but we're working up many angles. We know the people who took him are driving black SUVs, and we're trying to trace them through CCTV. I have others working to identify the suspects through travel records, and a forensics team is at the factory gathering evidence. There's not a lot more we can do at the moment.'

Thompson was about to question Ellis's statement when there was a knock on the door.

'We picked them up leaving the M25 at junction sixteen,' Solomon said. 'Eddie tracked them along the M40 to junction eight, where they took the exit towards Oxford. We've alerted the local police force and they have three armed response units on standby.'

Ellis was first out of the office, and Thompson followed her to Howes's desk. On the screen they could see stills of the two vehicles taking an exit at a roundabout. The next shot saw them turn left onto a minor road.

'Where are they heading?'

Howes brought up a map of the area and pinned it to the top-right corner of the screen. 'There's not much around there. A couple of villages, a few farms.'

'Sounds like the ideal place to hide someone,' Ellis said. 'Where did they go next?'

Howes clicked the map and brought up the next camera, which showed the main road in a small village. He synchronised the times, then flicked forward until the vehicles once again came into view. After marking their last known location, he searched for the next area to have CCTV coverage, but it wasn't good news.

'That's all we have in the area,' he said, and then expanded the map to show where coverage would be picked up again. 'All I can do from here is check each of these twelve cameras to see whether our guys drive past. If they do, we're back on their tail. If not—' He drew an imaginary circle around a vast expanse of land. 'They're in here somewhere.'

'Get checking,' Ellis said. 'Elaine, contact the local police and give them the coordinates of the area. I want a containment around it as soon as possible. No-one leaves the area.'

'You think they're still in there?' Thompson asked.

'If they were heading somewhere else, they wouldn't have used these back roads.'

Thompson nodded. 'Then I'm going in.'

Andrew Harvey watched his captors dining on home-made soup and had to admit that it smelled delicious. He was tempted to ask for some, if only to delay the inevitable, but had the feeling they weren't in a sharing mood.

Scarface dunked a piece of bread into his bowl and stuffed it into his mouth. 'You not scared? You think your friends will save you in "nick of time"?' he asked Harvey, making air quotes.

It was indeed something Harvey had been thinking about for the last thirty minutes.

'If I was back at the office, I'd have you surrounded by now. There are over eight thousand CCTV cameras covering Britain's roads, taking over twenty-five million pictures a day, so our journey here will have been recorded. They'll have helicopters up soon, and the entire area will be cordoned off. It's over.'

Scarface looked thoughtful. 'You think they track our vehicles?'

Harvey nodded. 'Don't be surprised if you get a knock on the door any minute now.'

A smile appeared on the scarred face. 'Then it was good idea to send cars to Scotland, no? Your people will be looking in wrong place, Andrew Harvey. When they find out drivers live here, we are already gone. Vanish.'

For the first time, Harvey thought about the owners of the farm. They'd driven the Russians' cars north? Why would English farmers be in league with Russian criminals? His puzzlement must have shown.

Scarface laughed. 'You think I am so stupid? You think this is my first mission in the field? No, we go soon, after Vasily practises on you.'

The conversation was interrupted by a phone, and Vasily answered it. He listened for a moment, then gave the handset to Scarface. The conversation that followed was brief, and Scarface tossed the phone on the table.

'Change of plan,' Scarface said to Harvey, then spoke to the others in the room in Russian. Three of them disappeared and returned five minutes later with their bags, accompanied by three others who looked like they'd just woken up.

Harvey assumed they'd be moving out immediately, but after gathering their belongings, the men simply sat around. Vasily dismantled his rifle and put it back in its case, while the newcomers helped themselves to the remainder of the soup.

It gave Harvey a modicum of hope. The longer they waited, the better the chances of Ellis containing the area and sending in a rescue team. The silence dragged on for minutes, until a shout came from one of the men near the kitchen window.

Scarface jumped up to take a look, then went to the door and opened it. Through the gap, Harvey could see two vehicles approaching – an estate car and a minibus. When they parked, two men climbed out of each vehicle and walked towards the building.

Scarface had an automatic in his right hand, hidden behind his back. He challenged the four men, but when they responded he waved them inside. Three of the visitors were young, no more than teenagers, while the other looked to be in his fifties and wore a suit under his heavy overcoat. He was carrying a leather bag that looked to be of the kind doctors used when they travelled.

'I'm going to prepare you for your journey,' the older man told Harvey, setting his bag on the table. Unlike the others, this man was English. He reached inside the bag and produced a hypodermic needle, which he filled with a clear liquid from a small bottle. He barked some instructions, and Harvey watched four men head out to the car and open the trunk. They pulled out a large, rectangular box, about seven feet in length. One climbed into the back of the car and retrieved a green case. The items were brought inside and laid out on the floor.

'What journey?' Harvey asked, his voice cracking ever so slightly. 'Where are we going?'

A bead of sweat appeared on his brow and lazily meandered down between his eyes, which were focused on the needle in front of him.

One of the men opened the box, and Harvey could see it was empty. As he looked at the box, the man with the needle slipped around behind him. He felt a sharp prick in his neck, followed by pain as a bolus entered his bloodstream. *A bolus of what, exactly?* he wondered. He turned to the English doctor to ask, but his tongue refused to obey his mental commands. His vision started to blur and he shook his head in an effort to counteract the drug, to little effect.

The last thing he saw was the doctor opening the green case and removing a tank of oxygen with a facemask attached, before his eyes finally gave up the fight.

Chapter 10

20 January 2016

The needle on Sarah Thompson's speedometer crept past ninety as she barrelled along the M40, her windscreen wipers working furiously to counter the spray thrown up from the vehicles in front of her.

She eased over to the inside lane as she saw the first markers for junction eight, then pulled off at the exit and killed her speed. At the roundabout she took the same route the SUVs had, her eyes peeled for roadblocks.

She found none.

Thompson's phone was synched by Bluetooth to the car's computer. She hit the Call button on the steering wheel and told the on-board system to dial Ellis's number.

'Where the hell are the local police?' she asked when the call connected. 'I'm seeing cars everywhere driving out of the area!'

'They're moving as many people into position as they can,' Ellis replied. 'They're also dealing with a pile-up at junction twelve, and that's drained their resources.'

'Then ask the Met for some men,' Thompson said. 'We're going to lose him!'

'They've already got four teams on the way,' Ellis assured her. 'ETA six minutes.'

'What about the chopper?'

'No point sending it up until containment is in place,' Ellis said. 'We've got nationwide surveillance systems looking for them, so even if they manage to leave Oxfordshire, they won't get far.'

Thompson hit the button to end the call. Her satnav was programmed with the location of the farm nearest to the motorway, and she followed the directions. Trees were a blur as she sped down the narrow country road, and she reduced her speed to fifty as she approached a little village. She was through it in seconds and, back on the empty roads, she pushed the needle past seventy.

'Turn left,' the electronic voice told her, and Thompson slammed on the brakes as the turning appeared in front of her. She spun the wheel and took to the dirt road, which rose ahead of her and disappeared over a rise.

She brought the car to a stop and climbed out. If Harvey were being held here by an unknown number of armed men, blazing into view would do neither of them any good. She locked the vehicle and drew her Glock. Satisfied that it had a round in the chamber, she placed it into her shoulder holster, then hugged the bushes as she crept up the hill.

At the top, she could see a long building made from corrugated iron, and to the right of it a detached house. A man came into view, wearing a heavy jacket and waterproof leggings, and she watched him wheel a barrow towards a huge pile of manure and empty the contents at the base. She saw him go back the way he'd come, and waited to see if anyone else showed their face.

Minutes passed, and the only person she observed was the one assigned the job of mucking out the horses as he made another journey to the dung pile.

It looked like business as usual, but Thompson wanted to be sure. She opened her phone and found the settings for the ringtone, then put it back in her pocket and crept back to the car. She drove over the rise and into the courtyard, just as a woman appeared from the house, wearing wellington boots, jodhpurs and a windcheater.

'Can I help you?' she asked.

Thompson removed her wallet from her pocket and flipped it open.

'Sarah Thomas, DEFRA,' Thompson said, showing an identity card bearing the Department for Environment, Food & Rural Affairs logo. It was a legend she'd created before leaving Thames House, one that would allow her to inspect any farm without rousing suspicion.

'I'm Jennie,' the lady said, looking concerned. 'We had an inspection two weeks ago. Was something wrong?'

'Not that I'm aware of,' Thompson told her. 'This is an unrelated matter. Do you mind if I have a look around?'

'Sure, but I'd appreciate it if you could tell me what this is about.'

'We have a case of foot-and-mouth disease less than thirty miles from here,' Thompson said. 'At the moment, we believe it's an isolated incident, but just in case it spreads, we're checking all nearby farms to make sure you have procedures in place to combat it.'

The woman's face was a mask of horror. 'Please tell me you're joking!'

'I wish I was,' Thompson said, 'but so far we have four infected cows and we're conducting further tests on the other livestock on the farm.'

A shell-shocked Jennie agreed to show Thompson around the farm, and explained her concerns. 'Back in 2007, my husband and I had a farm near Pirbright. We lost three hundred head of cattle due to that testing facility's damn negligence.'

Thompson nodded mechanically as she led Jennie to a Land Rover and inspected the wheels.

'How many vehicles do you have here at the moment?'

'Just this and my estate,' Jennie said.

Thompson had been looking for side roads and fresh tracks during their brief walk, but she'd seen nothing to suggest that Jennie was being anything other than honest.

She mentally crossed this farm off her list as she put her hand into her pocket and hit the button to test her ringtone.

'Excuse me,' she said, and held the chiming phone to her ear. She pretended to listen for a moment, then turned to Jennie.

'Sorry, but I've just been told about another possible infection. I'm going to have to cut and run.'

She walked quickly back to her car and sped off. The first farm had been a bust; six more remained in the area.

Andrew was in one of them, she was sure, and time was running out.

The Spetsnaz veteran with the scarred face picked up the chirping mobile and pressed the green button.

'*Da.*'

'What's your situation?' Bessonov asked.

'He's packed up and ready to go. We'll be at the airport in a couple of hours.'

'Just send the doctor,' Bessonov said. 'Tell him Polushin will meet him at the freight terminal.'

'What about the rest of us?'

'The news is reporting roadblocks in your area. There's no confirmation of what they're looking for, but we have to assume it's you. They have no reason to detain an English doctor, but ten Russians are a different matter.'

'We have that covered,' the soldier said. 'We sent the vehicles north on the motorway. Once they're spotted on camera, the police will send everyone to intercept them.'

He'd instructed two farmhands to get as far from the area as they could and, if spotted by the police, to flee for as long as possible.

'Good. I'll send someone to monitor the area. As soon as the police leave, get to the airport. We have a charter plane waiting to go.'

The soldier ended the call and told his men to load the crate into the back of the doctor's estate car. It took four of them to lift it, the MI5 agent's body making for a heavy load.

'Now what?' Vasily asked.

The leader gave the doctor his instructions and watched him climb into the vehicle and drive off.

'Now we wait,' he said.

Sarah Thompson negotiated another tight curve on the narrow country lane and stamped on the brake as she saw a green estate coming the other way. Both cars had to ease onto the grass to crawl past each other, then she hit the accelerator, following the directions for the third farm on the list.

When the satnav's electronic voice told her she'd reached her destination, Thompson pulled over and climbed out. Over a hedge, she could see an array of buildings and several head of cattle grazing in a nearby field, oblivious to the spitting rain. A two-storey house sat off to one side, and in front of it sat a minibus.

She immediately got the feeling something wasn't right. It wasn't the kind of vehicle she'd expect to see on a farm, and adrenalin started coursing through her veins as she realised she might have the right place.

Her first thought was to call for backup, but she hesitated. That would mean pulling one of the police cars off a roadblock, and if she were wrong, she'd be offering Andrew's abductors a way out of the area. She couldn't wait for a team to arrive from Thames House, either. There was no telling what they'd do to Andrew when they realised they were surrounded.

But what could one agent accomplish alone? Torn, she decided to take a closer look and get proof before making the call for backup.

She prepped her phone once more, then climbed back into the car and took the turning onto yet another dirt road. As she approached the main residence, she saw curtains twitch in the window, and when she pulled up a large man opened the front door of the house and made straight for her car.

Dan Fletcher stared into the teacup he was grasping tightly and wondered exactly how long the thugs were going to hang around.

It had been two years since he'd accepted the deal brokered by his brother-in-law from the City, and since then he'd made his payments on time, every month without fail. The twenty grand had been enough to satisfy his creditors and stop them declaring him bankrupt, which meant he got to keep his farm and had enough to tide him over during what had been a lean period.

The man he'd met seemed decent enough, and his English was very good. Fletcher hadn't cared that he was Russian, and he hadn't felt the need to do a background check on his benefactor. Had he done so, he would have steered well clear of him.

At first, the deal had seemed superb. He got the cash as well as a contract to provide milk for several of Bessonov's businesses. The price paid was better than the supermarkets were offering, and for the first time in years his business was showing a healthy profit.

Everything was rosy.

Until the phone call.

Why he had to provide temporary accommodation for ten men, he didn't know, but he guessed they weren't on holiday. He'd told Bessonov that there simply wasn't room to house them all, and that was when he'd learned the truth about his benefactor: if he didn't want to see his farm burn to the ground, he'd house the men.

The phone on the side table caught his eye yet again. He was tempted to call the police, but what could he say? *I accepted a business partner's request to let ten men into my home.* He hadn't seen anything on the news about a band of marauding Russians terrorising the country, but as soon as they showed up at the house he knew they weren't boy scouts. Still, what was he to do? Test Bessonov's threat?

The leader had treated him like a servant from the moment they met, ordering him to make tea for everyone and then get out of their way. His scarred face was terrifying enough, but when he'd produced an automatic weapon to emphasise his point, Fletcher decided it was a role he would happily play, if only temporarily.

They'd been in the kitchen for hours now, allowing him in only to refill his cup and make them something to eat, and their presence would have been fine if they'd let him carry on as normal. His cattle needed to be milked, but the scarred one had pulled his sons off that duty and sent them up to Scotland in the Russians' SUVs. His guest had made it clear that the police would be looking for the vehicles, but they were to lead them on a merry chase as long as they could. Otherwise: '*If police come and I still here*, boom, *father dead.*'

With Scarface's threat ringing in their ears, the boys had hugged their father and set off, the younger one with tears in his eyes. That had been hours earlier, and Fletcher was still trying to think of a way to explain his part in it without mentioning

Bessonov's name. *Well, officer, these ten men just turned up, asked my sons to go on a two-hundred-mile joy ride and I thought nothing of it.* He knew it wouldn't fly, but if he revealed the truth, he could kiss his livelihood goodbye.

He almost dropped the cup when the scarred man poked his head inside the room and barked a single word.

'Come.'

Fletcher got to his feet and followed the man into the kitchen. 'What is it?'

'You expect visitors?' He led Fletcher to the window and pulled back the corner of the curtain to reveal a Ford easing up the approach road.

'No,' Fletcher assured him.

'Get rid of them.'

Fletcher was pushed towards the door, and as he looked back, he saw the man pull the slide back on his automatic.

'You tell them we here, you get first bullet.'

Fletcher swallowed, despite his mouth being dry as a bone. He took a deep breath, then opened the door and marched out to meet the car. He could see just one person in the vehicle, a rather striking woman with long blonde hair and green eyes set above high cheekbones and a sumptuous mouth. On any other occasion he would have greeted her with a welcoming smile and invited her inside, but he knew the importance of getting her off the property as soon as possible.

'Yes?' he said brusquely as the woman began to get out of the car.

'Sarah Thomas, DEFRA.'

Fletcher glanced at the woman's identity card and felt his heart miss a couple of beats, then race double-time to catch up. Plan A had been to simply tell her to piss off, but that was no longer an option. Instead, he tried his best to smile.

'What can I do for you?'

Thomas told him about a case of foot-and-mouth disease in the county and asked if she could look around.

'Sure,' Fletcher said, and gestured towards the milking shed. He hoped to get her as far from the house as possible, but the woman wasn't in the mood to comply. She stood her ground and looked at the minibus.

'That yours?' she asked.

'My son's,' Fletcher said. 'He plays for the local football team, and he brings his mates here to train. They do a lot of cross-country work.'

Now looking towards the house, the woman asked a question that almost made his heart stop.

'Do you mind if I use your toilet?' Thompson asked.

She was desperate to get inside the house, to have a look around. There was something about the farmer that didn't smell right, and it wasn't the cow shit on the bottom of the man's wellingtons. When she factored in the fresh tracks leading up to the building, the minibus and the twitching curtains – which were drawn in the middle of the day – she was certain she had the right place.

'I'm afraid it's backed up,' the farmer said.

Was it coincidence, or did he just want to prevent her from looking around inside?

Thompson had seen enough. She was convinced she had the right place, and decided the time was right to call in backup. She made a note of the minibus's licence plate, then put her hand in her pocket to activate the phone, looking to make an excuse to back away from the area and let the armed response units do their job. But the phone rang before she had the chance, startling her.

She glanced at Fletcher, who was watching her carefully, then dug the phone out and saw Ellis's name on the screen.

'Please tell me the roadblocks are in place,' she said quietly as she walked away from the farmer.

'I've pulled them back,' Ellis told her. 'The SUVs were spotted just north of Wigan on the M6.'

'When?'

'An hour ago.'

'An hour! And we're just hearing about it now?'

'Greater Manchester Police chose to get their assets in place first. They only contacted us as an afterthought, and a junior analyst who wasn't aware of the significance took the call. I've ordered the chief constable to contact me directly from now on.'

An hour meant at least another seventy miles, so they would be approaching the Lake District by now. 'Keep me updated,' Thompson said as she climbed back into her car, the farmer already forgotten. 'I'm on my way.'

Scarface watched the exchange through the tiniest gap in the curtains, his index finger on the trigger guard of the automatic in his hand. The woman seemed to be paying too keen an interest in the house, but he was prepared to deal with her if she made a move towards the door.

He watched the woman take a phone call and climb back into her car and, once she'd disappeared from view, he opened the door and let the farmer back in.

'Who was it?' he asked

'DEFRA. They do inspections now and again.'

'That was quick inspection.'

The farmer shrugged. 'She got a call and buggered off.'

Scarface peeked through the window once more and, satisfied that the woman was gone for good, ordered the nervous farmer to go back and sit in the living room.

What followed was a tense hour as he waited for Bessonov to call with news of the roadblock. His men were ready to go, but until they knew the roads were clear, they had little choice but to sit it out.

When the call finally came, he ordered his men into the minibus and called the farmer through to the kitchen.

'Hide this well,' he said, pointing to the case containing Vasily's sniper rifle. 'Someone will collect it soon.'

The soldier joined the others on the bus and they set off for Heathrow. Once they cleared the area, he would gather the rest of the small arms, put them in plastic bags and dump them in a bin at a service station.

He felt a little sad that he hadn't had the opportunity to take part in the assassination, one that would have enabled his team to command a higher price on their next outing. But that was the way things went sometimes.

Two hours and some heavy traffic later, the minibus pulled into the long-stay car park and he led his men to the departure area. He found the Concord Air charter counter, where they picked up their tickets and made it through security without any issues.

Within the hour, his team and he were wheels up and on course for Moscow, where they would wait for the next contract to come along.

Chapter 11

20 January 2016

Dan Fletcher sat at the table next to the kitchen window, the open curtains giving him a view down the approach road. The sun had set just before 4.30 p.m., and he'd been staring into the darkness ever since.

He sipped a cup of tea that had grown tepid as he waited nervously. He expected the police to turn up at any time, and he went over his story once more, just to make sure the answers sounded credible in his own mind.

A set of headlights finally pierced the darkness, followed by two more sets, and Fletcher got to his feet and headed to the door. He opened it and squinted as the glare assaulted his senses.

'They're gone!' he shouted, raising his hands as high as he could. Armed police piled out of the first two vehicles, and Fletcher could see the outline of a woman approaching, her silhouette striding confidently, almost menacingly, towards him.

When the policemen ordered him to the ground, Fletcher eased himself onto his stomach and stretched out his arms. Two men patted him down and pulled him away from the door as four others crept into the house, their MP5s up and ready.

Fletcher was taken to a police car and told to sit in the back seat, his legs hanging out the side.

'Where are they?'

He looked up at the figure leaning over him. It was the woman who'd been at the farm earlier in the day.

'You're not really DEFRA, are you?'

'Where are they?' she repeated.

'I told you, they're gone.'

'When?'

'About two hours ago,' Fletcher told her. 'They tied me up and left. I eventually managed to free myself and call the police.'

The woman eyed him suspiciously. 'Why didn't you tell me about this when I was here earlier?'

'They threatened to kill me. You too. If you'd gone inside the house, we'd both be dead now.'

The armed officers emerged from the house and declared it safe. The woman turned and called over the scene commander and told him to get a forensics team in as soon as possible. She then pulled out her phone and brought an image up on the screen.

'Did you see this man among them?'

Fletcher studied the photo of a man in his forties, smiling as he posed on a beach somewhere. He shrugged. 'They had someone with them, but he had a bag over his head. I never got to see his face.'

The woman gazed off into the distance, as if searching for someone. Then she turned back to Fletcher. 'Tell me everything,' she said. 'From the moment they arrived.'

Fletcher went over his concocted story, telling her that they'd arrived early and surprised him as he answered the door. He and his boys had been having breakfast when the Russians arrived and forced them all into the living room, where he was tied up and the boys ordered north. From that point on he'd been left alone, apart from the time he'd been freed to get her off the property. The rest of the time had been spent in isolation, and after they'd left, it had taken a couple of hours to free himself and make the phone call.

He hoped the woman swallowed the story, and that his nervousness would be put down to his recent ordeal.

'I'm afraid you can't stay here tonight,' she said. 'Forensics will need to go over the place thoroughly. Is there someone you could stay with?'

Fletcher assured her he could stay at a neighbouring farm, but his main concern was for his sons. 'What about my boys? Did you find them?'

'They were stopped just south of Carlisle. They didn't do themselves any favours by failing to stop for the police.'

Fletcher told her about the scarred man's threat – that his boys were only fleeing to protect their father. The woman seemed to accept it but got an officer to come over and take his full account of the episode.

As she walked away, Fletcher had a feeling the man she was looking for was someone special to her, someone very close. Deep down he wanted to tell her that yes, he'd seen the man tied to a chair, and that he'd been taken away a couple of hours before the Russians left. If he did, though, his whole story would unravel, and as much as he wanted her to have her man back, he couldn't bear the thought of losing his sons.

Sarah Thompson walked back to her car and called Ellis with an update.

'It looks like they were here, but we missed them by a couple of hours. There was a white minibus parked here earlier. That's probably how they left.'

She gave Ellis the licence plate of the vehicle and told her to alert all forces to keep an eye out for it.

'Solomon got some hits on the inbound flights,' Ellis said. 'We've got six matches on the Interpol database. I'm sending the images to you now.'

Thompson waited for the pictures to arrive, then went back over to the police car and showed them to the farmer. 'Recognise any of them?'

Fletcher slowly scrolled through the mugshots, his head bobbing nervously. 'This is their leader,' he said, showing her the scarred face of Anatoly Potemkin. 'I didn't really get a good look at the others.'

That was enough for Thompson.

'Give the officer your contact details. I may need to speak to you again.'

She left Fletcher and climbed into her car, calling Ellis to confirm that they were on the right track. 'Put the names on the no-fly list as soon as you can, and notify all seaports and private airfields. These guys don't leave the country.'

She fired up the engine and sped off down the driveway, throwing up a shower of gravel as she took the turn onto the main road. For the first time, they had positive identification of the enemy, and she wanted to be back at Thames House when the sightings came in.

Traffic was light by the time she hit the M40, and she ate up the miles quickly. A set of roadworks temporarily slowed her progress, but she still made it back to headquarters in record time.

It was after seven in the evening when she entered the office. Howes and Solomon were engrossed in their work, and Thompson could see Ellis in conversation in her glass-walled office. She knocked on the door and entered just as the director put down the phone.

'Any sign of them?'

'Anatoly Potemkin and nine others boarded a chartered flight from Heathrow. It took off for Moscow thirty minutes ago.'

'Can we call it back?' Thompson asked.

'We tried that,' Ellis said. 'Air traffic control instructed them to turn around and land, but the pilot isn't acknowledging.'

'Then send a couple of fighters after them and force them to land.'

Ellis sighed and sat back in her seat. Thompson thought she suddenly looked a lot older than her fifty years.

Losing a couple of agents will do that to you.

'I just got off the phone with the home secretary,' Ellis said. 'The MOD won't scramble jets until we have concrete proof that Andrew is on that flight, and according to the flight manifest, he isn't. I even had Elaine check every passenger at the boarding gate against facial recognition, but no hits on Andrew.'

'But surely placing Potemkin at the farm is enough,' Thompson protested.

'It's enough for the home secretary to start extradition talks with the Russians, but not to send the air force after them. I tried explaining that Potemkin is our main lead to finding Andrew, but apparently the PM prefers to take this one through diplomatic channels. Tensions with Moscow are already strained to breaking point, and interfering with a legitimate flight is not going to make matters any better.'

Thompson knew the director general was just regurgitating the message passed down by her superiors; she could almost hear Ellis choking on the words.

'I say we bring Bessonov in and lean on him until he tells us where Andrew is.'

Ellis stood and folded her arms, pacing behind her desk. 'Bessonov is not to be touched,' she said, anger evident in her tone. 'I tried ruffling his feathers earlier today, and the message from on high is that unless we have evidence that he was on the scene at the time of Andrew's disappearance, we are to cease harassing him.'

Thompson put both hands on Ellis's desk. 'Are you serious? Bessonov and Potemkin are our only leads, and we can't get to either of them?'

'I'm afraid that's the situation as it stands.'

'Can you see it changing anytime soon?'

Ellis shook her head.

Thompson sighed and stood back. 'So what is the team working on?'

'Tracking the movements of the minibus Potemkin used. Andrew must have been dropped off somewhere before they caught their flight. We're checking every camera along the route.'

There was little else the team could do right now, not with Bessonov enjoying his diplomatic protection and Potemkin homeward bound. Thompson contemplated going home, but with Andrew missing, she knew she would drive herself crazy with worry.

'I'll go and see how they're getting on with the search.'

Chapter 12

21 January 2016

Andrew Harvey tried to swallow, but his parched mouth struggled to produce any saliva. His tongue felt like sandpaper against the roof of his mouth, and when he tried to move his head, blinding pain warned him to remain still.

He cracked open one eye, then the other, and found himself in unfamiliar surroundings. Paint was peeling off the once-white ceiling, and grey cinderblocks formed the walls of a room barely bigger than a walk-in closet. Opposite him, a metal door broke the symmetry of the brickwork.

Something tickled his cheek, and when he tried to swat it away, he found his arms unable to move. The restraints felt like leather, and he soon discovered that his feet had been similarly shackled.

The pain in his head continued to pound, and he closed his eyes, welcoming the slip back into unconsciousness.

When he woke again, the headache had subsided a little, but the thirst remained. He tried to remember what had happened, but all he could recall was being tied up in the farmhouse and sitting opposite Scarface.

Had they taken him to another location to work on him? The farm smell was no longer evident, so he assumed they must have.

He had no idea if it was night or day. There were no windows to give him any clues as to his whereabouts, only a single bare light bulb bathing the small room in its yellowish glow.

His stomach demanded food, but Harvey ignored the rumblings and instead tried to free his hands. He tried pulling and twisting, but all he managed to do was anger the skin on his wrists. He decided to save his strength. He couldn't escape his bonds, and even if he managed to break free, he could see no doorknob, which meant it must be locked from the outside.

Harvey lay still and closed his eyes. Memories began to rush back in, and he saw the English doctor with his leather bag.

Why had they felt the need to drug him? Had they taken him through a populated area and knocked him out to prevent him from raising the alarm? If they had, there was a good chance he was back in London. Ellis was sure to be turning over every business owned by Bessonov, and it was only a matter of time before she found him.

With renewed hope, he relaxed a little, though the lingering possibility of torture still niggled away at him.

The faint sound of voices drifted into the room, at first incomprehensible. But as they drew near he realised they were talking a foreign language. Harvey's attempts at becoming multilingual had ended when he'd dropped French as a subject in high school, so he couldn't be sure if they were speaking Russian, Polish or even Romanian. Probably the former, he told himself, as metal scraped and the door opened outwards. A man walked in, and if he'd been wearing a red suit, Harvey would have sworn he was Santa Claus. Instead, the man sported combat fatigues fashioned from Disruptive Pattern Material, topped off with a grey fur hat.

'Mr Harvey, I am Colonel Dmitri Aminev.' The man smiled broadly. 'Welcome to Hell.'

Chapter 13

21 January 2016

Veronica Ellis swiped her security card through the panel next to the door and walked onto the main floor. The scattered desks were mostly empty, just a couple of night shift operatives on watch, which was about what she expected at six in the morning.

She glanced over to the right-hand side of the open-plan office and saw Sarah Thompson at one of the hot desks.

'Have you slept?'

Thompson blinked a couple of times and looked up at her through red-rimmed eyes. 'I think I nodded off for an hour.'

Thompson looked like shit, but Ellis decided not to share such unladylike thoughts.

'Manage to find anything?' she asked instead.

'The minibus was a bust. It stopped off at some services but they were within camera shot the whole time. All they did was dump something in the trash can and drive off.'

'That doesn't make sense,' Ellis frowned. 'Any idea what they threw away?'

'Weapons,' Thompson said, stifling a yawn. 'I had a local unit check it out. And they found ten assorted automatic and semi-automatic handguns. Forensics are working them up as we speak.'

Ellis looked at the computer screen and saw a set of blueprints on display. 'What's this?'

'I took over from Gareth, checking out all of Bessonov's businesses to see if any of them have basements. I know it's a long shot, but there isn't much else to go on.'

Ellis could see genuine anguish behind the tired eyes. Harvey's disappearance had been a personal blow to his colleagues and her, but the pain must be magnified tenfold for Thompson. Ellis had never pried too far into their relationship, but Harvey had been like a man reborn over the last twelve months, so she'd assumed it must have been going well. Seeing Thompson pull an all-nighter and sift through probably worthless data only showed that she cared for him equally.

'The team will be back in at seven,' Ellis said. 'Go and get some sleep.'

The words sounded hollow as they left her mouth, but Ellis needed Thompson fresh and alert when they finally got a lead.

Thompson gave in to a yawn and nodded. 'I'll send this lot across to Gareth and head home for a couple of hours.'

'You do that. And make sure you call a taxi. You're in no fit state to drive.'

Ellis left her to collate the data and entered her own office. She dug the laptop out of her bag and mated it with the docking station, then went to make a coffee while it booted up. She came back to find the login screen waiting, and she entered her password and waited for the network to authenticate her credentials.

Once in, Ellis clicked the icon to open the internal mail client and once again entered her password. She was rewarded with the news that she had ninety-three new emails to deal with.

A typical Thursday morning.

She began going through them, moving weekly reports into the designated folder and deleting the offer of revolutionary penis-enhancement drugs that had slipped through the spam filter. By the time she'd pigeonholed the last of the emails, no new wars had broken out and, apart from the continuing threat from ISIS, no new terror organisations had popped out of the woodwork overnight.

Ellis returned to the weekly reports folder and printed each one, preferring hard copies to reading from a screen. As she dealt with each one, she visited the internal portal and added her electronic signature to sign them off.

She was halfway through the last one when her desk phone buzzed.

'Veronica, it's Gayle.'

'What brings you in so early?'

'I got a call from the night watch,' the Russian section leader said. 'It's something you need to see.'

Ellis promised to be down in a couple of minutes. She locked her computer and took the stairs down one level.

Cooper's door was already open, and she invited Ellis to take a seat before hitting the remote control for the wall-mounted television.

'This is a recording of a news item that played on Tagrilistan's national news channel early this morning.'

The screen showed a man in his fifties wearing a plain grey jacket over a shirt and tie. He was speaking Russian. Ellis asked for a translation.

'The Russian separatists in the country want to do a prisoner swap,' Cooper said as she paused the playback. 'They are willing to exchange their recent captive for the ninety-four Russian prisoners of war in Tagrilistan. They also want Milenko to cancel the signing of the trade agreement on the twenty-ninth.'

'Hardly earth-shattering news,' Ellis said.

'Wait until you see who the prisoner is,' Cooper said, and hit the Play button.

A battered face under tousled hair appeared on the screen to the right of the talking head. One eye was swollen, and heavy bruising had puffed up the lower lip.

Ellis's hand covered her mouth as she recognised the man on display.

'Andrew!'

'They claim he's a British spy caught operating illegally in their country, and they've set a deadline of five days,' Cooper said. 'If President Milenko doesn't agree to their terms by next Tuesday . . .'

There was no need to finish the sentence.

'I'll let the home secretary know,' Ellis said, trying to gather herself. 'Send me a copy of the recording and a transcript in English.'

'There's more,' Cooper said. 'We've got indications that the Russian withdrawal of troops back across the border appears to be nearly complete.'

'Meaning?'

'They could be paving the way for talks,' Cooper said.

'I thought Milenko was staunchly anti-Russian.'

'He is, but if he were no longer in charge of the country . . .'

It fit in with the assassination theory they'd been exploring, but Ellis wondered aloud why they would go to the trouble of kidnapping Harvey if they already had plans in place.

'Contingency?' Cooper offered. 'Or it could be that they know Milenko's stance. He'll refuse to negotiate with the terrorists, which puts a British citizen in harm's way. Just another way of destabilising the upcoming talks in London.'

Ellis didn't like the way things were playing out. Harvey was being used as a pawn in Moscow's game, a token to be discarded once it lost its strategic importance. She thanked Cooper for the input and hurried back up the stairs and onto her own floor, almost bumping into Thompson as she barged through the door.

'Sorry, Veronica. I was miles away. I'm heading home now.'

Ellis considered telling her the news, but decided it would be counterproductive. Thompson desperately needed sleep, and she wouldn't get that if she knew her lover was being held hostage in a war zone three thousand miles away.

'Take it easy,' Ellis said, and held the door open for her.

'What's wrong?' Thompson asked, and Ellis knew her face was betraying her.

'Nothing,' she lied. 'I just hate to see you like this.'

Thompson seemed to accept the answer, and put her hand over her mouth as yet another yawn escaped. 'I'll be fine. See you this afternoon.'

Ellis watched Thompson leave and felt bad for not levelling with her. But her focus was on getting the powers that be to heap pressure on Milenko to secure Harvey's release. She walked into her office and dialled the home secretary's mobile.

'Maynard,' she heard the familiar, no-nonsense voice say.

'John, it's Veronica. I have news about Andrew Harvey.'

She brought the minister up to speed on the situation in Tagrilistan.

'How the hell did he end up there?' Maynard asked. 'I thought you said they were holed up with him in Oxfordshire.'

'That's what we thought, but somehow they managed to get him out of the country. I'm working to establish exactly how they did it, but in the meantime I need you to ask the foreign secretary to put pressure on Milenko to accept their offer.'

'I'll mention it,' Maynard said, 'but don't get your hopes up. This deal has been two years in the making, and the PM isn't going to jeopardise it just because one of your boys got careless.'

Ellis could barely contain herself. *Careless?* Careless was dropping your phone. She desperately wanted to tear into Maynard for the insensitive remark, but she needed him as an ally, not an enemy.

'Andrew Harvey risked his life investigating the murder of one of his colleagues.'

'I appreciate that,' Maynard said, 'but I'm just letting you know how things stand. I'll take your request to the PM, but ultimately it's his call.'

Ellis thanked him and asked him to contact her as soon as a decision was made. She disconnected, knowing a political resolution was out of her hands, but there were other options to weigh up.

She walked quickly back down to Cooper's office and knocked as she entered the room.

'My team will be here in half an hour,' Ellis said. 'As soon as they arrive, I need you to do a presentation on Tagrilistan.'

'Sure. What do you need?'

The events leading up to the conflict were well known to anyone with a television or smart phone, so Ellis told her to skip that and go straight to the current state of play. 'I need to know which areas are controlled by the Russians, and your best guess as to where they might be holding Andrew.'

'The first part's easy,' Cooper told her, 'but we're talking about an area almost the size of England.'

'They must have a command centre. Start with that, then expand it to other possible sites.'

Cooper looked worried. 'Are you thinking about a military incursion?'

Ellis pursed her lips and gave the slightest shrug.

'That's not my call, but it might be our only option.'

Sarah Thompson stirred in a fitful sleep and reached over to Andrew's side of the bed. When her hand hit empty bedding, she cracked open an eye and looked around the room.

It took her a couple of seconds for the events of the last thirty-six hours to come flooding back, and she grabbed the spare pillow and hugged it, the faint scent of Harvey's cologne still lingering on the pillowcase.

She stayed like that for a few minutes until the alarm on her phone told her it was three in the afternoon. Time to get up, shower and return to the office to resume the search for the man she loved.

Half an hour later, she climbed into her car and stopped off at a garage on the way to top up with fuel and grab a couple of sandwiches to keep her going. She had no intention of leaving the office for at least the next twelve hours, longer if they found no leads.

Thompson arrived at the office after four and was disappointed not to see a hive of activity. Her new teammates were sitting quietly, looking at satellite images and making notes.

'Anything new?' she asked Elaine Solomon.

In response she got a look of utter sorrow and knew immediately that something had gone dreadfully wrong.

'Ellis said to send you in as soon as you arrive,' Solomon said, looking over to the boss's office.

'What is it?' Thompson asked.

'It's best if Veronica explains.'

Thompson strode over to the glass door and opened it. Ellis had seen her approach and was already walking around to the front of her desk.

'Something's wrong, isn't it?'

'Sit down, please.'

'I prefer to stand,' Thompson said, her hands on her hips. 'Where's Andrew?'

'Tagrilistan.'

Thompson walked unsteadily to the chair and flopped into it. 'How the hell did he get there?'

'We don't know. Our focus right now is on getting him back.'

Ellis picked up a remote control and played the video that Cooper had sent up that morning, now dubbed in English.

'What did Milenko say?' Thompson asked. 'Is he going to trade?'

'We're still waiting to hear,' Ellis said. 'I was told—'

Ellis's mobile phone chirped, and after checking the caller ID, she put a hand up and pressed the Connect button.

Thompson watched on, ears straining to hear the incoming voice, but Ellis was already walking back to her side of the desk.

'Okay, I understand,' Ellis said. 'What about a military response? My people have found three possible—'

Thompson was desperate to know what was being said. Ellis's face didn't exactly convey optimism, and seeing her cut off suggested it wasn't an argument she was winning. A sense of dread began to overwhelm her.

Ellis listened a little longer, then snapped off the phone and threw it on the desk.

'That was the home secretary. Milenko won't trade,' Ellis said. 'He flat-out refuses to negotiate. The PM summoned the Russian ambassador to Downing Street and warned him of the consequences if anything happened to Andrew, but he just reiterated the usual line about Moscow having no control or interaction with the rebels.'

'They're arming them, for God's sake! Everyone on the planet knows that!'

'I realise that,' Ellis said, 'but that's their stance and they're not budging.'

'So what about sending a team in to get Andrew back? Did he at least agree to that?'

'Military intervention has been ruled out.' Ellis sighed. 'They fear Russia will respond by mounting a full invasion and things could quickly escalate into all-out war.'

Tears welled in Thompson's eyes. 'So we just let him die? Our government has abandoned him and we're supposed to just sit and wait for confirmation of his death? Is that it?'

Ellis stared at her for a few moments, and Sarah spotted rare signs of anger creep onto the director general's face.

'The hell it is,' Ellis said, and picked up her desk phone.

Chapter 14

22 January 2016

Richard Notley swiped his Oyster card against the terminal and took a seat at the rear of the bus. He dug out his phone and checked his emails, then went to the BBC News website to see what had been happening to the world while he'd toiled for eight hours at the office.

Fresh fighting in Tagrilistan stole the headlines, with another strike planned by the fire brigade over pay and pensions. He selected the politics section, where the latest figures showed that waiting-time targets for A&E had been missed for the seventh week running, and the prime minister was promising to throw another few million at the problem.

Too late for that, Notley thought. *Too late for Marian.*

His wife of twenty-four years had gone in for the simplest of routine operations, yet understaffing on the night shift had meant she hadn't been monitored as often as she should have. No-one had noticed the internal bleeding until it was too late. He'd gone to visit her the next morning, only to find an empty bed and a very apologetic consultant.

Even as he thought back to that moment, he felt exactly the same pain as he'd done three years earlier. Like he'd been kicked in the chest by a horse.

Notley forced himself to take two deep breaths and stared out of the window, trying to dispel the memory of that terrible day, when he'd been stripped of his one true love. He turned his thoughts to the person responsible for Marian's death, and pure, unadulterated hatred replaced the grief he'd felt moments earlier.

Marian's death hadn't been a case of error in her care, as the inquest had decided. She'd been snatched away because of the actions of one man, and he was soon going to pay the price.

Notley reached his semi-detached house just before seven in the evening. It was a commute he'd come to despise, one with little purpose any more, but he had to do it. The visit from the police shortly after the Brigandicuum revelation had been a wake-up call for him, and it was important that he stick to his usual routine, giving no-one cause for concern.

He slipped the key in the lock and opened the front door. The house was warm, the central-heating timer having kicked in an hour earlier. He took his lunch box through to the kitchen and rinsed it out ready for the next day. Then he stuck a ready meal in the microwave and made a cup of tea.

While lethal waves nuked his supper, he wandered around the house, looking for anything out of place. The windows hadn't been opened, nor had the back door. The little telltale markers he'd put in place remained undisturbed. Just to be on the safe side, he went into the living room and woke his computer from sleep mode, then navigated to the surveillance app he'd installed. It recorded the feed from three hidden cameras dotted around the house, each activated by movement. He checked each folder, but apart from seeing himself leaving and returning, nothing else had been detected in the living room, hallway or upper landing.

Even if someone had been in the property, they would have found nothing here.

Not now.

His hard drive contained nothing incriminating, and that's the way it had been since the news about Brigandicuum had broken a year earlier. The panic that had gripped him at the time remained fresh in his mind, and he still got butterflies every time the doorbell rang.

His initial plan, on hearing about the invasive surveillance system, had been to trash the computer and get a new one, but that would have been too convenient, not to mention suspicious. Upgrading to a new computer days after the revelation that everything he'd ever typed on his keypad had been monitored would have set noses twitching, but thankfully he knew enough about computers to get round the problem. It hadn't taken long to buy an identical hard drive and clone his original drive, leaving out anything relating to his plan. The original drive had been smashed with a sledgehammer and dumped in the Thames, and he'd been forced to commit everything pertaining to the upcoming mission to memory.

By the time the knock came, months after the evidence had been destroyed, he'd had enough time to perfect his response to all of the questions he'd expected them to throw at him. They'd taken him in for questioning and confiscated his computer, but Notley had refused the offer of a lawyer. Instead, he'd answered their questions as calmly as he could, telling them he knew nothing about computers beyond sending email and surfing the Internet. When asked how Brigandicuum could have found those files on his computer, he told them he had no idea, suggesting that perhaps someone had been hopping on his Wi-Fi connection.

With no prior criminal record and no evidence to back up the Brigandicuum download, he'd been set free, though he knew that wouldn't be the end of it. There had been times over the last few months when he'd felt as if he were being followed, and a couple of times he'd seen a suspicious black van parked near his home.

Notley retrieved the chicken curry from the microwave and took it through to the living room, where he turned on the television and found the BBC News channel. He stuck a piece of unappetising meat into his mouth and listened as the talking head introduced an expert on fraud who explained why so many pensioners were being conned into investing their pension pots in non-existent schemes.

A pension was the last thing on Richard Notley's mind. He would have to live another fifteen years before being eligible for one, but if all went to plan, he would be joining Marian a lot sooner than that.

Chapter 15

22 January 2016

Tom Gray watched his daughter pull a face and spit out the cereal. Milk and brightly coloured Lucky Charms dribbled down her chin and onto the highchair table.

'That's another brand crossed off the list.' Gray sighed as he took the bowl away and cleaned up the mess. He hadn't noticed too much of a difference between the food in Florida and that back in London, but it was obviously a big deal for Melissa.

He put a pan on to boil and eased a couple of eggs in, then made a few rounds of toast. He didn't like to feed her eggs too often at such a young age, so made a mental note to get pancakes or waffles on their next shopping trip. Anything to add a bit of variety to her diet.

After three minutes of boiling, he removed the eggs and placed them in Peppa Pig egg cups, slicing off the tops and cutting the toast into little soldiers for her to dip into the runny yolk.

'Tuck in, princess,' he said, as she began eating contentedly. He had no issues with the American brands, but then Melissa had always been a fussy eater. She was, after all, the only human being he knew who couldn't stand the taste of ketchup.

The doorbell rang and Gray rose, expecting another visit from his neighbours, the Wilburns. He could see platinum hair through the mottled glass and thought he'd guessed correctly, but when he opened the door with a practised smile, he found himself face-to-face with someone he'd never expected to see again.

The smile quickly disappeared. 'Veronica?'

Ellis produced a smile of her own and looked over his shoulder. 'Mind if I come in?'

Gray nodded, dumbfounded, and stepped aside, letting Ellis pull her wheeled hand luggage over the threshold. He noticed a black Chevy Suburban with tinted windows sat in the driveway. Obviously her ride.

'Nice place you've got,' Ellis said.

But Gray was still in shock at seeing her. The director of MI5 didn't fly four thousand miles to pay a social visit. Something was deadly wrong.

Could it be Sonny or Smart? Had something happened to his two best friends?

'What are you doing here?' he asked. 'What's wrong?'

'You were always very direct, Tom. I don't suppose there's any chance of a coffee?'

Gray led her through to the kitchen, where Melissa had painted half of her face orange. Gray wiped her down and offered Ellis a seat, desperate to hear what she had to say, but at the same time dreading it. It would have taken her minutes to find his number and call, so he knew this wasn't the kind of thing that could be done over the phone.

That could only mean bad news, and as the only people he had left in his life were his two close friends and daughter, he prepared for the worst.

He placed the cup in front of his visitor and took a seat opposite her. 'Are you going to tell me what you're doing here?'

Ellis helped herself to milk and sugar, blew the hot liquid and took a sip.

'Hamad Farsi was hospitalised a few days ago,' Ellis said. 'It was a hit-and-run.'

Gray relaxed a little on hearing the news. He knew Hamad, but it wasn't as if they were lifelong buddies. Sure, they'd worked together on a couple of missions, but that certainly wasn't enough to get Ellis on a plane.

'I'm sorry to hear that,' Gray said. 'I hope he's okay.'

'He'll live.' Ellis sipped her coffee again.

'So how did it happen?' Gray asked, waiting for the bombshell to be dropped.

'He was trying to stop Andrew Harvey from being kidnapped.'

So there it was, the real reason for her turning up on his doorstep.

'They were checking out a possible assassination attempt when things turned ugly,' Ellis continued. 'Andrew was taken prisoner and Hamad was trying to stop them when he was hit by their car.'

'So someone has Andrew?' Gray asked, still not quite understanding why he was being involved. This was a matter for the UK authorities, not a semi-retired security consultant. That aside, he felt genuinely concerned for the MI5 operative.

'Yes, and we have four days until he's executed.'

Gray noticed for the first time that this Ellis wasn't the comfortable, confident woman he'd met a couple of times before. Her normally immaculate hair was a little unkempt, and her eyes told him that more than just a lack of sleep had taken its toll recently. She'd obviously taken Harvey's kidnapping hard. Gray felt much the same.

His relationship with Harvey couldn't have got off on a worse footing, with the MI5 operative trying to stop Gray's attempts to highlight his perceived inequalities in the British justice system. A year later Harvey had turned saviour, orchestrating the rescue of Gray and his friends from a government-sanctioned hit man. The friendship had bloomed since then, but until today he'd considered Harvey part of his old life.

Tom Gray's life.

He was now Tim Grayson, obscure engineer in a foreign land, trying to raise his daughter as best he could.

'Did you check that James Farrar is still locked up?' he asked.

Farrar had once run the government's black-ops division, until his operation was shuttered after he targeted British citizens, Gray and his friends included. He'd then absconded and masterminded the recent devastating attacks on Britain. Once again, Gray had been the target. Not only him but Melissa too.

'I check his prison record every single day. There's no way he's involved.'

'Well, I hope you find Andrew,' Gray said. 'He's a good man.'

'That's just the trouble. We already know where he is.'

Gray's eyes furrowed. 'And the reason you can't go in and get him is . . .?'

'Complicated.'

Ellis gave a full breakdown of events since Harvey had been picked up by the Russians, culminating in the video showing him held hostage in Tagrilistan.

'Sadly, our government sees this trade deal as more important than Andrew's life. They won't do anything to jeopardise it, and that includes sending in a team to bring Andrew home. If they do, and word gets out that British troops are on the ground in Tagrilistan, President Milenko believes Russia will launch a full invasion.'

That didn't leave many alternatives that Gray could imagine, making the reason for Ellis's visit clearer by the second.

Gray stood and took his cup over to the sink. 'I'm really sorry, Veronica, but you've had a wasted journey.'

'You're the only option I have left,' Ellis pleaded. 'I can't just leave him to die.'

'I know that,' he said. 'Trust me, I've been there. But what you're talking about would need someone with recent military experience. I haven't been into battle in years.'

'What about Malundi?'

'I got there about fifteen minutes before the end of the fight,' Gray said, 'and by that time it was barely even a skirmish. What you're looking for is someone straight out of the regiment. If you like, I can get Len Smart to look around for a few people who fit the profile.'

'This isn't something I can put through the books,' Ellis said. 'I've been ordered to accept the fact that Andrew's gone, so I'm out on a limb just being here. Whoever goes to get him will have to do it on their own dollar.'

That put a different spin on things entirely. Gray didn't expect any of his contractors would be willing to drop what they were doing and take on a pro bono mission, especially if it meant going into one of the fiercest war zones around. If Andrew were someone they knew – a former colleague – that would be one thing. To ask anyone to risk their lives for a stranger was another matter entirely.

Gray returned to the table and sat down heavily. Ellis had obviously been through all the options, and coming to Florida must have been her last resort. She'd made it clear on previous meetings that she wasn't Tom Gray's biggest fan, but he was the only person she knew who had sufficient ties to Harvey and the funds to make it work.

'I can put up some of the money,' Gray offered.

If any of his men were going to take on the job, they'd want more than the standard five hundred a day. It would take at least a dozen men, and he could probably get them down to ten grand each. Then there were weapons to consider, plus flights and other expenses.

It wasn't going to be cheap.

'Money isn't the real issue,' Ellis said. 'I need the right people.'

'As I said, I'll get Len to pick the best men we've got.'

Ellis cradled her fingers and rested her chin on the knuckles. 'I read your MOD jacket,' she said. 'Iraq, 1991. You led a team behind the lines to take out a communications unit hiding in a small town. What happened?'

Gray felt uncomfortable with the question. True, he'd been the squad leader at the time, and it had been his decision to abandon the mission. 'We'd been told that there were no more than twenty enemy troops in the area. When we got there, it was more like a hundred. If we'd pressed ahead, we'd all be dead.'

'So you pulled back and saved your men.'

Gray nodded. 'It's what any squad leader would have done. Where is this going?'

'You walked away when you knew things were too risky. I can't afford that to happen this time. Whoever goes in will have to have a personal stake in this. If you send a squad in and they don't like the odds, there won't be time to assemble another team.'

It was true. If one of *his* men had been held captive in that Iraqi town, he would have thought twice about pulling back. At the time, though, it had been an easy decision.

Ellis took out her phone and Gray watched her fingers dance across the screen.

'I already have two men,' she said. 'They both know Andrew and jumped at the chance to take part in the rescue. I was hoping you'd lead them.'

Gray's forehead furrowed. Andrew had been round to Gray's house plenty of times, and Gray knew just about everything there was to know about him. He'd never mentioned close friends with military backgrounds.

'Who are they?'

The doorbell rang, but Gray ignored it, waiting for an answer.

'I think you should get that,' Ellis said.

Reluctantly, Gray rose and walked quickly to the door, determining to get rid of the unwanted interruption. He pulled it open and found himself facing two smiling men – modern-day versions of Laurel and Hardy. One stood a couple of inches taller than Gray, with a balding pate and bushy moustache. He looked like a salesman or company director, with a lifestyle that included one too many burgers per day. The other was the complete opposite: a foot smaller and a hundred pounds lighter, with sandy blond hair and boyish good looks.

'See,' the smaller one said, hands on hips. 'I told you he'd forget us the moment he left the country.'

Gray had known Len Smart and Simon 'Sonny' Baines for years, having first served with them in 22 SAS Regiment as a twenty-six-year-old. Baines had looked seventeen at the time and, twenty years on, he still had to show ID to get into pubs. Smart, on the other hand, had always looked the typical soldier. That is, until he left the service. Almost immediately, his hair receded and his waist expanded a few inches, until he looked more at home in a boardroom than in a battle zone.

'What the hell are you two doing here?'

But as soon as the words left his mouth, Gray knew the answer. By getting Len and Sonny on board first, Ellis had played her trump card.

'What do you think?' Smart asked. 'Veronica told us about Andrew. We're here to plan the mission.'

It wasn't something Gray wanted to discuss on the doorstep, not with the Wilburns out tending to their garden next door. He ushered his friends inside and led them through to the kitchen, where Ellis sat looking like she'd been caught with her hand in the cookie jar.

'So, how soon can we ship out?' Sonny asked, stooping to give Melissa a peck on the cheek.

'Tom hasn't agreed to go along yet,' Ellis said sheepishly, drawing looks of confusion from the others.

Sonny straightened up and looked at Gray. 'Am I missing something, Tom? Andrew's in trouble and you need time to think about it?'

'I'm with Sonny,' Smart chimed in. 'It took me about ten seconds to agree to Veronica's request. What's the problem?'

Gray looked at his daughter. 'Melissa's the problem,' he said. 'If it wasn't for her I'd have jumped at the chance, and you know it. If I don't make it back, who's going to raise her?'

'I'm sorry,' Sonny said. 'From what Veronica told us, we assumed you were already in.'

'That's my fault,' Ellis said. 'I needed them to come with me and convince you to take part.'

'Why?' Gray asked. 'You've already got Len and Sonny on board. Why do you need me?'

'Because you're the brains behind things.' She stole a look at the pair. 'No offence.'

'None taken.'

Ellis focused on Gray. 'Back in 2011, you had the police, security services and SAS running around in circles trying to stop you from killing those kids. You made us look like the Keystone Cops.'

'First of all,' Gray interrupted, 'I was never going to kill any of them. Secondly, I had six months to plan that op. You've barely got six hours, and from what you've told me, you don't have a clear idea of the situation on the ground. You don't know his location, enemy strength or any of the dozen other things we need to start putting a mission together.'

'That's why I need your help,' Ellis pleaded. 'Your military expertise. We've narrowed it down to three possible targets, but we need a trained eye to figure out which is more likely.'

Smart shrugged. 'It can't hurt to take a look.'

Gray sighed and motioned for his friends to sit, while Ellis dug into her bag and pulled out a folder and a laptop. While she waited for the machine to boot up, she opened the file and spread three satellite photos on the table.

'We think Andrew is being held in one of these locations,' Ellis said, pointing to the first of the images. 'This one is Dubrany. It was the first town to fall to the separatists and has a high concentration of Russian civilians. The circles represent what we believe to be anti-aircraft batteries. The second is Milev.'

Gray picked up the next high-resolution photo and studied it closely. He could see a few dozen buildings, but most looked to be pockmarked by artillery fire. Rubble had turned the roads grey, and he could see little sign of life.

'What makes you think he might be here?' Gray asked.

'One of my staff, Gayle Cooper, works the Russia desk. She told me that the leader of the Russian separatists, Colonel Dmitri Aminev, was seen there two days ago.'

Gray turned to the last image.

'That's a place called Gornjy,' Ellis said. 'We marked it as a possibility because of the concentration of heavy weapons both inside the town and on the outskirts.'

Gray looked at the third image for a minute or two, then went back to the first.

'He'll be here, in Dubrany.'

'What makes you say that?' Ellis asked, looking at the other two men.

'Gornjy is too close to the front line,' Gray said. 'It would be madness to hold a high-value prisoner there. It looks like it's already taken a pounding, and with the concentration of heavy weapons, there's more to come.'

'These pictures are four days old,' Ellis said. 'We heard yesterday that all Russian heavy artillery is being pulled out of the area and back over the border.'

'Even then, the place looks like a wasteland. I'm betting the infrastructure has crumbled, meaning no electricity or water.'

'What about Milev?'

'Too remote. They'll want him somewhere with a large concentration of troops to discourage any rescue attempts.'

'Dubrany was our best guess, too,' Ellis said, as she typed on her keyboard. She turned the screen towards Gray. 'This is a live feed from a US satellite over the area. I had to call in a few personal favours to get access.'

Smart and Sonny gathered round as Ellis pointed out the first item of interest.

'According to Cooper, this is Aminev's headquarters.'

'What type of building is it?' Gray asked.

'It used to be a hotel. He occupies two adjoining suites on the top floor.'

'They'll be holding Andrew somewhere secure. Is there a prison or jail in the town?'

Ellis moved the cursor and panned the video to the left. 'This was the main police station until the fighting took hold. It includes a number of holding cells, but we've no idea if anyone's being held there.'

Gray studied the surrounding area, then asked Ellis to zoom in. The building was L-shaped and sat back from the road, completely surrounded by a wall that looked to be about two feet thick.

'Getting to the front door is going to pose a challenge in itself,' Gray said. 'Even if they make it that far, you're talking about a prison break. That would be difficult against a civilian target, but these guys are going to be armed to the teeth.'

'As I said, the Russians themselves have pulled back to the border. All we're facing now is the local militia.'

'How many?' Gray asked.

'Rough estimate is two thousand, but that's spread out over the entire front. We don't have exact numbers for Dubrany.'

Gray's face took on a pensive look. As Dubrany was the main town and housed the separatists' HQ, there was likely to be a high concentration of troops in the vicinity. Still, a small unit *might* be able to make it in undetected . . .

'What about exfil?' he asked. 'Once they grab Andrew, how do the team get back out?'

'Apart from the Russian forces to the north, the closest border is forty miles to the west. It shouldn't take long to drive.'

'Forget driving,' Gray said. 'Chances are, there'll be contact at some point. All roads in the area will be closed down within minutes. There has to be air support.'

'Out of the question,' Ellis said. 'Unless you happen to have your own helicopter.'

'I don't,' Gray told her, 'but I know a man who does.'

He got up and made a fresh pot of coffee, then took Melissa through to the living room and popped a DVD into the player. He also gave his daughter her prized toy piano to play with.

Back in the kitchen, Smart and Sonny were discussing ingress points.

'It doesn't matter which way we go in, we'll be exposed most of the way,' Smart pointed out. 'A large party will be too easy to spot, but a team of four might make it in a car.'

'What about jumping in?' Sonny asked. 'A HALO drop right into the compound.'

'Those anti-aircraft batteries tell me that's a bad idea,' Gray said, looking over their shoulders. 'I suggest the chopper drops you off a couple of miles outside of town and you find a vehicle to take you the rest of the way.' He turned to Ellis. 'Is there a way to get a street view of the area?'

'The Google cars never made it that far,' Ellis said. 'This is as good as it gets.'

It wasn't the first time Gray had had to come up with a strategy based on minimal intel, though with all the technology available today, he'd hoped those days were behind him. All they had to work with were overheads and GPS coordinates – the word 'clusterfuck' sprang to mind.

The sound of Melissa trying to coax a tune out of eight available keys drifted from the living room as the men turned their attention to the weapons and equipment they'd need. It didn't take long to decide on AK-47s. Apart from being extremely reliable, it was the ubiquitous assault rifle of the region. For close quarters, they selected the Glock 17 with suppressors developed by the Advanced Armament Corporation. Various types of grenades were added to the list, along with some plastic explosives, night-vision goggles and comms units.

'You said you knew a man who had a chopper,' Ellis said. 'Who is it?'

'Erwin McGregor. He was my first troop leader when I finished selection,' Gray told her. 'He led us for about a year, until a bad landing on a night jump brought an end to his career. He stayed in touch for a while and I saw him at the reunions, then one day he dropped off the radar. Long story short, he's been running his own flying school in Kazakhstan for the last five years.'

'Do you think he'll be willing to take part?' Ellis asked.

'He won't need to,' Gray told her. 'I know of at least five men on my books with enough hours to do the job. All we need is a chopper for them to fly. I'm sure Mac will help us out.'

Melissa toddled into the kitchen and declared her hunger. Gray was about to dig out a snack for her when the wall clock told him they'd been working up the plan for two hours straight. Instead, he put on more coffee and prepared a plate of sandwiches for his guests, while his daughter got the tin of spaghetti hoops she'd asked for.

The meeting was put on hold as Smart and Sonny got reacquainted with Melissa, even though it had only been a few weeks since they'd last seen her. She giggled as Smart's moustache tickled her cheeks, and howled with delight each time Sonny pulled a stupid face.

Gray called an end to the lunch break when Melissa started yawning and, after taking her upstairs for a nap, he joined the others in the kitchen.

'I just got the latest troop numbers from Cooper,' Ellis said as he entered the room. 'Nearest estimates are that there are only around four hundred men left in Dubrany.'

'Only?' Gray asked. 'So they'll *only* be outnumbered a hundred to one.'

'Dubrany is a pretty big place,' Ellis pointed out. 'Four hundred spread over an area the size of London's East End leaves lots of gaps.'

Gray could tell Ellis was determined to make this work, and he didn't blame her. He wanted Harvey back, too, but while Ellis tended towards optimistic, he was more pragmatic.

'What about civilians?' Gray asked, concerned about collateral damage. 'Are we likely to come across any?'

'Dubrany was the focal point of the fighting for many weeks. Most were evacuated early on, relocated farther inland or to other

Russian-held towns, depending on their allegiance. All you're likely to find there are the stubborn few who refused to be moved on.'

The situation didn't look as bad as it had six hours earlier, but it would still be far from easy. Getting the supplies would be crucial. Without them, the mission was over before they even left the ground.

'I'd better call Mac,' Gray said. 'If he can't help, we've got real problems.'

He took himself off to the other end of the kitchen and looked up McGregor's contact details on his phone. It had been years since he'd heard his old sergeant's voice, and wasn't even sure if he was still alive, let alone still in Kazakhstan.

The phone rang a dozen times before it was answered by a gruff Glaswegian voice.

'McGregor.'

'Mac, it's Tom Gray.'

'Who the fuck's Tom Gray?'

It wasn't how Gray had expected the conversation to go. He needed to get the giant Scot onside, but he couldn't have made a worse start. Without McGregor's help, the mission was a bust.

'You were my troop sergeant when I joined B-Squadron.'

'Gray, you say?'

'Yes, Tom Gray. We met at the reunion a few times. I've been out of the regiment for a while, too.'

'Aye, I remember someone called Gray. Nasty wee bloke. Never liked him.'

Gray started to panic. He couldn't think what he'd done to offend McGregor. They'd always got on well in the past, and he couldn't understand what had brought about such a change.

'You still there, wee man?'

‘Yes,’ Gray said, ‘I’m still here.’

‘Had you going there, Tom.’

Laughter erupted down the phone, and Gray silently cursed McGregor’s warped sense of humour. He was worse than Sonny, who went through life with a semi-permanent smile and was always up for a bit of mischief. Poor Len was usually the butt of his jokes, which led one to wonder how Sonny had survived so long.

‘Oh, you got me good,’ he told McGregor.

The big man laughed. ‘You always were too serious. Walking round with a stick up yer arse. You should take life lessons from that Baines kid.’

‘Fat chance,’ Gray said with a laugh. ‘We’re still waiting for Sonny to reach puberty.’

They spent the next few minutes catching up, then Gray explained the real reason for the call.

‘Just a hop-in-and-out, you say?’

‘That’s right,’ Gray assured him. ‘Drop off should be easy, but it might be hotter on the way back.’

‘That’s nae problem. I’ll charge you a thousand to drop you off and another grand to bring you home, plus you pay for fuel and any repairs.’

‘All I need is the chopper,’ Gray told him. ‘I have a man who can pilot it.’

‘No way, Tom. I heard all about you and Freddie Rickard down in Malundi, and I ain’t got that kind of insurance. I pilot the bird, end of.’

Gray had little inclination to argue. The price McGregor was quoting was a lot less than he’d expected to pay, though that was sure to rise if they didn’t get the helicopter back in one piece.

'I can only carry five,' McGregor added, but Gray assured him that was more than enough.

'What about the weapons?' Gray asked.

'The AKs are nae problem, but the rest could be tricky. I'll put the feelers out straight away.'

'Just get what you can,' Gray said. 'The lads will meet up with you in about thirty-six hours.'

'The lads?' McGregor asked. 'Yer no coming?'

'It's a long story.' Gray sighed.

'You surprise me. One of yer mates is in trouble and you send someone else in to get him? What the fuck happened to you?'

'I've got a two-year-old kid,' Gray said. 'If I don't make it back, what happens to her?'

'She grows up, you numpty. When she's old enough, someone will explain what happened to you and that she should be proud of yer loyalty and dedication to those who matter.'

'I tried that before and it cost me my wife,' Gray said. 'I'm not going to lose my daughter too.'

'Oh, get over yerself. What about the kids out in Afghanistan? You think none of them have got bairns? You think they don't have families? Yer a soldier. Start acting like one.'

'Easy for you to say,' Gray parried.

'Aye, it is. I lost my boy twelve months ago to an IED. They didnae find enough of him to have a proper funeral, so don't tell me how hard it is for you to leave yer wee 'un with a babysitter for a few days.'

Gray had known that McGregor had a son serving in Afghanistan, but he had no idea he'd been killed.

'I'm sorry, Erwin.'

A conciliatory grunt came from the other end of the line.

'As always, you make a sound point,' said Gray. 'I'll think about it.'

'You do that, because when yer friend gets out and finds you couldnae be bothered to go in and get him, he'll not be a friend for long.'

McGregor signed off, leaving Gray with some soul-searching to do.

Chapter 16

22 January 2016

'You sure you won't come?' Sonny asked as Gray walked them out to the SUV.

Darkness had descended a couple of hours earlier, though the temperature hadn't dropped more than a couple of degrees. Insects were already in mating mode, their shrills and chirps punctuated with the occasional croak of a frog in search of a partner.

'I'm sure,' Gray said, though he felt far from it. Until the conversation with McGregor, he'd been adamant that he would take no part beyond developing the strategy, but the last couple of hours had seen him battling internally.

If it weren't for Melissa, he'd have had no hesitation in signing up, despite the danger. It wasn't dying that troubled him. Death came to everyone, something he'd reconciled himself with a long time ago. What really held him back was the thought of Melissa growing up without a family.

He just couldn't shake the notion that a girl needed her father.

'We'll be in touch when we're out,' Smart said. 'Look after yourself, Tom.'

The trio climbed into the SUV and Ellis reversed out of the driveway, Smart's parting words weighing heavily. Is that what he was doing? Selfishly looking after his own interests?

And what of the man at the centre of all this? How would Harvey feel, knowing Gray had refused to help beyond offering advice and procuring weapons and transport?

Melissa began fidgeting in Gray's arms as he watched the SUV disappear around the corner.

'Bedtime for you,' he said, planting a kiss on her cheek. He carried her upstairs and changed her, then tucked her into bed and continued reading the epic saga that was *The Cat in the Hat*, a tale he'd been reading to her for the last few nights. As always, Melissa started out listening intently, but her eyes soon began to lose the battle. She was asleep before he'd managed to finish two pages.

Gray put the book down next to her water bottle and swapped the table lamp for the nightlight, but instead of retreating downstairs, he sat gazing at his daughter.

She looked so at peace, completely unaware of all the anger and hatred going on in the world around her, and it was his job as her father to protect her from it. He couldn't be so irresponsible as to go marching off to war when his real duties lay here with his little angel.

You think none of them have got bairns? You think they don't have families?

McGregor had a valid point. Ninety-five per cent of the soldiers serving in conflict zones had someone waiting for them to come home, and many had young children expecting Daddy to return safe and sound. On the sad occasions when that didn't happen, life went on. Sure, the families suffered intolerable grief, but it faded over time. Gray knew a few widows from his days in the regiment. Wives of brave warriors who'd lost their lives doing what they did better than anyone else. Some still attended the reunions, their now-grown children none the worse for their single-parent upbringing.

His case was different, though. If he failed to return, Melissa had no mummy to step up and shoulder the burden. His daughter would be sent to live with people she considered her grandparents, Ken and Mina Hatcher. They were actually his dead wife's aunt and uncle, but he referred to them as grandma and grandpa for Melissa's sake. Not only would he be denying his daughter a father; he'd also be imposing on his late wife's relatives for the next sixteen years, at the very least. That they would take on the responsibility wasn't in doubt, but they would be pushing seventy by the time Melissa reached the age of boyfriends and rebellion. Would they be able to cope with the pressure?

Gray ran a finger across the scar on his cheek, ironically gained after leaving the service. More than a decade in the armed forces, and the worst he'd suffered had been severe athlete's foot while on jungle exercises in Belize. In the last five years, though, he'd been almost killed in a bomb blast, seconds from perishing in the Philippine jungle, marked for death by a Malaysian human trafficker and shot down while flying over an African war zone. It was as if some higher power was telling him to quit playing Action Man and stay the hell away from trouble.

Your fighting days are over, Gray.

That was the easiest one to reconcile, which was why he'd abandoned the country of his birth in favour of retirement in a quiet community thousands of miles away.

But what if that wasn't what the universe had planned for him?

Trouble seemed to have no problem finding him, and the next time it reared its head, Melissa would be in the firing line once again.

Perhaps she'd be better off growing up in the quaint Italian village where the Hatchers lived, enjoying an idyllic life a world away from all the pain and suffering felt elsewhere.

Melissa turned and placed her hands together on the pillow, resting her cheek on them as if praying in her sleep. The serene image distracted Gray from his thoughts, and his throat tightened as tears threatened to overwhelm him.

He leaned over and kissed her gently on the forehead, then rearranged the covers before leaving her room and heading downstairs. He took a couple of Buds from the refrigerator and carried them through to the living room, where he sat in darkness and waited for clarity to strike.

Chapter 17

23 January 2016

Len Smart pulled his Ford into a bay in Heathrow's long-term car park and the team climbed out to retrieve their luggage from the back of the car. Along with Smart and Sonny were three others, handpicked for the mission.

Mark Howard was only four months out of the regiment and, like Sonny, had been an instructor in close quarters battle, specialising in fighting in urban situations. A Yorkshireman, he stood a shade under six feet and wore his black hair in a tight crew cut.

Sean Butterworth, also known as Doc, was a tall, wiry figure who brought language and first-aid skills to the party. He would be the squad's medic and one of two who spoke fluent Russian.

The other was Edgar Melling, who matched Sonny's diminutive physique but lacked his joviality.

Along with his personal luggage, Smart pulled a Samsonite suitcase containing the Sentinels, automated firing systems patented by Gray and used to good effect in Malundi a year earlier. They consisted of a modified rifle breech and two-inch barrel that was fed with up to two hundred rounds of 7.62 mm ammunition. The external casing of these particular units was designed to resemble stone, ideal for deployment to places such as Afghanistan. The satellite imagery had shown plenty of rubble on the streets of Dubrany, making them the perfect choice.

While Sentinels could be left in deploy-and-forget mode – the units opened fire when proximity sensors were triggered – they could also be controlled remotely. This enabled the operator to see approaching targets and manoeuvre the barrel to pick them off. Gray's company had tried developing an app for phones and tablets that would do a similar job, but in Wi-Fi and data blackspots the units refused to respond. They'd been able to achieve a little success using Bluetooth technology, but unless the handsets were adapted to use Class 1 radios, range bottomed out at around thirty feet.

The handsets in Smart's luggage allowed him to control up to eight units by toggling through a visual display and pressing a virtual trigger. The time lapse between firing and the bullet leaving the barrel was negligible, meaning the operator could take part in a battle while hundreds of yards from the action.

Having these handy weapons was one thing. Getting them through airport security was something else entirely.

Although the British armed forces had yet to decide if they wanted to take delivery of the Sentinels, Minotaur Logistics had been granted a licence to use them for training and demonstration purposes, which meant they could take them overseas. Unfortunately, each trip abroad required clearance from the government in the form of a Standard Individual Export Licence, or SIEL. These took up to four weeks to process and, as Harvey barely had a day before the deadline was reached, they'd had to improvise.

Ellis had instructed MI5's tech wizard Gerald Small to find his way into SPIRE, the government's export licensing system, and create a new permit. A printable copy had then been emailed to Sonny, who had used a previous permit to copy over the relevant signatures. While it looked authentic, and the soft copy was correctly entered on the government database, the ruse would fall apart if anyone cared to do a little digging.

Ellis had assured them that Small had covered his tracks, but if they got caught at the border, they were on their own.

Smart had seen it as an acceptable risk. Not only did the Sentinels more than double their firepower; they would also hold up any pursuers, aiding the team's escape.

After checking in the rest of their baggage, Smart led the squad to the security desk, where he handed over the permit with a smile. The woman behind the counter didn't reciprocate as she picked it up and studied it closely, occasionally glancing up at Smart, who did his best to remain calm.

'Bring it through,' she said, and opened a door so that Smart could wheel the luggage into a small room. He lifted the suitcase and placed it on a counter, then undid the combination locks and flipped open the lid.

'What are these?'

Smart took one of the devices from its compartment and quickly took it apart, explaining its purpose.

The woman asked him to put it back together, then counted the contents of the suitcase and compared it with the permit.

Just stamp the bloody thing, Smart silently urged her, but instead the clerk picked up the phone and began dialling.

Betty Hemmingway wanted to ignore the bleeping phone and get to the George and Dragon, where her sister was waiting to have lunch with her. Betty was desperate to know the results of the scan, but her supervisor was hovering near the water cooler and wouldn't take kindly to her leaving her desk five minutes early and ignoring an incoming call.

Hemmingway snatched at the handset. 'Department of Business, Innovation and Skills,' she said, trying to sound civil.

'Hi, this is Anne Pickering from Heathrow,' the caller said. 'I've got a SIEL here and would just like to authenticate it.'

Great, Hemmingway thought. A ten-minute slog back and forth to the archive, meaning a short lunch break. Not what she needed when her sister was going to give her the results of the oncology test.

Sorry to hear the bad news, sis, but I have to get back to work now.

'Okay, give me the number,' Hemmingway said, resigned to the fact that she would be late. She picked up her pen and pulled a notepad towards her, but an idea stopped her.

Verification was normally done against hard copies to ensure that the necessary signatures were in place, but there was also a database containing records of all permits issued. She checked the clock on the wall and saw that her lunch break started in two minutes.

Hemmingway glanced over to her supervisor, who was thankfully in conversation with the office Romeo and flirting like a teenager. She opened the SPIRE screen and typed the reference number into the box before hitting the Enter key.

'Issued to a Mr Leonard Anthony Smart of Minotaur Logistics on January sixth,' she said, reading from the screen. 'Eight Sentinel automated devices – whatever those are – and no ammunition.'

'Thanks,' Pickering said. 'That tallies with what we have here.'

Hemmingway put down the phone and saw that she was a minute into her lunch hour. She closed down the screen and locked her computer, then grabbed her coat and bag and hurried to the exit.

The fact that the name of the authorising clerk on the permit was Betty Hemmingway simply didn't have time to register with her.

'Thank you, Mr Smart. If you leave this with me, I'll make sure it's loaded onto your flight.'

Smart left the office and joined the four other men; he was finally able to release the breath he felt he'd been holding for the last five minutes.

'We good?' Sonny asked, and got a nod in reply.

'I think I need a beer, though,' Smart said.

They wouldn't be heading into Tagrilistan for another twenty-four hours, so it wasn't as if they didn't have time to sleep it off. Smart led them through customs and security, then found a bar that sold his favourite ale. He bought a round on the company credit card and settled into his chair.

'I can't believe Tom didn't come,' Sonny said, sipping his lager.

'I know,' Smart agreed. 'He's changed so much in the last couple of years. I can't say I blame him, though. Melissa's his world.'

'Who's Melissa?' Howard asked.

'Tom's daughter,' Smart told him.

The three newcomers had all met Gray during their interviews with Minotaur months earlier, though they knew nothing of his private life beyond what was available on the Internet.

'I heard his wife died a couple of years ago,' Doc said. 'Must be hard bringing up a kid alone.'

'He's doing a great job,' Sonny said. 'Maybe a little overprotective, but that's his prerogative. Still, with his mate in trouble . . .'

'Tom's been through his fair share,' Smart said. 'He deserves to call it a day.'

Melling asked when they'd receive further details about the mission.

'Once we land in Kazakhstan we'll be met by our pilot,' Smart said. 'We'll then have eighteen hours to go over the plan and get our kit sorted.'

Smart would have preferred another couple of days going over satellite imagery before setting off, but the countdown to Harvey's demise was ticking. He'd given the trio the basics – location, target, time frame – but the finer details would have to wait until they were on the ground.

Sonny asked the others about their backgrounds. He'd been the one to put them through their paces at the training facility as part of their interview, but that had only lasted a couple of hours and the point had been to test their skills, not delve deeply into their private lives.

Doc Butterworth, it turned out, was the only one who was married, though he admitted it had been on the rocks for a few years now. It was the typical story of soldiers everywhere: always being away from home, putting a strain on yet another military marriage.

Smart rose and got another round of drinks in, then sat back down and pulled his Kindle from his hand luggage.

'Hey,' Sonny said, nudging Smart's foot with his own. 'You're becoming a real antisocial prick in your old age.'

'If we make it out of this alive, you can sue me,' Smart said, flicking the device into life. 'But just in case we don't, I want to finish this book. It's an absolutely cracking read.'

'I didn't know *Playboy* made e-books.' Sonny nudged him again.

Smart sighed. 'I know you have trouble concentrating on anything for more than two minutes if it doesn't centre around naked women, but some of us are a little more sophisticated.'

'Okay, professor, so what does SpongeBob SquarePants get up to this time?'

'It's actually called *Killing Hope*, by Keith Houghton.'

'Never heard of him,' Sonny said.

'That's because you're an uncultured yob, but give it a couple of years and even you'll recognise the name.'

Sonny shrugged and turned back to the other men, leaving Smart to indulge his passion.

Smart wasn't left alone for long.

A holdall was dumped on the seat next to him, startling him, and he looked up to see who the culprit was.

'Tom!'

'None other,' Gray said. 'Where's my pint?'

'We didn't think you were coming, remember?'

'What? You think I'd leave Andrew's life in Sonny's hands?'

'So what made you change your mind?' Sonny asked, ignoring the dig.

Gray asked a passing waiter for a beer and took a seat. 'Hopefully, I've got another forty years left on this planet. I just couldn't spend every day between now and then knowing that I didn't step up when a mate needed my help. Especially one who'd already saved my life.'

'What about Melissa?' Smart asked. 'Who's looking after her?'

'I wanted to get her to Ken and Mina in Italy, but there just wasn't time, so I asked my next-door neighbour. Sue used to be a teacher, and as they're both retired, they were happy to take her in for a few days.'

'I don't want to sound the pessimist, but what if we don't make it back?' Smart asked.

'I've already spoken with Ellis,' Gray said. 'She has instructions to take Melissa to San Giovanni in Fiore, and Ryan Amos has my will. She'd be well looked after.'

'Well, I'm glad you're here,' Sonny said, glancing at Smart. 'It wouldn't be the same with Granddad in charge.'

Chapter 18

23 January 2016

Harvey heard the lock on the door being pulled back, and he forced himself further into the corner of the room, giving them as little of his body to aim at as possible.

For the last . . . he had no idea how long it had been – they'd been coming into his cell and beating him mercilessly. Not once did they ask any questions, they just set about him with their fists and feet. The assaults lasted just a couple of minutes, then they would leave, laughing as they slammed the door and locked it once more.

Harvey got himself into a foetal position and waited for the punishment to begin, but all he heard was metal scraping on the floor, before the door banged shut again. He waited a few moments, just in case it was a ruse to get him to drop his guard. He listened for breathing, and when his ears failed to register anything, he cracked open one bruised eye and surveyed the room. His head pounded when he moved it, but eventually his gaze came across the tray of food on the floor.

He couldn't remember the last time he'd eaten. He recalled having a late snack before going on the stake-out with Hamad, but how long ago was that? He'd spent at least eighteen hours at the farmhouse before he was drugged, and it took another ten to fly to Tagrilistan, plus the drive to the airport and the journey to his current location. That accounted for a day and a half, and then there was the time he'd spent in his cell.

Harvey eased himself over to the tray, his arms and legs aching from the beatings. Close to three days, he reckoned. He'd had a drink of water at the farmhouse, but nothing since. The liquid in the Styrofoam cup tasted like nectar as it slid down his throat, but there was too little of it. He used his parched tongue to extract every last drop, then turned to the rest of the fare. Two slices of hard bread sat next to a grey-brown mush that must have passed for stew to the locals. He sniffed at it, a pointless exercise as his broken nose was bunged up with blood and snot. Harvey scooped up some of the stew with a slice of bread and thrust it into his mouth.

He instantly regretted it.

As he bit down on the rock-hard bread, his broken incisor sent a lightning bolt of pain shooting through his skull. The food dropped from his mouth as he screamed, and he cursed himself for forgetting about it. It was one of two teeth that had been damaged during the assaults, the other a molar on the other side of his mouth.

Harvey abandoned the bread and scooped up the stew, sucking at any lumps before swallowing the foul-tasting mess.

Once he'd finished, he sat back and tried to take stock of his injuries. His arms were covered in bruises from his attempts to deflect the blows, and one or two of his ribs felt like they were broken. Blood caked the side of his head where it had been smashed against the brick wall, and both eyes were swollen almost shut.

All in all, he looked like crap and felt like shit.

Harvey slowly edged himself back into the corner, ignoring the more comfortable-looking bed. If they decided to rush in again, he wouldn't have time to get to the relative safety of the floor before they set about him again. It meant sitting on the freezing-cold stone floor, but a cold backside was better than leaving his internal organs exposed.

What concerned him most – above the pain and hunger – were the words Colonel Aminev had left him with.

You will be shot as a spy on Tuesday morning.

Harvey tried to focus his mind and work out what the hell he was doing here. Why would Bessonov have him sent all the way to Tagrilistan? Why not just kill him and dump him in the river, as he had done with Willard? If they really thought he was a spy, they would have dealt with him by now, so why wait until Tuesday?

Perhaps the British government had offered a deal to get him out, and a deadline had been set to secure his release. That would explain the delay, but what could Aminev want in return? It wouldn't be weapons, because Aminev was getting plenty of those from the Russians. Money, perhaps? A prisoner exchange?

If it were the latter, then he was in big trouble. Cooper had told him how much the Tagrilistani president, Viktor Milenko, hated Moscow, so there was no way he'd allow a single separatist prisoner to go free.

He had to pray that it was something else.

A deal that both sides could live with.

One that would be finalised before Aminev and his cronies finished him off.

Chapter 19

24 January 2016

A slate-grey sky and bitter winds welcomed Gray and his team to Kazakhstan. They passed through immigration without a problem, but Gray knew the real fun would start when they reached security.

'Are you sure this is going to convince them?' Gray asked Smart.

'Guaranteed.'

Gray didn't share his optimism. Planning is like a house of cards, and just one mistake can bring the whole lot crashing down. The concern on Gray's face didn't go unnoticed.

'I watched Sonny create it,' Smart said. 'It's a masterpiece.'

Smart explained how Sonny had taken a copy of a fax he'd received from the Kazakh interior ministry and doctored it to look like the certificate they needed. 'It was the PIC they sent us back in 2011, when we were protecting the BP people, remember?'

Gray did indeed. The Prior Import Consent document had enabled them to take their own weapons to Kazakhstan five years earlier, as part of a security detachment guarding oil workers who were operating near the Russian border at a time of high tensions. The certificate was the counterpart to the SIEL Smart had used to get the Sentinels out of the UK, with this part authorising them to be brought into the Kazakh capital, Astana.

'Sonny cut the header off the old one,' Smart said, 'you know, the bit with the sender and date stamp. He altered it, then stuck it onto a blank PIC and filled in the details. He then ran it through the fax machine on copy, and *voilà*.'

'Well, after what you told me about Heathrow, let's hope the guys here aren't as thorough.'

Gray needn't have been concerned. They produced the document at customs and, after a cursory examination of the luggage in a private room, the team were allowed on their way.

Out in the arrivals area, it wasn't difficult to spot McGregor. He towered above everyone else, his bushy black beard making him look like a grizzly bear.

'I see you found some backbone.' The giant smiled, grabbing Gray's hand with paws the size of dinner plates.

'I had some wise words thrown at me.' Gray winced as his fingers were crushed. 'Some of them must have stuck.'

Gray handled the introductions. McGregor already knew Smart and Sonny, having served with them before, but the rest were new faces.

'Looks to me like you can't count,' McGregor said. 'I told you I only have room for five.'

'I was a last-minute addition,' Gray apologised. 'It was too late to send one of the others home. Besides, I was hoping you could manage six, what with Sonny and Edgar being so small.'

'It's not about weight,' McGregor said. 'We'll be using a Bell Jet Ranger, and with your gear, there'll be no room for a sixth man, no matter how small they are.'

'We're not taking that much in with us,' Gray argued. 'Can't it go in the luggage compartment?'

McGregor shook his head. 'From here to Dubrany is two hundred and fifty miles and the chopper's range is only three hundred. I've had to fit an auxiliary fuel pod in the hold to get us there and back.'

That left Gray with an awkward choice to make. There was no way Sonny or Smart would stand down, which left the other three. Mark Howard's CQB skills would be much needed on the mission, but then so would the language skills of the other two.

He decided to keep Butterworth, mainly for his medic skills. With one Russian speaker chosen, it then became easier to pick the last member of the squad.

'Sorry, Edgar, but I'm going to have to send you home. You can keep the money I paid you up front, but you'll have to make your own way back to the UK.'

Melling looked a little deflated, but he nodded gamely. 'No worries. Five grand to take a couple of flights is no great hardship. Are you sure you don't want to keep me in reserve, though?'

Gray considered the idea, but not for long. 'If anything does go wrong, we'll be dead by the time Mac here manages to get you on the scene. No, go home, mate, and thanks for volunteering.'

Melling shook hands all round and wished them all a safe return, then threw his bag over his shoulder and headed for the ticket desk.

McGregor led the team outside, where a biting wind tugged at their clothes. Rain added to the misery, but thankfully they didn't have to walk far to McGregor's minivan. They dumped their gear in the back and piled in, then McGregor drove them past the glass-fronted terminal building with the huge blue dome on top and down Qabanbay Batyr Avenue. The road seemed to go on for ever, just a right-hand bend to break up the monotony. Eventually, they arrived in the capital, and Gray was surprised by the architecture. He'd expected block-like Soviet-era buildings everywhere, but the place was a mass of curves and spires. To his right he saw a pair of gold towers, and beyond that the blue-domed roof of the Presidential Palace.

'I must say, I wasn't expecting this,' he said to McGregor. 'This place puts London to shame.'

'It certainly is beautiful,' the Scotsman agreed. 'Now you can see why I left Glasgow behind.'

Twenty minutes and one left turn later, they were back in the countryside. Green rolled by on either side for another few miles, until the aerodrome came into view. McGregor turned down the approach road and pulled into a hangar, killing the engine. The men climbed out and found themselves sharing the space with a black helicopter, its engine port open and tools strewn on the floor. Spots of rust on the skids suggested it wasn't the newest of machines.

'Throw your things in the corner,' McGregor said, pointing to an area of the hangar that contained five sleeping bags. 'I'm afraid that's your digs for the night.'

The Scotsman led them over to the sleeping area and turned on two industrial heaters – Gray immediately felt the difference. Large pieces of cardboard had been spread on the stone floor to stop the cold from seeping upwards as they slept, and an ancient kettle stood next to coffee and tea canisters on a metal workbench nearby.

'What about the weapons?' Gray asked.

'On their way,' McGregor assured him. 'They'll be here tonight.'

'We'll need somewhere to prepare,' Gray said, as he dumped his bag on the floor and pulled out a file containing screenshots taken from Ellis's laptop. McGregor cleared a table and pulled it away from the wall so that everyone could gather round, then filled the kettle and produced some cracked and stained mugs, telling the team to help themselves.

Once everyone had a beverage, Gray outlined the plan.

'Mac will drop us off here,' he said, pointing to an open expanse to the east of Dubrany. 'Our approach doesn't take us over Russian-held territory, but there's still a chance the Tagrilistani army might want to take potshots at us. We won't be filing a flight plan, so both sides will probably treat us as hostiles.'

'You always start off with good news,' Sonny said with a wink.

'What happens after we land?' Howard asked.

'We'll be dropped off a couple of miles from the edge of town. Any closer and we risk someone hearing the chopper. From there we tab to this area.' Another spot on the map marked a disused petrol station, along with GPS coordinates. 'Sonny and Len will plant an incendiary, then we make our way around the town to our infiltration point. It's a six-mile hike, so I hope you've been staying in shape. We'll be going in at oh three hundred tomorrow, so we don't expect too many people to be around at that time. A few sentries at most. If we come across anyone, we try and skirt round them. If we can't, we take them out as silently as possible. Most of them should already be preoccupied with the explosion, anyway.'

'What weapons are we taking in?' Doc asked.

'AKs and suppressed Glocks,' Smart said, looking at McGregor, who nodded confirmation.

'I've also got half a dozen concussion grenades and a dozen frags, plus night-vision glasses, comms units and a block of C4. Everything Mr Gray asked for. I've even got a little surprise for you.'

'What's that?'

'If I tell you, it won't be a surprise.' McGregor tutted.

'On the way into town,' Gray continued, 'we'll set up the Sentinels along this route. Doc, you've used them before, right?'

'A couple of times.'

'Good. There's an alleyway here. I want you to remain there and control the Sentinels to cover our retreat.'

'That'll leave us a man short,' Sonny pointed out.

'I know, but it's not easy to control these things when you're running for your life. It'll only take four of us to go in and get Andrew. Two to carry him, if need be, the other two to provide cover.'

Gray showed them overheads of the police station where they believed Harvey was being held captive. 'We don't have schematics, only word that the building contains holding cells. So when we get inside we'll have to do our best to locate him. Once he's found, we make our way back out the same way and rendezvous with Mac at the drop-off point.'

'Sounds good to me,' Smart said.

'Yeah,' Sonny added. 'What could possibly go wrong?'

They all ignored the rhetorical question, knowing that plenty could send the plan sideways before they even landed in Tagrilistan.

All heads turned to the entrance as a truck pulled up. A man wearing jeans and white shirt climbed out of the cab, dark glasses on despite the sun having disappeared a couple of hours earlier.

Gray watched McGregor go out to meet him, and noticed the man wasn't exactly enamoured with having an audience. McGregor spoke to the man quietly, and his words seemed to have a calming effect.

Their host walked back inside the hangar and asked a couple of the men to help unload the vehicle. They happily obliged, and within a couple of minutes the boxes were stacked on the floor and the truck drove off into the night.

'Let's see what we've got,' McGregor said, using a screwdriver to prise open the largest box. Inside were five AK-47s.

Gray took one and examined it. 'Looks pretty new,' he said as he stripped it down to check for dirt.

'Marek only delivers the best,' McGregor said.

The rest of the boxes were opened one by one, until their armoury was accounted for.

'Here's your little surprise,' McGregor said, holding a box of 9mm ammunition. 'For the Glocks I got ya.'

'What the hell are these?' Smart asked, examining the strange-looking rounds. The bullet itself was hollow with a copper jacket.

It looked like someone had taken a thin blade and cut through the head four times, creating eight pointed prongs and a crown resembling the teeth of a saw.

'G2R RIP rounds,' McGregor said, turning a cartridge in his hand. 'Stands for "radically invasive projectile". See these little strips of copper? They shear off when the bullet strikes the target. The rest of the slug continues on like a normal round, but these fly off in eight different directions and give someone a really bad day. Hit someone in the centre of the chest and you damage the heart, lungs, liver, stomach, spleen – you name it.'

'Sounds like major stopping power.'

'It'll turn people to mincemeat,' McGregor said. 'Speaking of which, I'll go and get some food in. You guys clean those weapons and we'll test them first thing in the morning.'

Chapter 20

24 January 2016

Veronica Ellis looked out on the main office and saw a sea of empty desks. A light illuminated a corner of the room, where Thompson was predictably working late into the night.

Ellis turned off her laptop and secured it in her bag, then locked her office door and went over to see how her temporary section lead was getting on with the latest search. Following Harvey's disappearance, it hadn't taken long for the paperwork confirming Thompson's temporary reassignment to Five to go through, and her experience made her the ideal choice to take over the reins from Solomon.

'Still nothing on the inbound flights,' Thompson said.

Ellis knew that if Bessonov had sent his entire kill squad home, there was bound to be someone to replace them. Either that, or he'd decided to cancel the assassination attempt, which she didn't consider likely.

'Maybe you should expand the search to all flights from the East, not just Russia.'

'I already did that,' Thompson said. She sat back in her chair and ran her hands through her long blonde hair. 'Any news from Gray?'

'Nothing yet. They only landed a couple of hours ago, so give them time to get ready for the mission. Don't worry, Tom knows what he's doing.'

Thompson offered a weak smile. 'I know, I've seen him in action. It's different, though, with Andrew the one being held prisoner.'

Ellis felt the same. It was hard to stay detached when someone close was in danger.

'How's Hamad?' Thompson asked.

'Stable, the last I heard. I'll be going to see him tomorrow. Hopefully I'll get to talk to him this time.' Ellis put a hand on Thompson's shoulder. 'Don't stay too long. You need your sleep.'

She left the office, swiping her card at the door. It had been another long day, and further attempts to reach a diplomatic resolution had proven pointless, leaving Harvey's fate in Tom Gray's hands.

Richard Notley pulled off the country road and opened the gate to the field, then got back in the car and drove through, parking behind the tall hedge.

As with every journey he made in his car, he'd done his checks before setting off. Nothing under the hood and no tracking devices secured beneath the car. Still, he rolled the window down a couple of inches and waited for ten minutes.

Not a single vehicle passed his hiding place. Satisfied that he hadn't been followed or tracked, he got out of the driver's seat and climbed in the back, where his bag waited. He carefully took out the small device and laid it on the seat, then found the tube containing the detonator. It wasn't the most sophisticated bomb ever conceived, but tonight he would discover if it was enough to achieve his aims.

The small roasting tin had been filled with gunpowder taken from the fireworks he'd purchased at the end of October, just before Bonfire Night. He'd also added some screws, then used a soldering kit to weld a small metal plate over the contents, creating an improvised Claymore mine. On this test unit he'd forgone the hooks that would allow him to thread a string through and hang the device around his neck. If tonight were a success, it would be the last adjustment to make on the one remaining bomb, which remained safely stashed in his garage in a hole dug under a loose flagstone.

Notley put the detonator in his pocket, then carried the device and the bag into the night, sticking close to the hedge that ran away from the road. He took his time, with only the faint moonlight to guide his way. When he reached the far corner of the field, he climbed over a stile and into the next field, where a tree stood proud but naked, its leaves shed months earlier.

Marian had loved this place. He recalled how they used to picnic here during the summers, enjoying sandwiches and a bottle of wine before lying back and savouring the peace and quiet, far away from the bustling capital.

They'd planned to move out here once they retired. Get a little place of their own, perhaps grow vegetables and have a few chickens and goats roaming around.

That plan had been destroyed the day she'd been stolen from him.

Notley cleared away the image and concentrated on the job in hand. He placed the bomb at the base of the tree, then removed the detonator from its tube. Wires trailed from one end, attached to a small circuit board. He stuck the other end into the hole in the side of the casing, then took the watermelon from the bag and placed it on the ground ten feet in front of the tree.

Once he was happy with the angle, he walked back to the hedge and climbed over the stile once more, then took the phone from his pocket and turned it on. Turning it off earlier had been a necessary precaution to avoid blowing himself up as he prepared the test.

He listened once more for sounds of anyone in the area, but heard nothing but a few night creatures in search of food or love.

Notley found the preset number and hit the Call button.

He'd expected a loud bang, but not one that shattered the night. Seconds after detonation, he could still hear the echo reverberating around the valley below. Conscious that someone must have heard it, he quickly jumped into the next field and checked the scene.

The device was nothing but a lump of twisted metal, and a huge black scar adorned the tree where the bomb had been sitting. Screws embedded in the bark glinted as he examined the scene more closely. There was now little doubt that when he wore the other device around his neck and detonated it, he would not survive the blast.

That no longer mattered.

The good news was that the melon hadn't fared any better. It lay in a dozen pieces, ripped apart by the explosion and homemade shrapnel.

Notley quickly gathered as much of the evidence as he could and stuffed it back in the bag, then jogged back towards the car. A vehicle's headlights crested the hill a few hundred yards away, causing him to freeze in fear. Notley threw himself to the ground and watched the two white discs approach him.

Was it the police? Had they tailed him here, and were now closing in to catch him in the act?

The vehicle was nearing the gate, but instead of stopping, it maintained its speed and he watched its red tail lights disappear around the corner.

For the next few seconds, the only sound he could hear was the pulse pounding inside his skull. He forced himself to his feet and got back to the car as quickly as he could. After throwing the bag onto the back seat, he opened the gate and got behind the wheel. There was no sign of any traffic as he pulled out of the field and back onto the road, and he kept his foot to the floor, putting as much distance between himself and the blast site as quickly as possible.

Notley came to a main road a few minutes later, and he eased off the accelerator to stay under the speed limit.

Adrenalin continued to course through his body, though he felt a little calmer now that he was heading home. All he had to do was dump the bag somewhere. Then he could relax completely.

The test had gone better than expected, and only a few days remained before he would take his remaining device and give Marian the justice she deserved.

The sun was offering up its last rays when Ivan Zhabin walked into Ezeiza International Airport, carrying only a holdall containing two changes of clothes and a bag of toiletries.

He'd spent the fifteen-mile journey from his apartment on the outskirts of Buenos Aires on his phone, studying overheads of London. It gave him a starting point, but he wouldn't be able to get a proper feel for the location until he was on the ground, and able to walk around and see the buildings up close. Despite the advances in online map technology, he couldn't get a true sense of the angles, even using Google Street View.

At the check-in desk, he produced a German passport in the name of Alec Stutz. It was one of five identities he used, each belonging to a different nationality. Apart from his native Russian, he also spoke fluent German, along with Spanish, French and English. Languages had come easily to him as a child, and even now, in his late forties, he was expanding into Mandarin Chinese and Arabic.

After collecting his boarding pass, Zhabin was forced to suffer the boredom of airport security. Fifteen minutes later, he was browsing the duty-free shops, and a paperback about an American sniper caught his eye. It was a book he'd read the previous year, its military aspect mirroring his own experience, decades earlier.

Zhabin had been a wiry seventeen-year-old when he'd been shipped out to Afghanistan towards the end of the Soviet war. For one so young and inexperienced to be assigned to a Spetsnaz unit would have been unheard of if it hadn't been for the remarkable skills he'd shown with a rifle during basic training. After excelling with the standard AK-47, he'd been introduced to the VSS Vintorez, or 'thread cutter'. Grouping five rounds in a one-inch target had been a piece of cake, even at the outside of the rifle's effective firing range of four hundred yards. When tested with a Dragunov SVD, which had double the range, he'd managed to maintain his accuracy. Eventual progression to the KSVK 2.7, with a maximum range of two thousand yards, had seen him break numerous army records.

Zhabin vividly remembered his first kill, in the Panjshir Valley. It had been in 1985, when through a heat haze he'd watched five armed members of the Mujahideen snake their way through a mountain pass. He'd been on forward lookout, alongside a surly sergeant who'd made his dislike for the rookie well known.

Zhabin had tried to explain that it wasn't his fault he'd been parachuted into the Special Forces while everyone else had been forced to undergo months of specialised training, but his words fell on deaf ears. He'd soon realised that the only way to win the team's trust was to show his worth in combat, and that day on the ridge gave him the opportunity.

While the sergeant called in the enemy location and requested air support, Zhabin had picked the first of his targets: a bearded man with an American-supplied FIM-92 Stinger thrown over his shoulder. The shoulder-fired anti-aircraft missile had been responsible for bringing down more than two hundred helicopter gunships in the preceding six years. Zhabin's job was to take it out of the fight before it added another chopper to the list.

He'd calculated the range at seventeen hundred yards, adjusted for the slight breeze, and let loose his first round of the war. For a second nothing happened, until the bullet reached its target.

Zhabin's armour-piercing round penetrated the tube and struck the explosive warhead, vaporising the man carrying it. Before his companions could understand what had happened, another had fallen to a headshot, with a third struck in the chest as he dived for cover. The remaining pair had gone to ground by this time, only to be mopped up by a pair of MIL Mi-24 choppers a few minutes later.

The sergeant had grudgingly conceded that it had been a fine display of marksmanship, but Zhabin hadn't been looking for accolades. As long as they accepted him into the unit, he'd known that they would watch his back.

The war hadn't been about a glorious Soviet victory. Not for Zhabin, at least. He'd seen it as a legitimate way to hone his natural talent, which would one day see him earn more than $100,000 per kill.

The boarding announcement brought Zhabin back to the present, and he made his way to the gate. A blonde woman sitting in the departure lounge smiled as he walked past, clearly attracted to the lithe six-footer with the chiselled jaw and designer stubble. But Zhabin only had business on his mind.

Besides, she wasn't his type. He preferred brunettes, and the younger the better. Not illegal-young, but well before gravity and the ravages of time had a chance to ruin their bodies. There'd been many such women in his life, but he'd never been in a proper relationship with any of them.

He ignored the woman's gaze and took a seat a few rows away from her, then sat back and closed his eyes as he waited for his row to be called. The blonde's attention had stirred something in him, and his mind drifted back, as it often did, to his first sexual encounter.

It had been a few days after his first kill in Afghanistan, and the patrol had been tasked with clearing a small village suspected of housing Mujahideen fighters. They'd met no resistance, and only found two men capable of fighting, along with a dozen others of varying age. There was nothing to suggest they were anything than goat herders – no weapons or communication equipment – but that hadn't stopped his sergeant. He'd summarily executed the men and had his team round up everyone else.

A young girl, barely sixteen, had been discovered hiding in a locked cupboard in one of the ruined houses. Zhabin had been called in from his position on a mountainside overlooking the buildings, and after a thirty-minute hike to the village, the sergeant had handed her to him with a wicked grin.

'Time to lose your cherry.'

Noticing Zhabin's initial hesitance, his sergeant had drawn his knife and slashed the girl's clothing, then stripped her naked. To Zhabin, she'd looked exactly as he'd imagined a woman to look. He'd looked up at his sergeant.

'Quick, cherry, take her inside before your pants explode!'

Ignoring the jibes of the other soldiers, Zhabin dragged the girl into one of the houses, the hoots of laughter muted as he slammed the door shut and pushed her towards a bed, watching her hungrily as he fumbled at his clothing. He was naked in seconds and advanced on her, pushing her onto her back and forcing her legs apart. It might have been his first time, but he'd seen enough videos to know where everything went, and he pushed himself inside her, ignoring her cries. As he rode her, she clenched her eyes shut, her face turned to the side. It was only when he was close to climaxing that she turned to look at him. The raw hatred in her brown eyes was something he'd never forget.

That wasn't how it was meant to be. Nothing in the porn he'd seen had conveyed such a message, and he hated her for spoiling what was, for him, a special moment. His hands had gone to her throat, squeezing as he shouted at her in Russian to take it back, but the girl obviously didn't understand or was refusing to do so.

Zhabin had kept up the pressure on her windpipe, and it was only when the life had been drained from her that the hatred vanished. With it had come the most glorious explosion from the pit of his stomach, enough to make him see stars.

Around him now, passengers had begun walking to the departure gate. Zhabin realised he'd missed the announcement for his row. He hurried to join them, and promised himself that, although the trip to London was purely business, he'd find time to add a little pleasure.

Chapter 21

25 January 2016

Tom Gray sent another three-round burst downrange and waited for Sonny to call out the result.

'Still a couple of inches to the right.'

Gray made a small adjustment and tried again. This time he was rewarded with the thumbs-up.

With each man having zeroed their rifles and handguns, Gray set about putting Doc through his paces with the Sentinels. He set up four units and had Doc toggle between them to pick his targets.

'One, double tap!'

A second later, two rounds left the machine, scored chest shots in the improvised cardboard cut-outs.

'Three, single shot!'

It took Doc a few seconds to switch screens and adjust his aim, but he managed to get a round through the middle of a crudely drawn head.

Gray called out a dozen more commands, until Doc was able to go from one Sentinel to the next in under two seconds.

'Not bad for a nurse.' Sonny smiled.

'Ignore him,' Smart said. 'He's just jealous.'

'Len's right,' Gray added. 'That was good work. After we've had a bite to eat, we'll give it another go.'

McGregor had provided a picnic of breads and cold meats, as well as an icebox full of water and soft drinks. Gray made a sandwich and looked around, seeing nothing for miles in any direction. The entire area was flat, with just a few clumps of trees breaking up the horizon. The ideal place to get to know their weapons without interruption.

'So who's this Harvey guy?' Doc asked. 'I mean, I know he's a friend, but what's his story?'

Smart swallowed a mouthful of cold sausage. 'Remember a few years ago, when Tom was holed up in that building for a few days?'

'Who could forget?'

'Well, Andrew was the one sent to talk him down.'

'Seriously?'

'That's when I first met him,' Gray said, 'but later on, after I'd been living in the Philippines for some months, I was taken hostage by militants in the south. Sonny and Len came to get me, but on the way back there were elements of the government who wanted us all dead. Andrew stopped them. He saved our lives.'

'But to be fair, he didn't know who he was saving at the time,' Sonny said. 'Just that British citizens were in the firing line.'

'After that, we became close friends with Andrew,' Smart added. 'We've even carried out a mission together, in Cuba.'

'Andrew's a good man,' Gray said. 'He's one of the few I'd do this for.'

At Doc's request, Gray spent the rest of the meal telling them about his time in the Philippines, and how Sonny and Len had come to mount their own rescue mission, only to become targets themselves.

'Enough of the chit-chat,' McGregor said, breaking up the party. 'I need to get back soon. There's still some maintenance work to be done on the chopper before we go.'

They packed away the food and Gray gave Doc another thirty minutes of practice on the Sentinels. Ideally, he would have liked another hour, but apart from McGregor's concerns about time, they were getting low on ammunition. Of the two thousand rounds of 7.62 mm that McGregor had managed to get his hands on, a little more than a thousand remained. That gave them three thirty-round clips each for their assault rifles, plus a hundred for each Sentinel.

After gathering up the targets and spent cartridge cases, the team climbed into the van for the thirty-minute drive back to the airfield. Doc had his headphones on, listening to music, but the rest sat in silence, contemplating the battle ahead.

Tom Gray crept along the narrow street, keeping close to the wall. The night was one of the darkest he'd ever known, and even the night-vision goggles had trouble finding enough ambient light to illuminate the scene.

Behind him, Smart was checking the rooftops while Sonny kept an eye on the rear.

When he reached the building on the corner, he gazed out onto nothingness. They were on the outskirts of town, and where the man-made structures ended, a flat, endless expanse began.

Gray walked out into the black, his goggles now unable to even discern the horizon. Sonny and Smart followed, weapons seeking out targets that none of them could see.

Suddenly, the horizon appeared, the line between land and sky a single row of bright flashes.

'Incoming!'

Gray heard the staccato retorts of distant rifles, and watched immobile as tracer rounds began walking a path towards him, each one throwing up spurts of dirt as the bullets chewed the ground in front of him.

Tat-tat-tat-tat!

Closer, closer, until the first of them reached the toe of his boot.

Tat-tat-tat-tat!

Gray woke with a jolt, though he couldn't be sure he wasn't still dreaming. The *tat-tat-tat* continued, no longer just a memory of a distant time.

'Pissing down outside,' McGregor said, as he stirred a cup of tea.

Gray realised that the sound was large drops of rain bouncing off the corrugated iron roof of the hangar, not enemy gunfire.

'Bad dream?'

Gray looked up at the Scot. 'A night patrol in Iraq,' he said. 'The village was supposed to be cleared and secure, but as we passed through we came across a company of Iraqi regulars. Thankfully they weren't Republican Guard and couldn't shoot straight to save their lives. A few rounds came close, but we put down cover fire, retreated and called in the A-10s.'

'There's nothing like shitty intel to fuck up a stroll in the badlands.'

Gray couldn't agree more, and he knew that the mission they were about to undertake was based on best-guesses and shaky estimates of enemy numbers. The latest reports on the news had confirmed Ellis's report: Russian heavy arms were leaving Tagrilistan, despite President Demidov's insistence that there had never been any there in the first place. Whether they had all departed was the unknown factor.

If Ellis's numbers were correct and they only faced four hundred armed civilians, their chances of pulling it off were high. If the Russians had decided to leave a battalion behind, the odds of success nose-dived.

His watch told Gray that it was nine in the evening, two hours before they were due to set off. He woke the other four and told them to grab a brew, then get their gear ready.

As with the ride back from target practice earlier that morning, final preparations were done with minimal conversation. All thoughts were turned to the next few hours, during which time lives would be lost. Only by focusing could they increase the chances of not being included in that number. Even the normally cheerful Sonny was going about the job of securing his gear in silence.

Gray had nothing but Melissa on his mind. He began to doubt the wisdom of his decision to take part in this rescue attempt, but it was too late now. He was committed, and all he could do was pray that the information Ellis had supplied was close to accurate.

If it weren't, Melissa would likely grow up without the father she needed.

The sound of a motor broke into Gray's thoughts, and he looked towards the hangar entrance to see McGregor backing a small vehicle into the bay. He nudged it up to the nose of the helicopter, then climbed out and secured a metal arm from the back of the tow tractor to the wheeled platform the bird was sitting on.

'Stand clear while I take her out,' McGregor said, climbing back onto the compact machine. He slowly pulled the chopper out of the hangar and into the driving rain, then disengaged the tug and drove it out of the way. He then hit a button to lower the platform and rolled it back into the bay.

'Grab your gear,' McGregor shouted as he climbed into the pilot's seat.

Gray picked up his rifle and led the others out to their transport, a single line of figures dressed entirely in black. McGregor already had the engine cycling up, and the rotors on the tail and overhead began rotating, slowly at first, then faster as the mechanism got up to speed.

Gray climbed in the back and strapped himself into the seat, then put on a pair of headphones so that he could communicate with the pilot. Smart was the last aboard, and the skids left the tarmac the instant he slammed the door shut.

A gust of wind slammed into the chopper as it hovered above the pad, but McGregor expertly compensated and turned the nose ninety degrees, climbing quickly.

Within seconds, the ground was lost from sight, and Gray began to suffer from vertigo. With nothing to distinguish land from sky, up from down, his body couldn't be sure of its own orientation. It was something he'd experienced before, and to compensate he pulled the night-vision goggles down from his forehead and powered them up. It took a second for the unit to spring to life, but Gray was then able to make out the landscape below. Fields crawled past a thousand feet beneath them, and a swelling river cut a lazy path through dense woodland.

Once his body readjusted to the surroundings, Gray flicked off the NVGs to conserve the battery, then closed his eyes to try and grab some sleep. The constant whine of the engine and hypnotic *thwack* of the rotor blades as they sliced through the air produced the soporific effect he needed to drift off.

What seemed like only seconds later, McGregor's voice exploded in his headset: 'Fifteen minutes out!'

Gray was instantly alert. The others were already carrying out their final checks, ensuring rounds were chambered in their rifles and handguns, and that their grenades and knives were secure. Gray went over his own gear one more time, then put his face against the window. The rain was still lashing the bird, but through the rivers obfuscating the glass he could still make out lights on the ground in the distance.

McGregor let the altitude bleed off, then warned his passengers that they had ten seconds to exit the bird once they hit dirt.

Gray powered on his night-sights and braced himself, one hand on the door handle while the other gripped his AK-47. When the aircraft touched down, it was with a gentle kiss, and Gray threw the door open and jumped to the ground. He ran twenty yards through slick mud and brought his rifle up, searching for any signs that their approach had been detected. As he'd hoped, the landscape was clear.

Seconds later, the downdraught blew rain sideways as McGregor took their transport a safe distance from the landing zone. Gray waited for silence to return, then gathered the men and checked his GPS to guide them in the right direction.

The rain and sodden ground made it heavy going, and they arrived at their first port of call twenty minutes behind schedule. Gray was the first to see the canopy covering the petrol pumps and the small shop adjacent. The station was based on the edge of Dubrany, one of those last-stop-for-a-hundred-miles places before civilisation gave way to endless taiga. He ordered the men to take a knee and scoped it out. As expected, there was no sign of life. It looked like the fuel station had been abandoned, but there was still a chance some petrol remained in the underground reservoirs. If not, it would be the most pitiful diversion in history.

Sonny and Smart stooped and ran forward, while the rest of the team covered them. Gray watched them check the shop for signs of life, and then run to the two fuel pumps. Sonny extracted the first of the shaped charges and fastened it to the base of the dispenser, while Smart mirrored his actions on the other pump. Seconds later they were on their way back.

'We gave them an extra thirty minutes because of the conditions,' Smart said. 'We don't want them to go off too early.'

'Good thinking.'

Gray put Mark Howard on point and told him to set a decent pace. Normal walking pace was about three miles per hour, and they would need to manage at least double that to get to the kick-off point on time. The slippery conditions underfoot didn't help, and Howard soon had them all blowing as they covered the first mile in just seven minutes. By that time their clothes were saturated, and wind chill brought the temperature down to well below zero.

Howard suddenly stopped and raised a hand, causing the rest of the team to freeze. Gray went up front to find out what was causing the hold-up.

'Over there,' Howard said, pointing towards the town. They were skirting it at a range of five hundred yards, far enough away to have the rain dampen the sound of their passage.

Gray saw a light coming from one of the buildings. 'Looks like a fire,' he noted. His goggles showed a couple of figures standing around it, obviously trying to stay warm. The idea that everyone would be asleep when they attacked had been more in hope than anything else, and Gray warned the men to expect more sentries along the way.

'Let's move further out,' he told Howard.

The point man took them another two hundred yards from the nearest building before continuing to circumnavigate the town. It added a few minutes to the time, and Gray urged him to up the pace a little.

By the time they reached the insertion point, a few legs were suffering from the sapping march, but they'd made it a few minutes ahead of schedule. That gave them time to rub cramped calves and catch their breath.

They would be entering the town between two buildings, and for the first time they saw that a large chain-link fence stood in their way. It hadn't shown up on the overhead satellite images, but a closer inspection showed that it wouldn't be too much of a problem. The metal was rusty and there were several spots where it had pulled away from the supporting posts. Gray tugged at a corner and made a hole big enough for Smart to crawl through, then urged the others to follow. When the last man was through, he slipped into the gap and pulled the fence back into place as best he could.

Gray scanned the area, looking for an indication that someone had heard their approach, but all he saw were square silhouettes, and the only sound was the constant *pat-pat-pat* as the rain continued unabated.

He slapped Sonny on the back. 'Go.'

Smart followed, then Howard and Doc, with Gray taking up the rear. They moved cautiously, aware that at any moment a Russian militant could step out in front of them or, worse, spot them from one of the many windows they were passing beneath.

Smart stopped and pointed to an alleyway, and Doc came forward to take up his position. The medic quietly cleared a space between two dumpsters, then crouched and took the Sentinel control unit from his backpack. After a moment to let the machine power on, he gave a thumbs-up and slid back into his hiding place.

The others hung around, waiting for the diversion to kick off. Gray was checking his watch, and held up a fist as the second hand ticked towards the twelve. He was rewarded with a distant *Crump! Crump!* as the devices they'd planted at the petrol station shook the night.

Gray spread his fingers, indicating that they would give it five minutes before moving out. That would be enough time for anyone in the area to be alerted to the explosion and show themselves. Their rifles were pointed towards the mouth of the alley, but no-one sprinted past and no lights came on.

Gray moved to the entrance and checked up and down the narrow street, then waved for the others to follow. He took the lead, sticking close to the wall, the nose of his rifle darting in all directions as he sought a threat.

After a hundred yards he stopped and signalled for Smart to set up the first of the Sentinels in a pile of rubble. His second-in-command removed the first of the two devices he carried in his pack and set it down among the debris created by a long-ago mortar strike, then flicked it into life and used his comms unit to make sure Doc had a good angle of fire.

When the response was positive, Smart stood and joined the others. They continued their slow progress towards the police station, stopping every couple of hundred yards to plant more Sentinels.

Sonny was crouching to place the fourth when the sound of an engine froze him to the spot. Lights illuminated the end of the street, and a truck filled with armed men roared into view.

The men made themselves as small as possible, trying to blend into the shadows, and Gray let out the breath he'd been holding when the vehicle passed out of sight. He urged Sonny to hurry, then checked the GPS. They were still a mile from the police headquarters, and he wanted to get there before the fire on the outskirts was extinguished and everyone headed back into town.

Sonny got confirmation from Doc, and straightened as the sudden squeal of brakes resounded against the buildings. Red tail lights could be seen at the end of the street, their glow intensifying.

'They're coming back,' Gray warned, and sprinted to a doorway opposite. The others spread out, finding whatever cover they could. Sonny flattened himself behind the small pile of rocks he'd been using to disguise his Sentinel, while Howard and Smart dashed into the gap between two houses.

Shouts came from the end of the street and Gray wished he had someone who could translate, but Doc was well out of earshot, and Melling had been sent home. All he could do was hope it was someone looking for a place to take a leak, otherwise the mission was about to get noisy.

Gray leaned his rifle into the corner of the doorway and eased his other hand to his sidearm, slowly pulling it from its holster, while taking care not to expose any part of his body. He held the suppressed pistol by his side, silently praying for the approaching figures to turn and leave, but they kept advancing, their shadows casting eerie shapes across the wall opposite.

Gray hoped for a movie moment in which the bad guy gets called back just before he discovers the hero, but reality was firmly in charge. He watched the snout of a rifle come into view and knew he was a split second from being discovered. His pistol rose as he took half a step into the open, his other arm coming up to form a two-handed grip. The first two rounds took out the man nearest him and he spun to get the other figure in his sights. The speed of his attack had been enough to catch the second man off guard, and a double tap to the chest sent him sprawling backwards, the RIP rounds performing better than even Gray expected.

'We've got to take the rest down before they raise the alarm,' he said over the net. He'd already grabbed his rifle and was sprinting towards the sound of the idling truck. He heard footsteps behind as the others followed his lead.

At the end of the street, he stuck a quarter of his head around the building and saw the vehicle waiting ten yards away. Gray counted nine men sitting in the back, trying to stay dry, and whispered for Sonny to join him in taking them out. Howard and Smart were tasked with clearing the cab, and within fifteen seconds the shooting was over.

For the moment.

'Now what?' Sonny asked.

'We go back and pick up those bodies, then take the truck and dump it somewhere. We can't have people swarming all over here when we come back out.'

They made short work of retrieving the dead, and once they were loaded into the back of the vehicle, Gray got the team to pull down the heavy canvas side panels to conceal the gruesome cargo before climbing in among the dead.

Smart climbed into the driver's seat, pushing the previous occupant into the right-hand foot well. He gunned the engine and sped along the main street, past shops long since abandoned. At the junction, he stopped to let a small convoy of similar trucks pass, then tagged on to the rear of them. Two blocks later, he took a sharp right and after a hundred yards pulled into the car park of a city school.

Smart pulled around the back of the building and killed the engine. He jumped out and found Gray already on the ground checking his GPS and online map.

'We're about six hundred yards from the police station,' Gray said. 'The most direct route is round the back of this building, over the wall and turn right, but we'll have to cross two main roads.'

'There's no other way in, unless we backtrack,' Smart pointed out. 'That adds nearly two miles to the journey.'

Gray agreed. The rain had partially let up, but a ten-foot wall remained a significant obstacle to his team. With no viable alternative, he led the team to the barrier, where they found a metal gate offering access to the adjoining street. One broken lock later, they slipped onto a quiet road. They'd already taken much longer than anticipated, so Gray led them at a sprint towards the next major intersection. Here, lights shone in a lot more buildings than he'd hoped for.

He signalled for his men to stay hidden as another couple of vehicles roared down the street, heading in the direction of the fire that still illuminated the skyline despite the rain. Once the tail lights were far enough away, Gray sprinted across the road and into the doorway of a bank. He waited for shouts to announce that he'd been discovered, but thankfully none came.

Sonny led the others across the road, and the four men jogged down a side street. Gray halted them before the next junction and checked their progress on his GPS set.

'Once we cross the next road, there's only two hundred yards to the target. Everyone know what they're supposed to do?'

Nods all round.

'Okay. Here we go.'

Gray once again took point and edged towards the corner of the building. With no traffic on the road, he ran as fast as he could across the four lanes and pressed himself against a wall, consumed by the shadows. Seconds later, the team was back together and they could see the fortress-like police station looming in the distance.

It was hard to miss.

Floodlights painted the inner walls white, and outside the perimeter wall there were three vehicles surrounded by at least twenty men.

'It'll be impossible to get past them without things kicking off,' Smart said.

Gray had been thinking the same thing, and once the bullets started flying, it was inevitable that every available Russian and militia member would be called in to help quell the attack. It was exactly the scenario he'd hoped to avoid, but short of calling off the mission and abandoning Harvey to his fate, he was out of options. They had to go in, but their chances of success had greatly diminished. They had no cover, whereas the guards had the vehicles to hide behind.

Gray had the feeling it was going to be a very short encounter, and not one they were likely to walk away from.

'Tom, let's plant the remaining Sentinels here and flank them.'

Gray looked at Sonny, who'd suggested the idea.

'Place two here and the other two twenty yards farther back,' Sonny continued, 'then we backtrack and come at them from the adjacent street. Doc can keep them occupied while we get behind them.'

'Do it,' Gray said, glad that someone on the team was thinking clearly.

He relayed the plan to Doc and told him to wait for his signal before engaging the enemy.

The four devices were set up within two minutes. Smart, Sonny and Howard followed Gray back to the main road, then edged along the front of a burnt-out supermarket to the next corner.

Gray stuck his head round and saw the rear of one of the vehicles, a twenty-year-old Toyota Hilux pickup with a .50-calibre machine gun nestled in the flat bed.

Gray set his comms unit to Open channel, so he wouldn't have to click his throat mic every time he wanted to relay orders, then made sure his men were set. They edged forward silently, until they were within fifty feet of the gated entry to the police station where the Russians were gathered.

'Doc, light 'em up.'

Almost immediately he heard the sound of bullets pinging off metal as Doc opened up with the first of the Sentinels. Gray saw a man jump into the back of the Toyota and begin returning fire at an unseen enemy, spraying the huge rounds down the street and into the darkness.

Gray pulled a fragmentation grenade from his webbing, tugged out the pin and broke into a sprint as he sent the orb arcing towards the vehicle. It landed in the flat bed with a thud, and the Russian barely had time to look down before he was thrown ten feet in the air, his legless corpse landing on the cab.

'We're moving in, Doc. Pick your targets!'

Gray and Howard ran to the truck and used it as cover while Smart hugged the corner of the building and added his own fire to the mix. Half of the Russians fell in the first few seconds of the fight, the accurate fire of their assailants picking them off mercilessly.

Sonny broke from cover and ran towards the second vehicle, an open-topped Land Rover. Two men lay beside it, one of them with an arm raised in a plea for help, but there was simply no way they could afford to take prisoners. Sonny administered a quick shot to the head and took the man out of the equation, knowing the same would have happened to him if their roles were reversed.

The rest of the Russians were pinned down, caught between the unseen foe at their front and the black-clad figures picking them off from the rear.

Bullets ricocheted off the corner of the building as Smart lobbed another grenade towards an open-sided truck. It rolled beneath the vehicle and blew out the back wheels, crushing a Russian who had taken cover under the rear axle. Sonny added a grenade of his own, throwing it into the back of the truck and killing the two men who were hunkering down inside.

'Doc, cease fire!'

Gray cautiously moved around the back of the Toyota, seeking out new targets. But all he found were bodies. He instructed the men to follow him as he ran to the open gates and scanned for other threats.

Two men crashed through the front door of the police station, their rifles blazing. Gray and Smart cut them down and moved in, with Sonny and Howard following up.

'Wait,' Gray said, noticing the diesel-powered generator at the side of the building. He ran towards it and removed the pin from a fragmentation grenade, then wedged the explosive device between the power lead and the wall before retreating.

Three seconds later, the building was shrouded in darkness.

Goggles in place, Gray instructed Howard to use one of his concussion grenades to clear the hall behind the front door. The resulting bang was enough to rattle their teeth, but those inside fared worse. Gray was first through the door and found two men collapsed on the floor, holding their ears. He took care of one while Sonny dealt with the other, then scanned the reception area for a way to the station's holding cells. They found two doors, one to the left made of plain brown wood, while the other, straight ahead, had bars set into the glass. Gray signalled for Smart and Howard to clear the former while he slung his rifle in favour of his handgun and headed for the latter with Sonny.

He swung it open as a figure emerged from a side room and let off a volley with an AK-47. Gray's weapon quickly barked in reply, and he watched the man stagger backwards and collapse in the hallway.

'Fuck!'

Gray turned at the sound of Sonny's voice and saw his friend clutching his left shoulder.

'How bad is it?'

'I'll live,' Sonny said, urging him forward.

Gray checked the room the Russian had stepped out of and found it clear, then followed the long snout of his silenced pistol towards another door at the far end of the corridor. He pushed himself against the wall and nudged the door open with his toe, a move that saved his life as a burst of automatic fire shredded the air a few inches in front of his face.

Gray tugged the last fragmentation grenade from his webbing and tossed it through the gap, letting the door swing shut. As soon as he heard the explosion, he pushed the door aside and found himself in a stairwell. Below, his goggles picked out a shredded body that lay in the landing between floors. Gray stepped over it and continued down to the basement, where frantic voices bounced off the stone walls.

Gray got to his knees and stuck his head around the corner. He saw two green-tinted figures, one holding a rifle aimed towards the stairs while the other frantically fumbled in the darkness with a set of keys. He was about to take them out when he thought better of it.

Footsteps behind him signalled the arrival of Smart and Howard; he held up a hand for them to wait, his eyes still on the Russians. It took an agonising eternity for the man to get the cell door open, giving Gray his cue. The armed man dropped first, quickly followed by the other.

Gray hurried down the hall and stepped over the bodies.

'Thanks,' he said to the second corpse, who'd saved him the job of finding the right key. He stuck his head inside the cell and saw an empty bed, nothing more.

'Andrew?' Gray shouted as he stepped back into the corridor. The possibility that Harvey wasn't actually being held in the jail created a knot in his stomach. All this way for nothing, and time was running out to find him.

'Tom?'

The feeble cry came from inside the cell. This time Gray walked in and dropped to his knee. He saw Harvey curled up under the metal bed. The relief was immense, but short-lived.

Harvey looked to be in a bad way. Both eyes were swollen shut; lacerations, contusions and congealed blood covering the rest of his body told a tale of numerous beatings.

'Can you walk?' Gray asked, trying gently to pull Harvey to his feet. The movement brought a howl of agony, and Harvey grabbed his chest.

Broken ribs. Not good news with so much ground to cover on the way home.

Once upright, Harvey's first few steps were tentative; Gray could see he was in a great deal of pain.

'Sorry, Andrew, but we've got to get a move on.' Gray called Smart over and told Harvey to put an arm around each of their shoulders. 'This might hurt a little.'

They took hold of Harvey's trousers at the waist and lifted him a couple of inches off the floor, then told Howard to take point as they made for the exit. They encountered no resistance on the way out, but it was only a matter of time before the place was teeming with pissed-off Russians.

'Howard,' Gray barked, 'get that Land Rover started! Sonny, disable the Toyota.'

Sonny pumped two rounds into the front tyres of the Hilux and one in the rear for good luck, then joined the others as they crammed into the only serviceable vehicle remaining. Harvey was helped into the back seat, and when Sonny clambered aboard, Howard gunned the engine and steered around the truck, bouncing over bodies as he did so.

'Turn right at the end of the street, then take the second left,' Gray told him from the passenger seat.

At the intersection, Howard spun the wheel and narrowly avoided smashing into the front of a moving armoured personnel carrier.

'I thought those things were all pulled back across the border,' Smart said, as he looked back and saw the BTR-60 performing a clumsy U-turn.

'Let's hope that was the only dodgy intel,' Gray said. 'Step on it.'

Gray's prayer went unanswered as they took a left at high speed and found themselves facing off with a BMP-3 armoured fighting vehicle, its 100 mm gun pointing straight at them. It was fifty yards away and closing, and their Land Rover had nowhere to go.

'Back up!' Gray screamed, but Howard was already on it, throwing the vehicle into reverse and steering one-handed as he looked backwards. The moment he hit the main road he executed a J-turn, spinning the steering wheel while pulling the handbrake. Harvey groaned from the back seat as the vehicle spun ninety degrees and Howard slammed it into first, tyres squealing as they gained traction.

The APC was now on their tail, but at least it lacked the firepower of the BMP-3. Gray hoped that they could keep it between

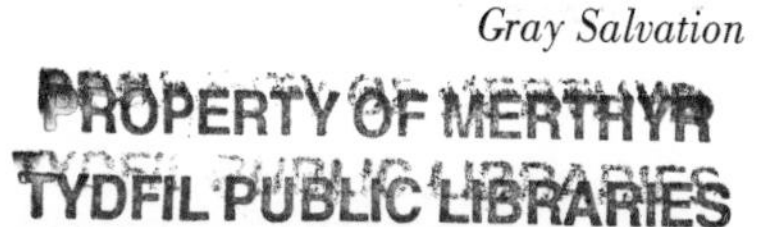

them and the mobile cannon, denying the heavy armour a clear shot. He'd seen one in action during war games a few years earlier: unlike conventional tanks that required reloading, this beast had a rapid-fire system much like an automatic rifle. If they got stuck in its sights, they'd be dead before they knew it.

Howard jinked the vehicle as gunfire erupted from the APC, chewing up the road a foot to their right. Gray tried to ignore it as he studied the GPS, looking for a way out of the rapidly deteriorating situation.

'Take the next right,' he said, and clung on as Howard followed his instructions, almost spinning out as he took the turn doing fifty. Rounds ripped into the wall a foot behind them as they disappeared into the narrow street, and a ricochet smashed into the windscreen, missing Gray by inches.

'Doc, we'll be on you in two minutes. Get ready to move.'

Gray got an affirmative in his earpiece, then contacted McGregor.

'We're coming in hot, Mac. Bring the bird in now.'

'Better move it,' Smart urged Howard from the back seat.

Gray swivelled to see the BMP-3 turning into the street behind them. Seconds later, the first of the large projectiles blew a hole in the wall behind them, showering their vehicle with rubble.

Howard had his foot hard down on the accelerator, snaking the Land Rover back and forth to make themselves a more difficult target. Another round flew past inches from the driver's door, creating a fountain of rubble as it struck a building twenty yards ahead of them. Howard slammed on the brakes as he reached the scene, and the truck pranced like a demonic stallion as they hit the debris in the road. It came back down on two wheels, and only Howard's expertise saved it from crashing onto its side. He nursed the Land Rover back onto all fours, and then gunned it again. The road ahead bent to the left, and Howard tested the car's handling to the limit, taking the bend just as the BMP-3 fired again.

Erwin McGregor sat in the cockpit of the Bell Ranger, checking his instruments for the tenth time. The rotors above him were stationary, but the engine was idling, ready for a quick take off.

Fuel was his only concern, the gauge looking a little on the low side. They certainly had enough to get out of the country and most of the way home, but whether they managed to get back to base was another thing. There would also be the added weight of the rescued hostage to take into account, but they'd already burnt up more than half of their Jet A-1, which just about compensated and kept them below the maximum flying weight.

'We're coming in hot, Mac. Bring the bird in now.'

When the words came over the headset, McGregor spooled up the rotors.

'Roger that. Be there in three minutes.'

As soon as the blades were up to speed, he pulled up on the collective until the aircraft left the ground, then used the pedals to ease the nose around. That was when the juddering started. It sounded like a kid banging on a biscuit tin with a wooden spoon, but McGregor instinctively knew that it was incoming gunfire.

Warning lights came on and alarms began shrieking as the oil pressure dropped and the controls became sluggish. The Perspex screen spider-webbed in a dozen places as round after round hit the cockpit, and freezing air blew in as a bullet finally found a way through. Another soon followed, hitting McGregor on the right wrist. The pain made him release the cyclic for a split second, and when he tried to grab hold of it again, he found his fingers unresponsive.

He knew it was futile to try to fly one-handed, and even if he managed to control it long enough to get out of the area, the damage done to the hydraulics meant it would be a short flight.

And a fatal one.

Out of options, he lowered the collective and bumped back down to the ground, killing the engine with his good hand. Outside he could see several figures advancing towards him, rifles raised and ready to give him the bad news.

McGregor raised his hands and remained in his seat, already working on his cover story. He was on a flight when he lost electrical power and got disorientated, so he landed to try and fix the issue. He wasn't armed, so it was a believable explanation.

'Tom,' he whispered into his throat microphone. 'I'm not going to make it. I'm surrounded by a dozen X-rays; the bird's shot to bits and I'm hit. You're on your own, son.'

He removed the comms unit and dropped it under the seat, silently wishing them luck.

He knew he'd be needing a big dose himself.

A concrete block the size of a shoebox flew past Gray's head as the next 100 mm round from the BMP-3 slammed into the wall a split second after they'd taken the bend.

Gray knew they had about fifteen seconds before the gun would reach the same point and have them in its sights once more, so he instructed Howard to take a right turn followed by a quick left.

The driver carried out the manoeuvre deftly, and two blocks later they were approaching the street where Doc and the Sentinels waited.

They weren't the only ones.

Another APC was disgorging troops as they approached their turn-off, and four were already taking cover in the very place Howard was heading, using the corner of the building as cover while they laid down fire at the oncoming vehicle.

'Doc, help us out!'

Gray shouted the order as he raised his own rifle and began peppering the entrance to the street with 7.62mm rounds. Smart and Sonny were also engaging targets, while Howard maintained his breakneck speed, aiming for Doc's side street.

One of the Russians firing from the corner suddenly dropped his weapon and keeled over, quickly followed by another. Gray saw the panicked look on their faces as bullets came at them from nowhere. One of them turned to fire back in to the darkness, and Gray took advantage, hitting the man in the thigh. The last of the men in the side street succumbed to a burst from a Sentinel, falling into the street.

'Doc, we're coming in, and we're on wheels. Once we get past the last Sentinel, set them to auto.'

'Roger.'

The wounded Russian lay in the road, but Howard didn't have time to avoid him. He ran over the stricken figure as rounds from their flank struck the frame of the Land Rover.

In the distance, Gray could see Doc's outline standing near the other end of the street. More rounds came their way as Russian troops surged into the street, bullets slamming into the back of the vehicle as Smart and Sonny returned fire.

The vehicle slowed to fifteen miles an hour and Gray helped Doc clamber aboard.

'Go, go, go!'

Howard didn't need telling twice. He floored it, heading for the fence that had marked the beginning of their journey. 'Hold on!' he warned, aiming for a point between two fence posts. The impact reduced their speed by half, but once the chain link gave, they were hurtling out into darkness.

'Kill the lights,' Gray said, powering his night-vision goggles back on. Howard did the same and turned the headlights off, using the green-tinged view to navigate the landscape and avoid wrecking their transport.

'Well, that was some hairy shit,' Sonny remarked.

Even Gray managed a smile at the understatement. 'How are we doing, Andrew?'

An exhalation and moan provided the answer.

'Looks like we're leaking,' Howard said, indicating towards the fuel gauge, which showed half a tank. 'It was nearly full five minutes ago.'

'That should be enough to get us to the rendezvous point,' Gray said, but his expression changed as McGregor's low voice came over the airwaves. He looked round at Sonny and Smart, who were hearing the same message.

'What is it?' Harvey asked from his prone position in the back.

Sonny was the one to deliver the bad news.

'We just lost our ride home.'

Chapter 22

26 January 2016

Ivan Zhabin woke from his nap feeling surprisingly refreshed, not something he normally experienced during long flights. He caught the flight attendant's attention and requested a bottle of water, then took it to the toilet to brush his teeth.

When he returned to his seat, he refused breakfast and fastened himself in, ready for the descent into London Heathrow. The plane shook as it breached the low cloud layer and landed heavily in the early morning darkness.

Zhabin made his way through immigration with no problems – his German passport facilitating speedy service – and with no checked luggage he made his way to the exit.

At the arrivals gate he saw a bald, middle-aged man holding up a sign with Alec Stutz printed on it. Zhabin walked over and introduced himself.

'Dimitri,' the man replied, leading Zhabin out into the freezing morning.

In the short-term car park, Dimitri used a fob to open a VW saloon and climbed into the passenger seat, letting Zhabin take the wheel. 'Here's everything you asked for,' Dimitri said, handing over a padded envelope from the glovebox.

Zhabin opened it and checked the contents. A Walter PPK with silencer and two clips of ammunition, a mobile phone and charger, the address where the rifle could be found, and a file containing details of the target.

Zhabin looked at the photograph and immediately recognised the man he was tasked with killing. Up to this point, he'd known only that the hit would centre on Whitehall. The information in his hand gave the target's itinerary and route, leaving Zhabin to decide the where. The when was 29 January, three days away, giving him plenty of time to pick a place from which to take the shot.

'If you need anything else, call me on that phone only. I will then pass your request on to the client.' He handed over a ticket for the car park. 'It's already paid.'

Dimitri exited the car and walked into the sea of vehicles.

Zhabin entered the postcode of the farm into the satnav, then drove out and followed its directions until he came to the M25. Even at dark o'clock in the morning, traffic was already building, though the junction for the M40 came soon enough. He pushed the car to sixty-eight and engaged cruise control.

An hour and a half later, he pulled onto the dirt track leading to the farm. The place was already a hive of activity, with cows being led back to a field after their morning milking. As he got out of the car, the smell of manure was overwhelming.

'Can I help you?'

The man asking the question was wearing thick, waterproof dungarees and looked senior enough to be the man in charge.

'Dan Fletcher?' Zhabin asked, reciting the name that accompanied the farm's address.

'That's right.'

Zhabin extended a hand and smiled. 'I'm Yuri,' he lied. 'You have something for me. A rifle.'

Fletcher shook his hand tentatively and nodded towards the house. Zhabin followed, taking in the surroundings. Only one other farm worker was in sight, but he would confirm the actual numbers later. First, he needed to make sure the weapon he'd been supplied with was good enough to carry out the mission.

Fletcher led him down the side of the building and into a Dutch barn, where straw and hay were piled almost to the roof. Zhabin watched as the farmer deftly removed three bales of straw and stuck his hand into a gap between two others.

'There you are,' Fletcher said, handing over the heavy leather case.

Zhabin rested it on a bale and flicked open the catches. The weapon inside looked almost brand new, which was good to see. He recognised the make, one he'd used in the past. Before he used it against Milenko, though, he'd need to make sure it was adjusted to his liking.

'I need to test it out,' he said to Fletcher.

The farmer looked pensive, clearly not liking the idea of such a monstrous weapon being used on his property.

Zhabin had already checked the surrounding area on his phone's map application, and knew the chances of the reports being heard by neighbours was low, but then he wasn't planning to hang around after sighting-in the rifle.

'It won't attract attention,' he assured Fletcher. 'Even if anyone hears it, they will think it is a shotgun. Very common here, no?'

The farmer, still reluctant, eventually gestured with his head for Zhabin to follow, and led him around the back of the barn.

'There's nothing for about three miles,' Fletcher said, pointing to a small copse way off in the distance. 'If you can aim towards those trees, you'll avoid my livestock.'

Zhabin could see sheep in fields to the right and left of where Fletcher had pointed, but they were too close to pose an obstacle.

The trees, however, looked to be about eighteen hundred yards away, the perfect distance to test the rifle's capabilities.

He began putting the rifle together, then looked up at Fletcher. 'So you run this place yourself?'

'No, my boys help me out.'

'Ah. Good to see a family sticking together. I have three children,' Zhabin lied. 'How about you?'

'Just the two boys.'

'Only three of you? I would have thought it would take many people to work a farm.'

'Ideally we'd like another hand.' Fletcher shrugged. 'But we just can't afford it.'

Zhabin continued to assemble the weapon, and looked around for a suitable target. He spotted something ideal for his purposes.

'Could you ask your sons to give me a hand with that big log?' he asked Fletcher, gesturing towards a large woodpile. The log looked to be at least six feet long and would weigh a considerable amount. 'It is the perfect size, but we will need to carry it a long distance.'

'Only one of my boys is here,' Fletcher said. 'The other stayed with friends last night.'

Zhabin shrugged. 'I can wait until he returns.'

'David won't be back until later on this afternoon,' the farmer said to him. 'Jake and I can help you with your target.'

'Okay.' Zhabin smiled.

He watched Fletcher walk away, and once the man was out of sight, he pulled the pistol and silencer from his jacket and screwed the two pieces together. When he heard footsteps behind him, he slipped the weapon between his knees and continued working on the rifle, sliding the scope onto its mounting and securing it.

Zhabin waited until the two men were standing over the piece of wood, then stood up, the pistol in his hand. Two sharp *pffts* broke the stillness of the valley, before silence descended once more. He walked over and checked the bodies, ready to finish them off, but his initial shots had proved fatal.

He returned to the rifle and fed three rounds into the magazine, then lay down and inserted it into the slot on the underside of the gun. After ramming the first round into the chamber, he put his eye to the scope and focused on an oak tree with a light patch where a branch had been shorn off. He pressed a button on the telescopic sight and the laser rangefinder indicated slightly more than seventeen hundred yards to the target.

Zhabin took a deep breath, then let it out slowly. Once the last of the air was expunged, he squeezed the trigger. The boom echoed off the distant hills, but he focused on the result of the shot. The round had embedded itself three inches high and a couple of inches to the left, which he put down partly to the trigger. It took a couple of pounds more pressure than he was used to, but it wasn't a game changer. He made a slight adjustment on the sight, and then squeezed off another round.

It landed an inch off centre, and given the wind swirling in the valley, it was as close as he could expect under the conditions.

Zhabin stripped the weapon down and put it back in its case, then collected the spent cartridges and put them in his pocket. Standing over the two bodies, he was torn between leaving them where they were and disposing of them. When the other son returned and discovered his family dead, the police would be called and a manhunt launched. That wasn't something he could afford, but the only other option was to wait for David to return and silence him, too. That presented other problems. Someone might come to investigate the sound of rifle shots, and the body count could quickly escalate.

Zhabin decided to hide the bodies as best he could and hope it was a couple of days before anyone found them. He went round to the front of the barn and began moving bales of straw. It took fifteen minutes to create a space deep enough inside the pile, then half that time to drag the corpses round, one by one, and stuff them into the hole he'd created. He found some tarpaulin and covered the father and son, then replaced the straw bales and got a bucket of water to wash away the telltale tracks of blood leading to their resting place.

When he was satisfied that the bodies wouldn't easily be found, Zhabin took out the phone he'd been given and looked on the map for the nearest Tube station. Having identified his destination, he dialled the only number in the contacts list.

'My car will be compromised,' he said, knowing CCTV cameras could easily track him in a country devoted to public surveillance. 'I will drop it near Uxbridge Tube station. Have someone pick it up and dispose of it, and have a replacement ready at my accommodation.'

Twenty minutes later, Zhabin was back on the M40 heading towards London. Once again, he stuck to the speed limit, acutely aware of the contraband in the back. If he were stopped by police, there would be no explaining it away, and the last thing he wanted to do was shoot a couple of cops. That would be the end of the mission and would put a dent in his reputation.

Zhabin followed the satnav until he saw the sign for the Tube station, then pulled into a side street and parked up, locking the vehicle and hiding the key under the front wheel arch. He carried the case to the station and used his phone to plan his route to the accommodation he'd been given, then purchased a ticket and climbed aboard the waiting train for the twenty-five-minute journey to Wembley Park.

The apartment was just a couple of hundred yards away from the station, above an Eastern European delicatessen. Dimitri, waiting outside, handed Zhabin the keys to another saloon.

'The other car is taken care of,' Dimitri told him. 'Is there anything we should be concerned about?'

'Just tying up loose ends,' Zhabin said.

Dimitri ushered him inside the shop and through to the back, where a staircase led to the first floor. The apartment was sparsely furnished, with a small bedroom, living and kitchen area, and toilet with shower. It was far from the most luxurious place he'd ever stayed in, but would suffice for the next couple of days.

'Call me if you need anything else,' Dimitri said before disappearing down the stairs.

Zhabin put the leather case under the single bed and locked the bedroom door, pocketing the key, then descended the stairs and walked back to the Tube station. He purchased a ticket to Westminster, and then walked up Whitehall, getting a feel for the location.

It soon became apparent that there was little chance of taking the shot while his target was here. The tall buildings on either side of the road were likely to be inaccessible, and besides which, they stood too close. He needed to be a sufficient distance away that he could make the kill and clear the area before the police arrived, but there were no buildings in the distance that would give him a clear line of sight.

If he were going to take out Milenko here, it would have to be while he was still in his car, but that was something Zhabin preferred to avoid. The Tagrilistani president was sure to be conveyed in an armour-plated limousine, and even if Zhabin had the firepower to breach the vehicle, it still meant making a headshot at a moving target. Even for a man of his considerable skill, that was a tall ask.

With Whitehall ruled out, he found a pub and ordered a sandwich and a glass of water, then took a seat in a corner and checked Viktor Milenko's itinerary. The president was due to sign the trade deal on Friday, but was arriving the day before for a banquet with business leaders eager to endorse the new trade agreement.

Zhabin used his phone to find the location of the dinner. It turned out to be a hotel on the bank of the Thames, and he immediately sensed that he'd found a promising opportunity. He finished his food and took a stroll to the hotel, soaking in the surroundings.

When he reached his destination he saw that there were plenty of tall buildings on the opposite side of the river, and the steps up to the building where the Tagrilistani president planned to dine would give him a few seconds to get the target in his sights.

It looked promising, so Zhabin continued down the embankment and over a bridge that crossed the Thames. From the other side of the river he could barely see the steps to the hotel, but a higher vantage point would give him the perfect shot.

All he needed to do was get access to one of the buildings, and a nearby sign offered a simple solution.

Gray kicked the side of the Land Rover in disgust. Three bullet holes in the bodywork indicated where the last of the fuel had drained away, leaving them stuck in the middle of nowhere.

Howard had managed to put some distance between themselves and their pursuers by heading off-road and into a wooded area, skilfully weaving between trees that the heavier Russian vehicles could not navigate. The team had begun to feel safer until the engine coughed a couple of times and gave up.

As if to compound their misery, the rain had intensified, huge drops making the puddles dance like a Las Vegas showpiece.

'How far to the border?' Sonny asked.

'Too far for Andrew to walk,' Doc said, taking stock of Harvey's injuries.

'Agreed,' Smart added. 'If we're gonna get out of here, we need transport.'

'We could just get on the sat phone and call for help,' Howard pointed out.

'Aren't we forgetting something?' Gray asked, drawing blank stares from his colleagues. 'Mac risked his life getting us in. We can't just abandon him. And if I call it in now, we'll be ordered home.'

'To be fair,' said Howard, 'we all knew the risks when we signed up, Mac included. Don't forget we've still got an armoured unit on our tails.'

Gray didn't entirely agree with Mark Howard's assessment of the situation. 'Sure, we knew the risks, but we never said anything about leaving men behind.' He took out his phone and bent over it as he studied the map, trying his best to keep the rain off the screen. 'According to this, there's only one road between Mac's lay-up point and Dubrany. The GPS says it's two hundred yards to our right. My guess is they'll bring him in that way.'

'If they come by road,' Howard argued. 'Intel was wrong about the BMPs, so who's to say they haven't got choppers, too?'

'We'd have heard them by now,' Smart said. 'The road's the only logical choice.'

Gray did a quick mental calculation. 'Mac radioed in ten minutes ago, and we're about three miles from his last known location. Adding in time to secure him and call it in, I'm pretty sure they haven't come through here yet.' He checked his watch. 'I reckon we've got ten minutes at the most. We need a plan.'

'We can expect company from Dubrany, too,' Sonny said. 'I suggest we stall them somehow.'

'Those BMPs will take a lot of stopping,' Smart pointed out, 'and we're down to a few rounds each.'

'Plus we don't know what they'll be transporting Mac in,' said Howard. 'Could be a Land Rover or another light infantry vehicle.'

Gray had to concede that it didn't look good, but then no combat situation ever did. Despite this, he wasn't about to give up. There had to be a way of halting the vehicle carrying their pilot while stopping the Russians from Dubrany crashing the party.

'Could we block the road with a couple of trees?' Harvey asked from the back of the Land Rover, speaking slowly to articulate the words through his injured mouth.

'Those BMPs are like mini tanks,' Sonny said. 'They'd roll over them like matchsticks.'

'How about blowing a crater in the road? In this weather, it would soon fill with water and look like any other puddle.'

'Aside from the noise that would make, BMPs are amphibious,' Sonny told him. 'We'd have more luck holding up a sign reading "Halt".'

'I think it's a moot point,' Gray said, as the sound of diesel engines invaded the night. He ran towards the road and crouched behind a tree, just in time to see the BMP-3 trundle past. It was obviously searching for them, and would soon meet up with the convoy transporting Mac to Dubrany. Behind it came the BTR-60 and another three armoured vehicles.

Gray waited until the vehicles had passed out of sight, then stood and rejoined the others.

'Looks like we'll have to come up with an alternative,' he said, letting the others know what he'd seen. 'There's no way we'll be able to stop six vehicles.'

'If you were in their shoes, what would you expect us to do?' Sonny asked.

'Head for the nearest border,' Gray said, and the others nodded in agreement. 'They'll probably send every spare man east to cut us off, while a small contingent forces us into the trap.'

'They might think we're a local Tagrilistani army unit and try to stop us getting back to our own lines,' Doc suggested.

'Not dressed this way,' Smart said, 'and the locals would see no value in rescuing Andrew. Tom's right. They'd assume we'd head for the border.'

'So the last thing they'd expect would be for us to head back into town,' Sonny said, a cheeky grin stretching his face.

'You want to go back to *Dubrany*?' Howard asked, looking from man to man. 'Are you crazy?'

Gray held up a hand. 'Sonny has a valid point. They'll be scouring the countryside for us, not the town.'

'Okay, they might not being expecting us,' Howard persisted, 'but they'll sure be on alert by now.'

'For a team dressed in black,' Gray countered. 'We can take the uniforms from the first group we took down back in town. That means getting to the truck we hid, then driving it to the jail.' Before Howard could protest, he added, 'We'll have their weapons and ammo, too.'

'The place'll be packed!' Howard said. 'Everyone's gonna want a piece of Mac.'

'Then we improvise,' Sonny said, clearly determined to press ahead with the rescue effort.

Howard shook his head. 'I'm used to firmer plans than "we'll improvise",' he said. 'It sounds like a suicide mission to me.'

'Then you stay behind and take care of Andrew,' Gray said. 'We can't take him in with us. We'll find a place closer in for you both to lie up until we come back out. Doc speaks Russian, so we'll need him with us.'

Howard seemed happier with that suggestion, and Gray told the team to set about fashioning a crude stretcher to carry Harvey.

They did so with two sturdy tree branches and a waterproof coat they found in the back of the vehicle, then collected their weapons and started the long slog back towards Dubrany.

Chapter 23

26 January 2016

Sarah Thompson sat impatiently at the red light, silently pleading with it to change so that she could continue to the office. She considered blowing through it, certain she'd get away with the minor transgression at five in the morning and with no other cars in sight, but after checking her rear-view mirror and seeing a police car pull up behind her, she thought better of it.

Eventually she got the green light and pulled away quickly, though not so fast that she drew attention to herself. If the cops pulled her over she could easily explain her way out of any ticket, but she didn't want the hassle. It would simply take up too much time, and she was desperate to get to Thames House to hear the latest news about the mission to rescue Andrew.

When she eventually pulled into the underground car park, she was glad to see Ellis's Jaguar parked in the spot reserved for the director general. Thompson ran up the stairs and swiped her card at the office door. Inside she found the room in near darkness, the only light coming from Ellis's glass palace. Thompson walked straight in, and her boss looked up from her laptop for a brief second before beckoning her over.

'Any word?' Thompson asked.

'Nothing yet,' Ellis said. 'I was just looking over the satellite feed. It's a few hours old, but it's all we have.'

Due to the secrecy of the mission, they hadn't been able to task the satellite to maintain a position over the conflict zone, instead relying on the few brief minutes when it passed overhead on its continuous orbit high above the planet.

'How does it look?'

'There's a lot more activity than there was yesterday,' Ellis told her. 'Whatever Gray did, it appears to have stirred up a hornet's nest.'

'That doesn't inspire confidence.'

'Wherever Tom Gray goes, this kind of thing happens. We can only hope they're already on their way out.'

Thompson leaned closer to get a better look. 'Those look like tanks,' she said, pointing to two shapes heading away from Dubrany. 'I thought the Russians pulled them all back.'

'It seems Gayle Cooper got that wrong. Or perhaps they were just well hidden.'

Thompson wondered what else they'd missed. Hopefully not much, because the odds of rescuing Andrew were slim enough as it was. The last thing they needed was more surprises, especially of the large and armoured variety.

'Wait!' she said, and Ellis paused her scrolling. 'Go back.'

Ellis tracked the image back, and Thompson pointed to the cross in the corner of the screen.

'That's a helicopter.'

Ellis looked at the summary Cooper had given her. 'According to this, the Russian forces never shipped any to Tagrilistan. It must be Gray's.'

Thompson's heart sank. She could see a few men standing around it – but if they were Gray's team, they'd be climbing aboard and coming home. They wouldn't be relaxing and taking in the view.

'Something must be wrong,' she said. 'Why are they just hanging around?'

Ellis's face told her they were in agreement. 'Either there's a problem with the helicopter, or that isn't Gray down there. Whichever way you look at it, the mission appears to be over.'

'But what about Andrew? We have to send someone else in.'

'Gray was our last chance.' Ellis pushed back from her laptop and rubbed her eyes wearily. 'Sending him in was always a risk – if it turns out he's failed, there'll be questions to answer. News of the rescue attempt is sure to leak, not least from the Russians, and the PM will want to know my role in this. I'll keep your name out of it, but as for Andrew, I'm afraid we've done all we can.'

Colonel Dmitri Aminev looked up as the door burst open, unhappy at the late arrival of the captain. He motioned for the man to sit at the table, making a mental note to have him disciplined once things returned to normal.

'As I was *saying*,' he growled, looking at the tardy officer, 'there appear to be five of them. They took the Englishman and made off in a Land Rover. Their last known location is here.' Aminev stabbed at the map with his pen, highlighting the place where the intruders had crashed through the chain-link fence to make their escape.

'A Tagrilistani unit?' the late officer asked.

'Clearly not. If you had been here on time, you would know that we managed to capture their helicopter pilot. He's British, which tells me that we're facing Special Forces, probably SAS. They operate in small groups, and they hit hard and fast.'

'With their air transportation compromised, they'll be forced to drive to the border,' a young lieutenant observed. 'That means crossing the river, and there are only three bridges. If we can get men there first, we can stop them.'

Aminev liked the way the junior officer thought. There were two units in the area that could split up to hold the crossings while his main force drove the insurgents towards them.

'Contact the commanders of these posts,' Aminev said, pointing to the locations on the map, 'and tell them to stop anyone who tries to cross the river.'

While an officer disappeared to relay the orders, Aminev gave instructions to gather the rest of the troops and get them mounted up. He had more than fifty vehicles under his command, enough to carry a large percentage of the five hundred men at his disposal. He decided to leave fifty behind and send the rest on the chase, with those who couldn't fit into the vehicles following on foot, as they carefully swept the countryside.

'Sir, don't you want to leave more men behind?' another officer asked. 'What if the Tagrilistani army tries to recapture the town while we're out searching for the British?'

Aminev dismissed the suggestion with a wave of his hand. 'We've both been observing the ceasefire, so there is no reason for them to attack. Besides, our men will be travelling *away* from enemy lines, so they won't even know we're gone.'

In truth, the last thing he cared about was losing the town. He knew the war was almost over, and that by the end of the week the pro-Europe president would be gone, replaced by someone sympathetic to the Russian cause. How exactly that would be achieved, he didn't know, but he'd learned about it at the same time that Andrew Harvey had been put under his control. Tasked with looking after the English prisoner, Aminev had demanded to know why the man couldn't simply be shot in the head instead.

He was their bargaining chip, the Russian envoy had told him, to be kept alive until Moscow deemed him surplus to requirements.

The penalty for failing to stick to the brief had been made all too clear, which was why Aminev was throwing almost everything he had at getting the prisoner back.

'Will you be leading the search?' asked the sharp young lieutenant.

'No,' Aminev said, rising from his seat. 'I will interrogate the helicopter pilot when he arrives. I want to know exactly who we're up against.'

Chapter 24

26 January 2016

Despite Ellis's assertion that they'd done all they could, Sarah Thompson wasn't about to let things lie. Apart from being her lover, Andrew Harvey was a damned fine operative, and to be cast aside by the government he served was unconscionable.

Thompson was sitting at her desk, the search for a replacement killer going nowhere. That didn't surprise her, because she knew she wasn't giving it her full attention. When she tried to concentrate, thoughts of Harvey kept jumping into her head, distracting her from the job in hand.

She rose and began pacing the room, trying to stem the anger boiling inside her. She couldn't believe Ellis expected her to simply get on with her job when Andrew was facing certain death, but that was what she'd been told to do. Carry on and get the name of the person sent in to carry out the assassination.

Easy orders to give when it wasn't your soulmate languishing in a filthy prison thousands of miles away.

Thompson glanced over at Ellis's office and saw her boss on the phone. She stood, checked her watch and decided that her moment had arrived.

'I'm going for lunch,' she said to Elaine Solomon as she headed for the door, getting a sympathetic smile in return. It had been the same for the last couple of days – condolences for her imminent loss, lots of tiptoeing around her. None of them knew about the rescue attempt, and they were clearly under the impression that Harvey's fate had already been sealed.

Not if she had anything to do with it.

Thompson rode the elevator down to the underground car park and climbed into her Ford, knowing that what she was about to do would probably mean kissing her job goodbye.

To her surprise, she found that she didn't care.

Over the last year, only one thing had come to mean anything to her, and that was Andrew Harvey. If he died, there would be little of value left in her life. She certainly wouldn't continue serving a government that had relinquished him so readily.

She drove out of the car park on autopilot, her mind concentrating on the upcoming encounter. She had to admit that she hadn't thought it all through and had no idea how it would turn out, but the one thing she *did* know was that she couldn't sit idle while Andrew's time ran out.

She hardly registered the details of the drive, and before she became fully conscious of it, she found herself parked outside the Petrushkin, still uncertain as to what she would do once she got inside.

She decided to play it by ear.

As she got out of the car, a traffic warden approached her.

'You're parked on double yellows,' he said, opening his pad to begin writing a ticket.

Thompson was conscious of the Russian thug standing watch outside the restaurant, and moved closer to the warden, her back to the building.

'MI5,' she whispered, flashing her temporary ID.

'You'll still have to shift it,' the man said, noting down her licence plate, 'otherwise it'll be towed.'

Thompson leaned in closer, looking at the warden's name badge. 'Jeff,' she said in a slightly harsher whisper, 'if I come out and my car has moved one inch, I swear I will shoot you in the head. You can either call this in and report me, in which case the black-ops team I run will hunt you down and destroy you, or you can stop scribbling and walk away. I'm working a case, and if you blow my cover or cost me my transport, life for you will turn very shitty, very quickly.'

Thompson turned her body so that the Russian on the door could see her smiling at the traffic warden, hoping he saw it as an attempt to flirt her way out of a ticket. Of more concern was Jeff, who looked like he was about to soil himself.

Thompson leaned in and gave him a peck on the cheek. 'Last chance,' she whispered, and was relieved to see him pocketing the ticket book as he walked away. She walked in the opposite direction, giving the bouncer her most dazzling smile as she pushed the restaurant door open.

As she'd expected, Bessonov sat inside, waiting for his regular meeting with Polushin. Two more of his thugs were sitting near the window, instantly alert to her presence. Behind the bar, a less imposing figure slowly polished an already clean glass.

Thompson strode to the rear of the room, where Bessonov was finishing off a bowl of borscht. The Russian watched her approach, offering the slightest glance to his henchmen as she neared the table.

'Where's Andrew Harvey?' Thompson asked, standing across from the mobster with her hands on her hips. She both heard and felt the footsteps behind her but kept her gaze on Bessonov, who looked up at her impassively.

In the mirror above the corner booth, Thompson could see the two bodyguards getting closer. The one in front was at least a foot taller than she and had to weigh twice as much.

Perfect.

As a meaty hand clasped her on the shoulder, Thompson grabbed the wrist and took half a step backwards, arching her back and pulling down on the arm. Her opponent's weight worked against him, and he flew over her shoulder and landed on his back with a thud. Thompson immediately dropped to her knees, one of them coming down on the man's face with all of her weight behind it. She heard the satisfying crunch of broken cartilage but didn't have time to savour the moment. Her hands were already inside the man's jacket, and a second later she was standing with the bodyguard's Makarov jammed in Bessonov's windpipe.

'Call off the dogs,' she said evenly.

Bessonov remained calm, raising a hand to halt the advance of the second bodyguard, who already had his own pistol aimed at Thompson's head.

'I'm warning you, tell them to back off or this'll be the shortest meeting you ever had.'

Bessonov carefully articulated a curt order, and his henchman stowed his weapon before helping his injured colleague to his feet. Thompson found herself on the receiving end of a fierce stare, but she wasn't there to win friends and influence people.

She waited until the pair had retreated a sufficient distance, then turned her attention back to their boss.

'Andrew Harvey. Where is he?'

'Never heard of him.'

With lightning speed, Thompson struck the mobster across the face with the butt of the Makarov.

'Remember him now?' she asked, ramming the barrel back into the side of his neck.

'You were warned to stop harassing me with these unfounded alleg—'

Thompson's free hand came up in a flash, her fist catching Bessonov's eyebrow with a glancing blow. The ring on her finger cut a gouge in his skin and blood immediately began seeping from the wound, but the mobster's tone didn't change.

'As I said, I've never heard of this Andrew Harvey.'

Thompson was beginning to lose her cool. Short of shooting him, there appeared little she could do to get him to talk.

At least, not here.

But the moment she took the weapon off Bessonov, his goons would draw down on her.

'Up!' she ordered, reinforcing the directive with another jab of the gun's barrel.

'If you walk away now, I'll forget this ever happened.'

'Oh, it's happening,' Thompson snarled, 'and this is the fluffy part. Trust me, it goes downhill from here.'

She grabbed his collar and jerked him upright, then pushed him ahead of her, the gun poised at the nape of his neck while her other hand gripped his shoulder.

Bessonov walked agonisingly slowly, and she got the impression he was stalling.

'Move it,' she urged, but Bessonov maintained the sedate pace.

What seemed like an age passed before they finally reached the door. The two goons were seated back in their usual positions, one emotionless while the one with the broken face glared daggers in her direction.

Bessonov stopped at the door.

'Open it,' Thompson ordered. 'Slowly.'

The mobster did as he was told and took a couple of steps outside, before tripping and stumbling to his knees. Thompson realised too late that he'd done it on purpose, and in her haste to get him into her car, she'd forgotten about the third henchman standing guard in the street.

Her gun hand exploded in pain as a ball-bearing-filled cosh crashed down on it, quickly followed by a fierce punch to the temple. Like an outclassed boxer, she felt her legs turn to jelly and collapsed to the ground face first. Her nose took the brunt of the impact, and blood began pouring onto the concrete. A crimson pool began to form as she felt herself being dragged back into the building, and the last thing she saw before she blacked out was Bessonov's equally bloody face, his dead eyes signalling the terror and pain to come.

'Easy, now,' Gray said as he helped Harvey down the narrow wooden staircase.

They'd come across the small farm twenty minutes earlier and he'd sent Sonny ahead to check it out. Fortunately, like many dwellings in this civil-war zone, it had been abandoned for some time, and it hadn't taken them long to find the cellar. Its door was set into the floor of the barn, and it made the ideal place for Harvey and Howard to wait while the rest of the team went back into Dubrany to rescue McGregor.

At the bottom of the stairs they found a damp floor and very little else. Gray called to Smart and had him throw down a few bales of straw, which would at least give the pair something dry to sit on while they waited for the others to return.

Doc and Sonny appeared at the trapdoor. They'd been outside with bowls to collect some of the falling rain, and had poured their catch into two bottles. Sonny had also brought a couple of old blankets and some dry clothes from the house.

'We should be back within six hours,' Gray said to Howard. 'If we're not, it'll be your job to get Andrew across the border to safety. I'm expecting another ruckus at the jail, and that should draw their troops back into town. That'll be in your favour.'

Gray began to climb the stairs.

'Tom . . .'

He looked back at Harvey, who cut a pitiful figure as he huddled inside a quilt-work blanket.

'I just wanna say—'

'Save it,' Gray said. 'We're not home yet.' He managed the faintest of smiles. 'But when we get back to London, you owe us all a few pints.'

'Deal.' Harvey tried to return the smile, but only succeeded in cracking open the wounds on his lips. 'I really need to speak to Ellis. It won't take long.'

'The battery on the sat-phone is really low, mate. It'll have to wait. Just do exactly what Mark says.' Gray turned to Howard. 'Get him home, no matter what.'

Speech over, Gray climbed out of the cellar and closed the trapdoor. He helped the others to gather loose straw from around the barn and use it to cover the hatch. Once he was satisfied that it was sufficiently camouflaged, he took a bearing on the GPS and led the others back out into the rain. Sonny picked up a rake on the way out and swept away any sign that they'd been there as they retraced their footsteps from the farm.

They soon reached a small stream, and Sonny hid the rake in some rushes before Gray led them up the riverbed, water lapping up to their knees. It made heavy going, but the important thing was to distance themselves from the farm while minimising the trail back to Harvey.

Night began to give way to a battleship-grey morning, but the rain refused to yield entirely, the earlier bombardment reduced to a steady drizzle.

It wasn't long before they encountered the enemy.

They were a mile from the outskirts of Dubrany, trekking through a mudbath. Vegetation was scarce, but ahead they saw a treeline and beyond that, the outline of the taller buildings that made up the war-torn town. They first heard, then saw, the BMP-3, its tank tracks making light work of the terrain. It came crashing through a small thicket, upending young trees and trampling bushes.

The vehicle was moving close to its top speed and Gray knew that meant the occupants didn't expect to find them so close to the town. Thankfully, it was maintaining a steady course that would take it two hundred yards to the right of them, putting it behind them in a couple of minutes.

Gray threw himself into the muck, closely followed by Smart and Sonny. Gray slowly turned on his back, getting a curious stare from Doc.

'Cover yourself in mud,' Gray whispered. 'Camouflage.'

Soon, all four of them blended into their environment. It wasn't perfect, but there was little else they could do under the circumstances.

And not a moment too soon.

Ahead, Gray saw an open-topped Land Rover approaching, five men on board, and moving on a much closer course to their location. Gray slowly moved his body from side to side, not so quickly as to draw attention to himself, but enough to sink another inch into the sodden ground. His men followed suit, becoming a part of the landscape as best they could.

The last thing Gray wanted to do was have to engage the vehicle, and he was relieved to see it travelling as fast as the armoured BMP-3, the driver keen to get to the border, passengers staring straight ahead.

As soon as the vehicle's roar had faded into the distance, Gray turned to Sonny.

'I was right. They're racing to close the border.'

It was good news, but they weren't safe yet. There was no telling how many Russian soldiers remained in Dubrany, and now their incursion would occur in broad daylight. Hardly ideal circumstances, but Gray had to play the hand they'd been dealt. Waiting until midnight would have been the preferred strategy, but that would have given the enemy plenty of time to realise they'd fallen for a feint. It would also have meant leaving McGregor in their hands for close on twenty-four hours.

Gray waited until the vehicles had disappeared from sight, then got the others to their feet and continued the march towards town. The landscape changed, with trees and bushes replacing the stark mud plains they'd had to endure. Once Gray could make out individual windows in the buildings on the edge of town, he took another reading from the GPS, altered course a few degrees and ordered the men back onto their bellies for the last few hundred yards.

It took more than an hour to reach the hole they'd created in the chain-link fence. Gray was the first to break cover, sprinting for the gap while the others prepared to lay down cover fire. Once he was through, he planted himself against the wall of the nearest building and urged the next man forward. One by one they joined up, and Gray used the GPS to find the location where Smart had stashed the truck.

'I just hope it's still there,' Smart said.

'If it isn't, we'll just have to go in on foot,' Sonny answered.

They walked slowly through now familiar streets, sticking to smaller avenues and avoiding major intersections. It took another thirty minutes to reach the rear of the school, and they were relieved to see the truck almost exactly as they'd left it.

The only difference was the stench of death filling the interior.

Working in pairs, they dragged the corpses from the cab and flat bed, then identified bodies with builds similar to their own. Luckily, there were plenty of puddles around, allowing them to wash off the bloodstains. Smart, being the largest, had to settle for a combat smock that he could barely button up.

'Time to lay off the pies.' Sonny laughed, patting the big man's belly.

'Knock it off,' Gray warned.

He forced open the school door and ordered the bodies to be pushed down a stairwell, then climbed into the passenger seat. Wanting a Russian speaker up front with him, he had Doc get behind the wheel, and gave him directions.

'Next left,' Gray said, taking them onto the main street that bisected the town. It initially looked to be deserted but Gray could see a car in the distance, and it was getting closer.

'Carry on, or turn off?' Doc asked, as the vehicle drew nearer, two hundred yards away and closing fast.

'Carry on,' Gray said. 'If they stop us, tell them you're low on fuel and need to top up before you join the others.'

'And if they don't buy it?'

There was really little alternative. 'We take 'em out. At your signal.'

He relayed the message on the comms, getting double-click replies from the pair in the back.

At a hundred yards, the car began flashing its headlights. Gray told Doc to ignore them, but the estate car driver yanked the wheel to the left and came to a halt fifty yards in front of them. A large man with a barrel chest climbed out and strode purposefully towards them. Gray prayed that he'd choose the driver's side. It looked for a moment as if he'd be disappointed as the approaching figure fixed his gaze on Gray, but Doc rescued the situation by leaning out of the window and calling out in Russian.

The man changed direction and went to Doc's side of the truck, waving and shouting, and even though Gray only knew a couple of rudimentary words, he could tell the Russian wasn't happy.

Gray watched Doc's fingers tighten around the silenced pistol on his lap, and knew they were seconds away from an unwanted firefight. His own hand moved to the door of the cab, ready to leap out and unleash hell on the other occupants of the car.

All he needed was Doc's signal.

When it came, it wasn't in the form of a bullet to the Russian's brain. Instead, Doc snapped off an awkward salute and put the truck into gear as the enemy soldier walked back to his own conveyance.

'What did he say?' Gray asked.

'Only that my mother was a whoring baboon, and that we should catch up with the others sharpish.'

'I have to disagree with the second part,' Gray said with a chuckle. 'Take the next right.'

Doc followed the directions, and three minutes later Gray ordered him to pull over. The police station was only two streets away, but he'd already ruled out driving straight up to the front gate. The first thing he wanted to do was to try to confirm that McGregor was actually being held there.

'Doc, you and Sonny get as close as you can to the jail and let us know what you see. If you come across anyone, try to talk your way out of it, but if it goes pear-shaped, we'll be thirty seconds behind you.'

Gray crawled over to the driver's side as Doc got out with Sonny. 'Don't forget, eyes on *only*. No hero shit.'

Doc Butterworth and Sonny walked casually around the corner, the dead Russians' AK-47s carried casually in their hands. Lurking in the shadows would have drawn too much attention, but walking the streets in full uniform made for perfect camouflage.

They didn't come across anyone as they neared the street in which the police headquarters stood, but when they turned the corner they saw major activity. Russians were carrying their dead out into the street, overseen by a large man sporting a grey beard. Five bodies lay on the ground, and Doc could see another being brought out of the building.

'Lots of activity here,' Sonny said into his throat mic. 'They're clearing out the dead and seem to be in a hurry.'

'Any sign of Mac?' Gray replied.

Doc watched the bearded man, who continually looked at his watch and seemed agitated. 'It looks to me like they're still waiting for him to turn up.'

'Give me numbers,' Gray said.

'I count fifteen here. There could be more inside.'

'Roger that. Wait one.'

Sonny backed away from the corner, signalling Doc to follow.

'I prefer the idea of taking them out in the open,' Doc said.

'Me, too,' Sonny agreed, 'but it's Tom's call.'

It had been sheer luck that none of them had been killed storming the police station hours earlier. Doc had dressed Sonny's shoulder wound, which hadn't been as bad as first thought, but they didn't dare push their luck by storming back into the bowels of the police building.

'Sonny, Doc, on me. Now!'

Both men broke into a sprint. 'What's happening?' Sonny asked as he ran.

'There's a truck approaching,' Gray said. 'Hopefully with McGregor in it. We're going to stop it and we'll need Doc to do the talking.'

Doc turned a corner and saw Gray and Smart standing near their own vehicle, which had been moved to form a roadblock. In the distance, a similar vehicle was approaching.

'When they stop,' Gray told Doc, 'tell them the building was booby-trapped and is out of commission. You've been ordered to take the prisoner back to Russia.'

'Can do,' Doc said, walking towards the approaching truck and waving it down.

Sonny walked over to one side of the road with Smart, while Gray took the other.

Doc held his Kalashnikov across his stomach, hiding the bullet hole in the jacket that he'd taken from one of the corpses, and continued to wave with the left hand. The truck pulled up in front of him; the front passenger jumped down, clearly irate.

'What the hell are you doing?' he shouted in Russian. 'The colonel is already pissed off that we're so late.'

'How come?' Doc asked.

'We had a puncture and some thieving hound had stolen the tool kit. We had to wait for someone to bring us a replacement.'

'Just as well. Those bastards left a bomb in the police station,' Doc told him. 'It killed ten people and the building is unsafe. We've been ordered to take the prisoner back to Moscow.'

The Russian's eyebrows narrowed. 'I've never seen you before. What's your name?'

'Markov,' Doc told him confidently. 'We were sent in from Orsk when we heard about the attack. Do you have the prisoner or not?'

The Russian pulled a radio from his pocket. 'I'll call the colonel and confirm it with him.'

'Don't waste your time,' Doc said. 'He was one of those killed in the blast.'

Doc silently urged the man to believe him, knowing that if the call were made, the charade was over. By this time, three men had jumped down from the back of the truck and two of them were walking towards Doc, demanding to know what was causing the hold-up. The other was shouting at Gray, who merely shrugged his shoulders. The situation was falling apart, but when the first Russian placed the radio to his mouth, Gray knew the ruse had failed completely. In seconds the truth would be out, and every enemy soldier in the area would converge on their position.

Doc brought his rifle up and sent a round through the chest of the Russian closest to him. The radio clattered to the ground as the man clutched his chest, and Doc was already shifting to the next man.

Almost simultaneously, Smart took out the passenger in the cab while Gray made short work of the Russian who'd been walking towards him. Sonny helped mop up the other two foot soldiers and ran to the back of the truck. Two more men were jumping out, but rounds from Sonny and Smart ensured they were dead before they hit the ground.

'Mac, stun grenade!' Sonny shouted.

Seconds later, the canvas sides of the truck billowed out as the blast assaulted the senses of those in the back. Sonny had already discarded the rifle and had his silenced pistol in his hand as he clambered up the tailgate. He saw McGregor, arms secured behind his back, with his foot against a Russian's throat, pinning him to the opposite seat. The dazed Russian was trying in vain to reach his rifle on the deck. McGregor, who appeared to be immune from the concussive blast, looked little the worse for wear, though he'd taken a bloody injury to his wrist, which hadn't been treated and so bled freely.

'What're you waiting for?' the big man growled.

Sonny's pistol popped, ending the struggle, then he ushered McGregor to the rear of the truck.

'Len, give me a hand!'

Smart appeared instantly and together they helped the Scotsman over the tail and onto the pavement, taking care not to jostle his wounded arm. Two of the other men lay in the back, groaning, and Sonny wasn't about to let them back in the fight. Two pops rang out and the moans stopped.

Sonny grabbed what weapons he could see and threw them out, then searched the Russians for ammunition. What his team had would soon run out, and there was no telling what battles lay ahead.

'Sonny,' Gray called out, 'time to go.'

Sonny leapt out of the truck and at Gray's order, shot out the truck's tyres, effectively disabling it. Gray was already in the passenger seat of their own vehicle, with Smart behind the wheel.

Doc and Sonny gathered up the arms he'd taken from the Russians and threw them into the back. Sonny was first to climb up, and as Doc was pulling himself into the cab, a bullet slammed into the bodywork.

The next one caught him in the forearm, and he lost his grip, dropping to the ground in agony.

Colonel Aminev was growing increasingly irate as the minutes ticked by. The last he'd heard, the prisoner had been fifteen minutes out. That was twenty minutes ago, and still no sign of them.

'Yakov, call Andreyev and find out where the hell they are.'

The private saluted and disappeared outside, leaving Aminev to reflect on the damage that had been done by the small British unit. Forty men confirmed dead, power to the police station disabled. But most importantly, the MI5 agent was gone.

If Moscow found out, he knew the penalty that waited him. If he were lucky, he'd get a bullet to the head, but he'd been a soldier long enough to know that was wishful thinking. His superiors were unforgiving, and would make an example of him, of that there was no doubt. He himself had come up with some particularly heinous ways of dealing with prisoners of war, and none of them particularly appealed as a way of leaving the planet.

'Sir, I hear a truck approaching!'

Finally.

Aminev bounded up the stairs. If he could make the new prisoner talk, there was still a chance they could get Harvey back before anyone heard about the rescue attempt.

And he knew plenty of ways to get a man to open up.

As he stepped out into the drizzle, he heard the sound of an engine, but it was idling a couple of streets away.

What are they waiting for?

The answer came in the guise of small arms fire, and Aminev instinctively knew something had gone dreadfully wrong.

'Follow me!' he yelled and, with more than a dozen soldiers in his wake, ran as fast as he could towards the battle. He heard the sound of an explosion as he tore through the side street, and a minute later he emerged onto the main thoroughfare, where two trucks stood.

Six of his men lay dead, and another wearing the same uniform was climbing into the back of one of the vehicles. He looked for the enemy, but there seemed to be no sign of them.

Until what appeared to be two of his men emerged from the back of the wagon, pushing a figure in black towards the second vehicle. As he watched, two men jumped out of the first truck, and one of them began spraying lead at the wheels.

Confusion gave way to rage, and Aminev brought his weapon up. He fired as the last of the attackers climbed into the truck and was rewarded with a scream as the man fell to the ground. He urged his men to open up, and they began peppering the vehicle with automatic fire.

It wasn't long before they began to come under fire themselves, and he was conscious of men falling all around him. The British were picking them off at an alarming rate, and he ordered his men to find cover as he retreated to the corner of the building. Metal pinged off the masonry around him, but he stuck his head around the corner and began firing at the tyres. If they managed to get their wounded man and drive off, there was no way he'd be able to catch them.

'Aim for the wheels!' he shouted. 'Don't let them escape!'

The men followed his lead, but the unerring accuracy of the enemy was taking a vicious toll. He was down to three soldiers, and another cry went up as one of them took a round to the chest.

Aminev began to panic. If he let the intruders escape, he'd be lucky to live until sunset. He shifted his aim to the man on the ground, but hesitated.

These people had come to get one of their own. Having rescued him, they came back for their pilot. It struck him that they wouldn't go while one of their men lay injured on the street.

The man in his sights got to his feet, cradling his arm as he staggered to the back of the truck. Aminev couldn't afford to let him climb aboard. He let loose two rounds, aiming for the man's legs, and was satisfied to see him go down.

That might stall them for a few more minutes, but Aminev had only two men against a highly trained unit.

'Yakov, get on the radio and order everyone back here, now!'

Aminev pressed himself further against the wall, offering as small a target as possible, then poked the snout of his rifle around the corner and let off another burst at the truck's cab. The firing pin came down on an empty chamber, and he switched magazines, conscious of the fact that ammunition would be crucial in this battle of attrition. Fortunately, the dead soldiers around him would no longer need the bullets they'd carried.

All he had to do was keep the enemy pinned down long enough for the cavalry to arrive.

Veronica Ellis slammed down the phone and stormed out of her office. On the main floor, the team were working feverishly, still filtering airline manifests and comparing the passenger names with known criminals.

'Where's Sarah?' she asked Elaine Solomon.

'She went out to lunch.'

Ellis consulted her watch and saw that it was just after three. 'What time did she leave?'

'Just after twelve, I think.'

It didn't seem like Thompson to take so long for her lunch break. Most of the time she just had a colleague fetch a sandwich and ate it at her desk. Ellis dug into her pocket for her phone, a sense of unease threatening to overwhelm her.

The call to Thompson's mobile went straight to voicemail. She hung up and tried the landline number she had in her contacts list, but after a dozen rings she gave up.

'Is it anything I can help with?' Solomon asked.

Ellis put her concerns for Thomson aside for a moment. 'As I expected, the video of Andrew hit the Internet soon after it was first aired in Tagrilistan. Several of our news outlets have finally picked up on the story and are asking what the government plans to do about it.'

'Maybe that's a good thing,' Solomon said. 'Perhaps now they'll send someone in to get him.'

'I doubt that very much. The deadline to organise a swap is today, so there's no time to assemble a team. Once news gets out that we knew he was being held hostage and did nothing about it, the media will have a field day. The opposition leader has already been asking searching questions, accusing the PM of putting money before lives.'

'Well, he's right, in a way.'

'He certainly is,' Ellis told her, 'and that's the galling part. The PM casts Andrew aside, then denies any knowledge. According to his statement, this was the first the government had heard about Andrew's kidnapping.'

'Which happens to be utter bollocks.'

'Crudely put,' Ellis said, 'though highly accurate. On top of all that, the Kazakhstani president wants to know why the Russian rebels are massing on his border. The home secretary just called me to ensure we stick to that script, especially if I'm called before the ISC.'

The Intelligence and Security Committee was a panel of nine MPs and Lords who oversaw the work of MI5, MI6 and the Government Communication HQ – not a friendly bunch at the best of times. Ellis could expect a tough time, particularly at the hands of the opposition members.

That would come later, though. Her priority was to find out where the hell Thompson had gone.

'Give me a list of all known contacts for Sarah,' she told Solomon. 'Email, social media, phones – the lot. We need to find her.'

Chapter 25

26 January 2016

'I'm getting low,' Gray said over the comms.

He was crouching behind the wheel of the truck, which offered more protection than the thin metal of the cab door. Beside him, Len Smart checked the contents of his last magazine and shook his head, and from the rear wheel Sonny reported that he was almost out, too.

'We have to get Doc to cover,' Sonny added. 'He's taken another hit. He'll be dead in seconds.'

Gray peered around the side of the tyre and saw Doc writhing on the ground. His forearm was covered in blood, and he had another nasty-looking wound to the left leg. A glance at the Russian defensive position showed him that the enemy had all the opportunity in the world to take out Doc if they wanted to.

'I don't think so,' he told Sonny. 'Looks like they want him alive, maybe to slow us down.'

'Either way, we've got to get him out of here. He needs a medic.'

'Then we need to finish these guys off.' Gray took out his GPS and quickly worked out a route to get behind the Russians.

'Len, you keep them pinned down. I'll take Sonny round the back of them.'

Before Smart could object, Gray ran over to Sonny's position and tapped him on the shoulder. They both backed away, keeping the large wheels between themselves and incoming fire. When Gray's back touched concrete, he crabbed to the corner and broke into a sprint, Sonny close on his heels.

At the end of the street, he took a left and ran two hundred yards to the third junction, then took another left, which brought them out onto the main drag. In the distance he could see the two trucks, and he signalled for Smart to keep up the sporadic gunfire to hold the Russians back while he and Sonny crossed the road. Small arms fire erupted as the Russians responded to Smart's shots in frustration, enabling Gray to lead Sonny across the street in a hurry. Another left turn and a short sprint later, he came upon the side street where the Russians were dug in. Only three of them. A welcome bit of good news.

'I'll send a grenade in first,' Gray said, tugging the pin from the explosive but keeping a tight grip on the handle, 'then we clean them up.'

Sonny gave a quick nod and had his rifle up to his shoulder, ready for action. The pair crept slowly towards the enemy, sticking close to the wall and planting their feet carefully. When they got within twenty yards, Gray motioned for Sonny to stop and push himself up against a doorway, then lobbed the grenade towards the Russian trio. It bounced once a couple of yards behind them, and then filled the air with shrapnel, cutting them down. A quick glance at the bodies told him there was no need to check for survivors.

'Clear, Len. We're coming out.'

Gray ran out into the street and over to Doc, who now lay still. He put his fingers to Doc's neck and found a faint pulse, but the widening pool of blood didn't bode well.

Sonny and Smart helped to lift Doc into the back of the truck, where McGregor was lying flat on his stomach, his arms still handcuffed behind his back.

Gray brought up a screen on the GPS and tossed it to Smart. 'You drive. Green is our current location, red is where Andrew and Mark are waiting.'

Smart climbed out of the truck and ran to the front, starting the engine and jerking the vehicle around to point in the right direction. In the back, Gray used a knife to rip two strips of cloth from Doc's smock to use as tourniquets. The truck bounced at every pothole and was running low on one side, where the tyres had been shredded by the Russians. Still, Smart was able to keep it going, and Gray much preferred the rough ride to walking.

'Any chance you could get these things off me?' McGregor asked, his head banging against the metal floor every time Smart drove over anything bigger than a pebble.

'You'll have to wait until we stop,' Sonny said. 'If I try to shoot them now I'll end up blowing a hole in you.'

To ease the man's discomfort, Sonny helped him upright and sat him down on the bench that ran the length of the flatbed. Sonny removed a field dressing from his pocket and tended to the wound on Mac's wrist.

'What's your plan?' McGregor asked Gray.

'Get out of town, then make a phone call.'

'I thought you said we were on our own. No backup.'

With the state the truck was in, there was no way they'd make it to the western border, and they couldn't head east without being spotted by the large concentration of Russian troops assembled there.

'We only have one real option left.'

Ellis was growing increasingly concerned about Sarah Thompson. There had been no word for four hours, and she hoped Thompson hadn't done anything stupid. The last they'd spoken had been in her office, when it looked as if Tom Gray's mission had failed.

Had Sarah taken that too hard? Had she decided she couldn't go on without Andrew?

Ellis dismissed the thought. Thompson was a strong woman. There was no way she'd consider harming herself, despite the circumstances.

The phone almost made Ellis jump, and she snatched up the handset.

'Ellis.'

'It's Gray. We've got Andrew.'

'Oh, thank God for that! How is he? Where are you?'

'He's fine, but we've hit some major problems.'

Ellis listened as Tom Gray gave her a condensed version of the events that had unfolded following their incursion into Tagrilistan.

'What do you need?' she asked tentatively. She'd already done all she could, and going back to the defence minister and admitting she'd ignored orders and sent a team in would mean a swift end to her career.

'We lost the chopper and reaching the border is out of the question. We need you to contact the Tagrilistan president and arrange safe passage.'

'Can't you just drive to their capital?' Ellis asked.

'The only transport we've got is a Russian truck. The moment they see us they'll blow us apart. That's why we need you to contact the Tagrilistan army and warn them that we're heading their way.'

'How long until you reach their lines?' Ellis asked.

'At the rate we're going, maybe ninety minutes.'

'Consider it done. I'll go and see their ambassador now and get him to pass the word along. I'll get back to you.'

'Hurry,' Gray said. 'The battery on this phone's almost out.'

Ellis ended the call and slipped into her coat. The relief that Harvey was so close to freedom was immense, but the one person desperate to hear the news was nowhere to be found. She walked out on to the main floor and over to Solomon's desk.

'I have to go out for an hour. If Sarah comes in, get her to call me straight away.'

Ellis swiped her security card and walked down the stairs, hoping the Tagrilistani government's wheels spun a little quicker than they did in Westminster.

Erin Potter ended one call and went straight to the next in the queue. As with every day, the phones rarely stopped ringing, though a glance at the clock told her that the shift at Thames House would be finished within an hour, when the night receptionist would take over.

Potter answered the next call with her usual greeting.

'Er . . . Hi. I'd like to report a kidnapping.'

Potter was used to crank calls, and went through the normal procedure of putting a trace on the call. Unusually this was from a landline, whereas most time-wasters preferred untraceable mobile phones.

'Can I take your name, please?' she asked politely. Sometimes they responded honestly to this question, but only on rare occasions.

'Jeff Swinton. I'm a traffic warden. I saw a woman being kidnapped earlier today.'

'Sir, you do realise that's more a matter for the police,' she told him.

'I know, but she told me she was from MI5.'

Potter instantly went on alert. She knew from her friend Elaine Solomon that Sarah Thompson had been strangely absent for most of the afternoon, and this could explain why. 'Can you describe the woman?'

The caller reeled off the description, as well as the time and location of the incident, and Potter typed up the details with lightning fingers, and had just put the caller on hold when she saw Veronica Ellis walking through the lobby.

'Miss Ellis!' she shouted, drawing the director general's attention.

Ellis quickly strode over to the reception desk and leaned over it. 'What is it?' she snapped, looking at her watch.

'I have a traffic warden on the phone—'

Ellis straightened, clearly annoyed. 'I don't have time for this. If he's going to give me a ticket, let him.'

She walked away, and Potter called after her. 'But he said it's about—'

Ellis waved her away, disappearing through the door.

Having tried her best, Potter reconnected the call and took the man's contact details, promising someone would be in touch in the next few minutes, then sent off an internal email to Elaine Solomon.

Ellis decided to walk to the Tagrilistani ambassador's residence, which sat in a side street just off Millbank, the street running parallel to the Thames. It was only a ten-minute stroll, but she made it in half that time, almost jogging. A phone call would have been quicker, but she felt something this important should be handled face-to-face.

She knocked on the door of the residence and it was answered by a staffer, who took her MI5 pass and made a call upstairs. Seconds later the reply came, and she was shown up to the first floor and along the corridor to a set of double doors.

'Please,' her escort said, opening the doors for her before closing them behind her.

Ellis found herself alone in the room with the ambassador, Mikhail Greminov, a thin man in his fifties who stood from behind his lavish oak desk and offered her a seat.

'Thanks you for seeing me, Mikhail,' Ellis said. 'I apologise for not calling ahead.'

'Not at all,' Greminov said. 'What can I do for you today?'

'It's regarding Andrew Harvey.'

Greminov's face screwed up in disapproval at the mention of the name.

'I think President Milenko has made his position regarding your missing operative quite clear.'

'I appreciate that, but there has been . . . a development. One of Harvey's friends heard about his predicament and took it upon himself to launch a rescue mission. He managed to get to Andrew, but he needs help getting out of the country.'

'And just who is this friend of his?' Greminov asked. 'I assume it isn't his tailor.'

'His name is Tom Gray. He and four friends managed to spring Harvey from a jail in Dubrany, but they have casualties. I need you to inform your troops that Gray will be approaching your lines in –' she studied her watch – 'about eighty minutes. I'd appreciate it if you could guarantee them safe passage and a flight home.'

'I must say, President Milenko is going to be less than pleased when he learns about a military incursion into our country. He specifically said he wanted no action that would anger Moscow.'

'Tom Gray isn't active military,' Ellis said. 'He retired years ago. This wasn't sanctioned by our government.'

Greminov eyed her quizzically. 'Are you telling me he had no help whatsoever?'

'None that our cabinet ministers are aware of,' Ellis said truthfully.

'The fact remains that armed Britons are operating on our soil without our permission. I think the first person we should notify about this should be your prime minister. It would be interesting to hear his thoughts on the matter.'

'Interesting, perhaps,' Ellis conceded, 'but in the meantime, Gray and his men are heading towards your troops – in a Russian vehicle. I think we both know how your countrymen will react if we don't forewarn them.'

'I still think—'

'No,' she said, standing and cutting him short, 'let me tell you what *I* think. I think the PM is going to find it very difficult to sign any trade agreement with Milenko when the public learns about this. I could explain to the media how a few brave civilians did what our governments refused to do, and how you were willing to sit back and let them die at the hands of your own troops. The story will hit the headlines within five minutes, Mikhail, and they'll want a quote from you. You can either confirm that you won't help, or make a humiliating U-turn and place the call to your ground commanders.'

'Miss Ellis, you have much to learn about diplomacy.'

'Fuck diplomacy! There are people's lives at stake!'

Greminov sighed and looked at his watch. 'This simply isn't my decision to make,' he said. 'President Milenko will be landing at Heathrow in about twenty minutes. I'll speak to him when he gets off the plane.'

'Do that,' she said. 'In the meantime, I'll prepare a press release. And if I don't hear from you within thirty minutes, I'll send it out.'

Before Greminov could protest, Ellis picked up her handbag and walked out of the room, leaving the doors open behind her.

Chapter 26

26 January 2016

'How much farther?' Sonny asked for the umpteenth time.

'At this rate, another ten minutes,' Gray said, as anxious as anyone to get to the relative safety of the Tagrilistani front line. Their conveyance was crawling along on two good wheels and two bare rims, having lost the last shreds of rubber miles back. It made for a lopsided and uncomfortable journey but, most frustratingly, it was slow-going.

'The Russians can travel about five times faster than this,' McGregor pointed out, though Gray needed no reminding. He'd been doing the maths for the last hour, and knew the pack would be closing in.

What's more, his men and he were heading into the unknown. The satellite phone had died thirty minutes earlier with no follow-up from Ellis. Worrying about whether she'd succeeded wouldn't do any good, though. All they could do was stick to the plan and pray the gods of war were in a pleasant mood.

He soon learned otherwise.

A shell flew past the truck and exploded at the side of the road a few yards ahead of them, causing Smart to veer sharply to the left.

As he did so, the bare metal of the wheel rims dug into the tarmac and the vehicle flipped over onto its side.

Gray found himself pinned to the door with Smart on top of him.

'Everyone out!' Gray shouted, as he pushed Smart upright and began kicking at the windscreen. It gave on the fourth blow, and Gray scrambled out and took a defensive position near the front of the truck, using the engine block as protection.

He looked back down the road and saw the outline of the BMP-3 half a mile behind; flanking it were four open-topped pick-ups, two of which had .50-calibre machine guns mounted in their beds.

Sonny and McGregor appeared around the back of the overturned truck, carrying Doc between them. Harvey and Howard were the last to show, the MI5 operative hobbling over to Gray with an AK-47 in his hand.

'You know how to use one of those?' Gray asked.

Harvey removed the magazine, checked how many rounds it contained, rammed it back into the housing and checked to ensure there was a round in the chamber. 'Set for three-round bursts.'

Gray smiled. 'You missed your calling, mate.'

As multiple rounds hit the underside of the truck, Gray leaned to the side and sent a few bursts towards the advancing Russians. All he managed to do was get the big guns to open fire, the .50-calibre rounds punching holes through the top of the chassis.

'Shouldn't we get away from here?' Harvey asked. 'If that tank hits the truck, it'll be game over.'

Gray understood his concern, though he suspected the Russians had other plans. 'They've been in position for a couple of minutes now. If they were going to take the shot, they would have done it by now. I think they want us alive.'

'Then why are they shooting?'

'To make us shoot back and exhaust our ammo.' Gray crouched for cover as another salvo came from the Russian ranks, the rounds hitting the truck well above their heads with others peppering the ground to their left and right.

'So what's the plan?'

'Good question,' Gray said. In normal circumstances he would make a managed retreat, half the team firing while the others leapfrogged them away from the confrontation. With Doc so badly injured, though, he knew that would be impossible. 'All we can do is try to coax one of those vehicles in closer and take the occupants out. That would at least give us some wheels.'

He stuck his head around the side of the truck and let off another quick burst, and saw that the Russians were holding their position. To make matters worse, three more tracked vehicles had joined the fray. The enemy were refusing to be drawn in, and it was only a matter of time before they'd be completely surrounded.

'We need to get out of here,' Sonny urged. 'They'll be all over us in a couple of minutes.'

Gray didn't need reminding.

To their rear was a small wood, around three hundred yards away. If they could get that far, they would have a chance of making it all the way to the Tagrilistani lines.

As he considered the long odds, his thoughts turned to his daughter. He so wanted to watch her grow up, to have as normal an upbringing as possible, to see her go to her own prom and graduate college. There were so many fatherly things he'd been denied when his son Daniel had been snatched from him years earlier, and it broke his heart to think he wouldn't be able to share those precious moments with Melissa, either. But with all other options exhausted, he made his decision.

'Len, you and Sonny take Andrew and get as far away from here as you can. We'll keep you covered.'

'No way,' Sonny countered. 'We all go or we all stay.'

'There isn't time to argue. Andrew is the mission. You need to get him home.'

As if to force his point home, the ground around them erupted in dirt and flame as a round from the Russian BMP-3 exploded a few yards to the left of their cover.

Gray shook his head to clear his ears and brushed dirt from his hair and forehead. 'Go!'

He stood, leaned out and raked the enemy vehicles with his rifle, then turned to see what progress Len and Sonny were making. Both men were crouching in their original positions, looking up at him.

'What don't you understand?' Gray shouted as he knelt back down.

'We all go together,' Sonny repeated. 'End of discussion.'

Smart looked Gray in the eye and nodded solemnly.

Another light artillery round exploded, but this one was farther away – closer to the Russians, in fact. It was swiftly followed by several more, and Gray looked to his rear to see four T-72 tanks emerging from the tree line and bearing down on them.

More *whooshes* from the tanks and Gray felt the air shake as the massive rounds coursed past them and into the Russian ranks. He spun in time to see a BMP-3 explode, its small turret ejected into the sky atop a column of flame. The smaller vehicles next to it were tossed into the air like toys, the occupants' arms and legs flailing as they were thrown in all directions.

Gray realised the T-72s belonged to the Tagrilistani army, but whether his men and he were in danger or not remained to be seen. To be on the safe side, he ordered his men to throw down their arms and kneel with their hands in the air.

The battle subsided as the heavily outgunned Russians beat a hasty retreat, and an open-topped Jeep raced towards Gray and his team.

'Stay alert,' Gray warned the others, 'we still don't know if Ellis got the message through in time.'

Three men jumped out of the Jeep as it slewed to a halt in the mud a few yards from them, their weapons to their shoulders. One man took a few steps towards them and aimed his rifle at Gray.

'Name?' the man barked.

'Tom Gray.'

The man lowered his rifle and said something in his native language, which made his comrades stand at ease.

'We are told to take you to Kazakh border.'

Gray lowered his arms. 'Thank God! We have injured men,' he said, reaching for his rifle.

'Leave it,' the soldier warned. 'You don't need again.'

Unhappy as he was at being in a war zone unarmed, Gray did as he was told. These people were here to help. It wouldn't do to piss them off.

'Quickly,' the soldier said. 'They come back soon.'

Gray didn't need telling twice. As he ordered his men to carry the wounded to the Jeep, an armoured personnel carrier pulled up alongside it. Gray got the others to load Doc into the APC, where a medic looked over his wounds. He and Harvey took their places in the back of the Jeep.

'We at hospital forty minutes,' the driver said as the small convoy set off.

Gray looked back and saw the tanks maintaining their position, glad to know that a mighty buffer now lay between his team and the Russians.

'I really need to speak to Ellis as soon as possible,' Harvey told Gray. 'There's going to be an assassination attempt on President Milenko, and I know how they plan to do it.'

Gray tapped the Tagrilistani soldier on the back. 'We need to make a phone call,' he said, using the international sign to make his point.

The soldier shrugged. 'At hospital.'

Gray looked to Harvey, who nodded wearily. It had been a long shot, hoping to contact England while still in the field.

'Tell me everything,' he said to Harvey. 'When we get to the hospital, I'll call her while they patch you up.'

Veronica Ellis was still fuming at Greminov's attitude as she hurried back to the office. It amazed her that people in his position could use the lives of others as a way of scoring points in a game of political one-upmanship. The man would have been happy to let Harvey and Gray's team perish simply because saving them wouldn't provide any tangible benefit.

She could only hope that her threat would be taken seriously, otherwise . . .

Her phone vibrated on her hip – caller ID told her it was Solomon.

'What is it, Elaine?'

'Where are you? I've got possible news about Sarah.'

'I'm five minutes away. What have you heard?'

'Someone reported a woman who claimed to be MI5 and who matched her description being attacked and dragged into Bessonov's restaurant,' Solomon said.

Damn it! She should have guessed Sarah would go after Bessonov. He was, after all, at the heart of all this.

'Check local CCTV for confirmation and get SO15 on the phone. I'll be there in two minutes.'

Ellis ended the call and quickened her pace, hitting the Speed-dial button for her superior's mobile.

'It's about Alexi Bessonov,' she began without preamble.

'We've been over this,' the home secretary said. 'You're—'

'Just listen, please.' Ellis summed up the new information in ten seconds. 'I want to send SO15 in to get her.'

'Do you have absolute proof that Bessonov is involved?'

'Nothing beyond what the witness reported. I've got my people going over the CCTV to confirm it.'

'Fine,' the home secretary said, 'but unless you see him taking part in any crime, you don't touch him. You don't even speak to him. Am I clear?'

'Crystal.'

Ellis snapped the phone shut and prayed the Russian had been careless enough to let himself be captured on film.

She walked into the lobby of Thames House and jogged up the stairs, then swiped her card to gain access to the main office.

Elaine stood as she entered and handed her a couple of sheets of paper. 'This is the report we got from the traffic warden who saw the woman being abducted.'

Traffic warden. That must have been what the receptionist had been trying to tell her. If only she'd taken a few seconds to listen, they could have been working this for the last half hour.

She scanned the notes. 'It says he saw it happen just before one this afternoon. Why did he wait until four to inform us?'

'I asked him the very same thing. It seems Sarah – if it is Sarah – threatened and belittled him before she went into the restaurant. He said his first thoughts were that it served her right, but his conscience got the better of him.'

So a traffic warden's hurt feelings could be the difference between finding Thompson alive and in one piece, or . . .

The alternative wasn't worth considering.

'Who's working the CCTV?' she asked.

A hand went up and she walked over to Gareth Bailey's desk, where a black-and-white image was being refreshed every second. Bessonov's restaurant, the Petrushkin, could be seen at the top of the screen, and a large figure was standing outside the front door, but the footage was grainy and it was difficult to distinguish facial features.

'Ask Gerald to run it through a filter and enhance it,' Ellis said.

'He already did,' Bailey told her. 'This is the result.'

'That's all we have available?'

Bailey nodded. 'There's no other coverage in the immediate area. This one is from a traffic camera two streets away. It's as if he chose the location for the privacy.'

'Or used his influence to get any existing cameras removed.'

Ellis watched the screen as a dark saloon pulled up outside the restaurant and the occupant got out. If the coverage had been a continuous feed it wouldn't have been so bad, but all they had was a still shot taken every second, making it difficult to get a real feel of the events unfolding on the screen.

The occupant of the car appeared to have light hair, much like Thompson's, and was soon joined by someone who looked to be wearing a high-visibility jacket.

'Is that the traffic warden?' Ellis asked.

'We think so,' Bailey said. 'The time frame matches.'

The pair stood together on screen for the next dozen frames, then split up as one went inside the restaurant and the other disappeared out of shot. Three minutes passed before the door opened once more and two figures emerged, one in front of the other. As the screen flicked to the next image, the figure at the front was on the ground and the one at the rear appeared to be falling, apparently from a blow delivered by the large doorman. In the next frame the blonde lay prone on the ground; three frames later she had been dragged back inside.

'Run that part again.' Ellis leaned in closer in an effort to establish if the figure in the foreground was Bessonov, but it was impossible to tell.

'I've got SO15 on the line,' Eddie Howes said, holding up his handset.

Whereas SO1's remit was to protect British and foreign ministers, their counterparts in SO15 formed the Counter Terrorism Command and worked closely with the security services in situations where armed police were needed. Ellis picked up the phone in front of her and hit the button to connect the call.

'Commander, this is Veronica Ellis.'

She made a signal for Bailey to run the sequence one more time.

'We're ready to go on your word,' said the SO15 commander.

Ellis said nothing as she watched the scene play out a third time, yet still couldn't be a hundred per cent sure if Bessonov was the man on the screen.

'Ma'am, my team are five minutes out.'

Ellis knew she'd used up enough lives to put a dozen cats to shame, and if she screwed this up, the home secretary would be looking for her replacement before teatime. That said, it would be a lot easier to find another job than to live with Sarah's death on her conscience.

'Tell your men to hold position. I want to be there when you take him down.'

Ellis beeped her horn as the car in front crawled along at fifteen miles an hour – she was desperate to meet up with the Metropolitan Police's armed counter-terrorism unit.

Thompson had last been seen over four hours earlier; each second in Bessonov's hands was one too many. Ellis only hoped they could find her in time. She'd left instructions for Bailey to continue monitoring the CCTV feed to see if Bessonov or Thompson had emerged at any point, but so far there had been no news. That meant she was either still inside, or she'd been spirited out of the rear entrance. If that were the case, they would be back to square one, with no real evidence and Bessonov's lawyer crying foul once more.

Her phone buzzed and she hit the button on the steering wheel to connect the call via Bluetooth.

'Ellis.'

'It's Gareth. Still no sign of anyone leaving, but we did see someone come out and throw water on the pavement and scrub it with a brush. It could be that whoever was knocked over lost some blood, and they were cleaning it up.'

Finally, some encouraging news.

She winced at the thought of Thompson being injured so badly, but it could prove a blessing in disguise.

'I want a SOCO standing by.'

'Already alerted,' Bailey said. 'Just give the word.'

Ellis thanked him for the good work and disconnected, then steered around the slow-moving car in front and sped past.

Ten minutes later she saw the firearms team: three cars occupying a bus stop a couple of streets from Bessonov's restaurant. Ellis pulled in behind the last car and got out. The passenger in the lead car decamped and walked over to her and checked her credentials.

'Sergeant Bury,' he said, shaking her hand, and explained what they were about to do.

'Do you know how many people are inside?' Ellis asked.

'We've been liaising with Gayle Cooper from your office,' Bury told her. 'They usually have one man stationed outside the front door. We're estimating three possible hostiles inside, plus wait and kitchen staff. We'll be going in front and back simultaneously.'

Ellis took out her phone and opened the gallery app. 'This is our main suspect,' she said, handing it over with a recent picture of Alexi Bessonov on the screen. 'I'd like you to take him alive, if possible.'

'That's usually the plan,' Bury said, clearly piqued by the suggestion.

'I appreciate that, but these people are always armed. Make sure your men are aware of that.'

The officer gave her a look that said 'we know what we're doing' and walked back to his car, but he stopped halfway and spoke into his radio. Ellis couldn't hear his words but guessed he was passing on her information.

Either that or some disparaging comment about women in authority.

When Bury reached his car, he turned back to her. 'When we stop by the rear of the building, hang back until I come and get you.'

'Suits me,' Ellis said, and walked back to her car. This was one time she was happy to leave it to others. Others who were armed and ready to kill if necessary.

The convoy took off, with Ellis bringing up the rear. Each time they approached a traffic light, the police cars lit up like Christmas trees, though they refrained from using their sirens. Ellis assumed they didn't want to announce their arrival, a prudent move when about to tackle armed mobsters.

Her adrenalin was pumping by the time the lead car stopped forty yards from the corner where the restaurant was situated, and the fire teams poured out from their vehicles and took up positions, with the third car in the convoy parked sideways to block the street. While she waited for them to strike, Ellis called Bailey and told him to send the scenes of crime officer in five minutes. She hoped the takedown wouldn't result in a hostage situation, but if it did, they could just hold back until it was resolved.

Night had already fallen as Ellis watched the four-man squad that had been designated the task of breaching the rear of the building. One of them slowly tested the round doorknob and shook his head, then lifted up his Enforcer – a portable red, steel battering ram. He stood ready to launch it at the door as one of the other officers signalled their status over the radio.

Further down the street, Ellis could see a team of six lined up against the side of the corner building, ready to go.

When the signal came, the lead squad disappeared around the corner, and she heard shouts as they tackled the doorman. The team at the rear were also in motion. It took two attempts with the Enforcer before the door crashed inwards and the men piled in with their MP5 machine guns raised. Ellis heard more shouts as the kitchen staff were ordered to the floor.

Then came the sound she was dreading.

Gunfire.

She closed her eyes and prayed that neither Sarah nor Bessonov had been on the receiving end of the rounds.

The wait for news was excruciating. She was tempted to jump out of her car and see for herself, but appreciated the danger involved in rushing into a scene full of pumped-up men carrying firearms.

After an interminable wait, the senior officer appeared at the corner of the building and motioned for her to join him.

Ellis reached him in seconds.

'I heard shots. What happened?'

'Some guy came out of the toilet with a pistol in his hand. He was ordered to drop it but he aimed it at my officers. They took him down.'

'Was it Bessonov?' Ellis asked.

'No, he's been secured.'

'What about Sarah? Any sign of her?'

'None,' Bury said. 'We've got seven males, including the one who was shot.'

Ellis's heart sank. They must have taken Thompson out through the rear entrance at some point.

'I need to see Bessonov,' she said.

Bury looked less than impressed at the idea. 'It's my crime scene,' he said. 'I'm afraid I can't let you in.'

Ellis hadn't expected this, so caught up in events that she hadn't considered police protocols.

'I'm going to have to override you,' she said, and then quickly explained how Thompson appeared to have been injured in the CCTV footage, making it likely that they'd find her blood on the premises.

'SOCO's a few minutes away,' she added. 'I need them to check the place with Luminol, but first I need to speak to Bessonov.'

Bury got on the radio and passed her request on to the commander, and a minute later she was given the go-ahead.

'Have they been read their rights?' she asked, getting an affirmative response.

She brushed past Bury and walked to the entrance of the Petrushkin just as the wail of an ambulance siren pierced the early evening traffic noise. Inside she saw a body lying in the narrow hallway at the far end of the room, where two officers were packing away a first-aid kit.

Tables had been pushed aside, and six men were lined up in seating positions against a wall, all handcuffed. Ellis kept to the side of the red carpet that ran the length of the room and walked over to the prisoners.

Bessonov faced her, looking as if he were waiting for a bus. Not a flicker of emotion, not even mild irritation at the damage done to his restaurant. Gayle Cooper had told her that he was a cool customer, and she had the unenviable job of trying to break through his nonchalant façade.

'A blonde woman came here earlier today,' she said. 'Where is she?'

'I have no idea what you're talking about. I just arrived for something to eat.'

'Nice try, Alexi, but we've got you on camera arriving hours ago.'

'I would say that was an intrusion into my private life, Miss . . .?'

'Veronica Ellis. I'm the director general of MI5, and I'm here for one of my operatives.'

'Ah, yes, Ellis. Good to finally put a face to the voice. Speaking of which, I believe I'm entitled to a phone call.'

'Not when you're being arrested under the Terrorism Act,' Ellis said. 'Now tell me where Sarah Thompson is.'

'Never heard of her.'

'But you did see a blonde woman here earlier, didn't you?'

Bessonov stared into her eyes. 'I think I'll wait for my lawyer before I say anything else.'

Ellis's only surprise was that he'd said anything at all. She'd expected him to remain silent under questioning, and now he wasn't disappointing her. She stared back at him for a couple of moments, until the scene of crime officer put his head through the door.

'Ma'am?'

She walked over to the entrance and the man introduced himself as Gary Bryan.

'I'm hoping there's a trail of blood on this red carpet,' Ellis told him. 'I need you to take samples and see if it matches a profile we have on record.'

All operatives had DNA samples stored on a secure database, and with modern methods Ellis was hopeful of establishing a match within a couple of hours. If they could, it would be enough to place Thompson at the scene and put Bessonov atop some very thin ice.

Bryan passed the instructions on to his team. Within minutes they had blacked out the windows with tarpaulin to blot out the glare of the street lights and, after turning off the lights inside, begun spraying the floor with Luminol. Immediately, a small blue fluorescent trail appeared. Bryan put down markers and took pictures before the next section was sprayed. A second technician followed Bryan, collecting samples of the blood they'd discovered.

The faint traces of blood suggested someone had cleaned the carpet, but the Luminol was able to pick it out as the chemical reacted with the iron in the haemoglobin.

'When we match this blood to Sarah, you're going down,' Ellis said to Bessonov, who simply shrugged his shoulders.

'If anything happened here, it was without my knowledge.'

Ellis found his demeanour frustrating but wasn't about to admit defeat. She walked over to the first technician and took the bottle from his hand, then went back to the Russian and stood in front of him.

'This should be illuminating,' she said, and began spraying him from his shoulders down to the top of his shoes.

She expected to see blue spots all over him, but was sorely disappointed.

'I expect you to pay to have this suit dry-cleaned,' Bessonov said, offering his first sign of emotion in the form of a smug grin.

An exasperated Ellis handed the bottle back to the SOCO so that he could continue his work. She went to the door to speak to Sergeant Bury.

'He must have changed clothes,' she told him. 'Get your men to search every inch of this place.'

'We already have.'

'Even upstairs?'

'There isn't one. At least not one that can be accessed from inside the restaurant. Trust me, we've checked every door.'

Ellis felt a terrible weight in the pit of her gut. It meant Sarah was definitely gone, and the chances of finding her alive diminished with every passing second.

'Mr Bryan,' she called, 'can you please check for bloodstains at the rear door, inside and out?'

The SOCO nodded but carried on with his work, laying down more markers next to glowing samples.

'It's urgent,' Ellis stressed. 'I need you to do it now.'

Bryan looked over to Bury, who simple gave a shrug that said 'she's in charge'.

Clearly upset at having his routine interrupted, Bryan stood and took another bottle of Luminol from his forensic kit, then walked along the side of the carpet and through to the kitchen, stepping over the corpse on his way.

Ellis followed, careful to follow in his footsteps to avoid contaminating the crime scene. The kitchen was small, with two aisles separated by a stainless-steel workspace. Under the workspace were a couple of ovens and storage space. The rear door was open, with an officer standing guard outside.

Bryan turned out the lights and began spraying the floor near the opening, and Ellis held her breath as she waited for the telltale signs to emerge.

Nothing.

'It's clear,' Bryan said, then went outside and repeated the task.

'Anything?' Ellis asked from inside.

'Not a trace.'

'Could they have cleaned it up?'

'Not completely,' Bryan said. 'If there was any blood here today, we should at least see a sign. There's nothing.'

The discovery left Ellis both elated and confused. It meant Sarah probably hadn't been taken out that way, but then where could she possibly be?

'Gary, you need to see this.'

Bryan followed the sound of his technician's voice to the hallway separating the dining area from the kitchen.

'What is it?'

'The traces follow a line from the door to here, and then . . . stop.'

Ellis looked back through the building and saw the lines of markers snaking from the front door. The blue glow from the Luminol was no longer visible as it only lasted around thirty seconds, but Bryan's square markers showed where each trace had been found.

The most recent ones were also losing their luminosity, but Ellis could clearly see them reach a certain point and turn towards the wall before stopping. The wall consisted of several wooden panels, some of which contained framed pictures of Russian landscapes.

'There must be a switch somewhere.' Ellis tried tapping the wall to find a hollow spot, but the sound was consistent across its width. She then ran her hands along the edge of a panel, but it appeared solid.

'Everyone, look for a button or anything that might be a door release.'

The SOCO team made way for two police officers, who joined Ellis in the search. They covered every inch of the wall, from top to bottom, but found nothing out of the ordinary.

'It must be here somewhere,' Ellis muttered as she walked back into the dining area.

She looked under the corner table where Bessonov always sat, but it was clear. She then walked behind the bar, flicking all the switches on and bathing the room in light. None of them triggered any secret passages.

Now that she could see better, Ellis checked all of the shelves under the bar. They were full of glasses, but it was the undersides she was most interested in.

It didn't take long to find what she was looking for. Her fingers tripped across a small recessed button, and when she pressed it she heard a click come from the hallway.

'Sarge, we've got something,' one of the officers said.

Bury walked over and saw the small opening. It had opened barely an inch, and he gave it a little push inwards. The light from the hallway partially illuminated the interior, revealing a set of stairs to the first floor as well as another leading underground.

Already at his side, Ellis whispered, 'I don't hear anything,' not wanting to alert anyone who might be inside.

'I'm not taking any chances,' Bury said, leading her away from the hidden entrance. He signalled for the other two officers to follow and called two more over to join the huddle.

'We don't know what's inside,' Bury told them, 'but chances are the woman is in there somewhere.'

He divided the men into two teams, assigning one the upstairs and the other the basement.

The officers checked their weapons and ensured their flak jackets were secure, then walked to the hidden door and stood ready for the go signal.

'Get these guys out of here,' Bury said, indicating the six prisoners.

Ellis watched Bessonov being helped to his feet, his smug expression now gone. Instead, a bead of sweat clung to his brow, and he looked both defiant and extremely pissed off.

'If you've harmed her, you'll wish you were dead,' Ellis said, and motioned to the police officer to get the Russian out of her sight.

Bury waited until they'd all been led outside, safe from any gunfire, before sending his men into the darkness.

Sarah Thompson hadn't experienced pain like it in her life.

She'd once broken a tooth while eating pork crackling and bitten down on the exposed nerve, but that was nothing compared to her current state.

They'd started by pummelling her face and body, taking turns to land excruciating blows, and after getting bored with that game they'd moved on to her fingernails, one by one, twisting the nail out with pliers before pouring surgical alcohol onto the exposed flesh. She'd screamed at the top of her lungs, but no-one had come to her rescue.

Instead, the two giants had gone about their business as if stacking shelves in a supermarket. No emotion whatsoever, not even a hint of a smile to indicate that they enjoyed their work.

Next, they'd focused on her thighs. One of them cut deep grooves, almost down to the bone, and the other had pulled the skin apart and placed salt into the gaps. Half a dozen of them on each thigh, as though preparing her as the main course for a barbeque.

The electric shocks had come next. They'd stripped her naked before securing her to the chair, and after dousing her with water, they used a makeshift cattle prod all over her body, including her most intimate areas.

Thompson didn't know how long she'd been going through the ordeal; she only wanted it to end. If that meant a bullet to the brain, so be it.

Anything to stop the pain.

The two tormentors were currently taking a break, having a drink while smoking and chatting in Russian. They could have been discussing football or classical music for all she knew, but she suspected they were working out which method to use next on her tortured body. She closed her bruised eyes and prayed that both men would die of acute lung cancer, or even simply clock off for the rest of the day. But fate had other ideas.

She heard a chair scrape and opened her eyes to see them approaching her once more, one of them holding an industrial-sized power drill.

Thompson knew what was coming, though it was just a case of which part of her battered body got the treatment. She screamed, more out of fear than in the hope that someone would hear her cries. She struggled against her bonds, but it was no use. Her time had come to an end. A relief, really, she told herself.

The Russian knelt down in front of her and looked up into her eyes as her screams reduced to sobs.

'Please, don't do this.'

He ignored her, unmoved by her pleading.

Thompson watched the drill inch closer to her kneecap, and she bit down hard on her lip and screwed her eyes up, waiting for the pain to strike.

Thompson immediately opened them again as the door crashed in and shouts echoed throughout the small room. She saw two figures in black pointing firearms at the Russians, ordering them to drop to the floor.

The one kneeling in front of her spun around and quickly got to his feet, and in just a couple of steps he was almost on top of the police officer, the drill buzzing away in his hands.

Three bullets hit him high in the chest, the sounds of the shots magnified in the confined space, but still he advanced, bringing the drill up and aiming at the policeman's head. Two more rounds struck him, one in the throat and the other under the chin as the shooter dived out of the way of the whirring tool.

The Russian collapsed to the floor, but his twin was only getting started.

Howling at the demise of his brother, Aslan Beriya leapt at the nearest policeman and knocked the muzzle of his gun sideways before stabbing at his throat with a stiletto. The cop spun out of the way but the knife found its mark, slicing an inch into the side of his neck. Both men were off balance, and the Russian's momentum sent them crashing to the floor, knocking the other cop down in the process.

Beriya pulled his arm back for another strike, but before he could deliver it, the back of his head exploded outwards. A third officer stood in the doorway, weapon up, calling in the all-clear.

Thompson was stunned by the ferocity of the sudden onslaught, and she could barely control herself when Veronica Ellis appeared at the doorway. Tears flowed down her bloodied cheeks at the sight of a friendly face, and her boss came over and removed her jacket, using it to cover Thompson's naked body. She then went to the side table and got a knife to cut Thompson free.

With her bonds removed, Thompson tried to get to her feet, her body refused to obey her commands.

'Just stay there,' Ellis said. 'We'll get an ambulance crew down here.'

Ellis passed the instructions to Sergeant Bury, who called up the stairs for the paramedics. They entered the room a couple of minutes later, and after assessing Thompson's state, put her on a stretcher and carried her up the narrow stairs and out into the cold January evening.

Ellis climbed into the ambulance and sat next to her as they set off through the rush-hour streets.

'What the hell were you thinking?' Ellis asked, as the paramedic inserted a cannula into Thompson's arm and hooked up an intravenous drip.

‘I guess I wasn’t,’ Thompson said, wincing as a dressing was applied to her hand. ‘I just felt useless and angry. Andrew’s stuck in Tagrilistan and we know Bessonov’s behind this. I just wanted to . . .’

‘I know.’ Ellis sighed.

‘The deadline must have passed by now,’ Thompson said, and fresh tears began to flow.

‘Enough of that,’ Ellis told her. ‘I spoke to Tom Gray a couple of hours ago. He managed to snatch Andrew from the Russians, but they’re still stuck in-country. I asked Greminov to help get them out.’

Thompson tried to sit up, but the paramedic eased her back down.

‘What did he say? Will he help?’

‘We don’t know yet. He passed it on to President Milenko. We should hear something soon.’

The ambulance made rapid progress despite the traffic, and when they reached the hospital Thompson was wheeled straight into the trauma unit. Ellis tried to follow but was asked to step outside. Not even informing them of her position was enough to convince the consultant on duty, so she asked how long it would be before she would be able to see her colleague again.

‘At least three hours,’ the man in scrubs said.

It was a long time to spend kicking her heels, so Ellis ordered a taxi and had it take her back to the Petrushkin.

The front and rear of the restaurant had been cordoned off with police tape, and Ellis found her car where she’d left it. A couple of uniformed policemen were standing guard outside the building, and after flashing her badge she was allowed access.

Inside, she found Bury with a phone to his ear. He put it away when he saw her enter.

'Just the person I was looking for,' he said. 'We found a small apartment upstairs.'

'Hardly earth-shattering news.'

'I know, but in it we found several changes of clothes as well as a plastic bag containing a bloodstained suit and shirt. They look to be a good fit for your suspect.'

That perked her up. She'd feared that Bessonov's lawyer could explain away his presence at the crime scene as legitimate, and that any evidence was circumstantial. With nothing but inconclusive CCTV in her favour, she'd have a hard time making a conviction stick. Bury's discovery of the bloody clothes put a new spin on things.

If only they could match the blood to Thompson.

'I'll get my office to send a sample over to you. If you identify a match, please let me know as soon as possible.'

Her phone rang, and she stabbed at the Connect button.

'Veronica, it's Tom.'

Gray sounded practically next door. No gunfire, at any rate.

'Sweet Jesus, you made it! Are you guys okay?'

'We're fine. The locals are looking after our wounded. Andrew should be fit to fly home tomorrow morning, but my guy will be here for a couple of weeks.'

'Do you need anything?' Ellis asked.

'Some post-dated medical insurance wouldn't go amiss.'

With the mission being off the books, she doubted the government would foot the bill. That said, involving Greminov and Milenko practically ensured that her superiors would find out soon enough. She only hoped securing Harvey's release and a conviction against Bessonov would placate them.

'I'll see what I can do,' she promised.

'Thanks. I'll ring you once our flights are confirmed. In the meantime, Andrew wanted me to pass on some information about an assassination attempt on President Milenko.'

'We're working that,' Ellis said. 'Their team skipped the country, and we're looking for likely replacements.'

'Andrew said you need to be looking for a sniper,' Gray told her. 'He was being held at a farmhouse and heard the Russians order the farmer to hide their rifle.'

'Hang on a second.'

Ellis called Bury over and explained what she'd just heard. 'Send an armed unit to check it out, and bring the farmer in for questioning.'

She returned to her call. 'The police are on it, but we've already ruled out a sniper as a viable option.'

'I'm just passing on the information,' Gray said. 'No need to shoot the messenger.'

'Sorry, I didn't mean to sound harsh. There's a lot going on here at the moment.'

She considered telling Gray about Thompson's ordeal, but decided it could wait until they got back, giving Sarah a little time to heal, both physically and emotionally.

'I'm really grateful for everything you've done,' she said.

'Andrew's safe, that's the main thing. You can owe me one.'

The call ended, and Ellis put the phone back in her pocket. She had one last look around the room, then went to retrieve her car.

A lot had been resolved in the last twenty-four hours, but if Harvey were correct, President Milenko remained in grave danger.

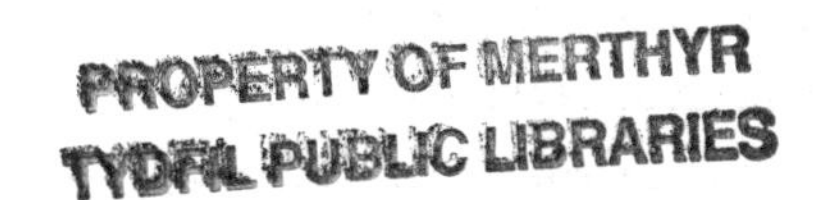

Chapter 27

27 January 2016

Ivan Zhabin dialled the number on the estate agent's website and stared out of the apartment window as he waited for the call to connect. The view was underwhelming, but at least the area was quiet and the room was relatively clean, though much smaller than he was used to. It was certainly better than some of the dumps he'd had to stay in throughout his career, but he still craved his expansive apartment on the outskirts of Buenos Aires, with spectacular views and a living room the size of a basketball court.

'Parry and Mason,' the chipper female voice said, interrupting his thoughts.

'Hello, I'm calling with regards to the property for sale on the Ashcroft development.'

'Certainly, sir. Can I take some details, please?'

Zhabin told her his name was Alfred Baume, spelling it out for her, and that he was a manufacturer from Frankfurt looking for a London property ahead of opening his UK branch.

'We could show you around at two this afternoon, if that's convenient.'

'Sorry,' Zhabin said, emphasising the German accent, 'but I will be in meetings for the next three days and have to fly home on

Thursday. Would it be possible to arrange for an evening viewing? Say, tomorrow at seven?'

This was the third estate agent he'd contacted, and the other two had refused his request. They were obviously confident of shifting their properties during normal business hours, but he hoped this smaller firm was willing to go the extra mile for a sale.

It was a tense few moments as he was put on hold, but the woman came back to the phone and said her colleague could accommodate him and would meet him in the lobby at the agreed time.

'And is the waterfront apartment still available?'

'It certainly is,' she assured him.

'Excellent! Tomorrow at seven, then.'

Zhabin hung up.

From what he'd seen of the property listing, he'd have to take the shot at an angle of about thirty degrees, but it was still well within his comfort zone. The weather forecast for the next day called for overcast skies with a slight chance of rain. Not ideal conditions, and when he factored in the early sunset, a night shot would make it a little more difficult. That said, Viktor Milenko was no longer a young man, and wouldn't be bounding up the stairs to the hotel. He should have plenty of time to get his sights on the president of Tagrilistan.

With the arrangements made, he had more than twenty-four hours to do with as he wished, and only one thought crossed his mind. He opened a new browser window and searched for red-light areas in London. The results told him his best chances of finding a woman were in King's Cross and Soho, so he searched both areas using the online maps.

An hour later, he decided on Soho, but there would be a lot of preparation before he could go and enjoy himself. He put his suitcase on the double bed and unzipped the top compartment, then removed the hidden panel to reveal his make-up kit. Inside the small bag were the false beard and prosthetic nose he used to disguise his features.

He applied the nose first, using alcohol to remove the natural body oils that would prevent the Pros-Aide prosthetic glue from adhering to his skin. Next, he used a Q-tip to apply the adhesive to both the foam latex and his skin, and once it had cured, he carefully stuck the new nose on top of his own. Once he was satisfied with the look, he used a small brush to finish sealing the edges to his face with spirit gum.

It took twenty minutes to get to this stage, and he then began the more laborious chore of applying layers of prosthetic make-up to match his own skin colour.

Zhabin eventually studied himself in the mirror and thought the transformation was remarkable, even though it was something he'd done many times. The final touches included a thick, black beard and a pair of horn-rimmed glasses.

Gone was the forty-eight-year-old with the chiselled looks, and staring back at him was a man in his sixties with a nose that suggested years of alcohol abuse. Zhabin topped off the look with a well-worn trench coat and fedora, and the figure reflected in the full-length mirror looked to be a complete stranger.

With the disguise complete, Zhabin returned to his laptop and searched for hotels in the area. He quickly eliminated anything above three stars, then narrowed it down to the seediest joint available. He dialled the number and got through to a surly receptionist. She spoke in a clipped tone, her words barely audible over the television show blaring in the background. Zhabin explained that he needed a room for a couple of nights but didn't have a credit card, and asked if he could pay cash. He was told that he could, though he would have to show a passport. He assured her that wasn't a problem and booked a room in the name of Ferrera. It was one of three false passports he carried that bore the image of him dressed as he was now, though none of them was of good enough quality to facilitate international travel. They were perfect for this type of thing, though, as he never used them in their supposed country of origin, and he doubted the receptionist would be able to spot a fake Venezuelan passport from the real deal. Once used, he would discard it, as he had done with many others over the years.

Zhabin put a small bottle of make-up remover in his pocket, then walked down the stairs and out into the street. He took the Tube to King's Cross and walked to the hotel he'd booked earlier. It was a miserable-looking place, but ideal for his purposes. There was an alleyway leading to the back of the four-storey building, and Zhabin took it. He passed dumpsters full of rubbish as well as piles of empty cardboard boxes until he found what he was looking for.

The emergency fire exit snaked down the side of the building, with a gantry on each floor. It was just what he was hoping for, but more importantly, there didn't appear to be any CCTV cameras.

Satisfied with his escape route, Zhabin retraced his steps and arrived at the Tube station, where he took the Underground to Piccadilly Circus. Once he emerged into the early evening throng, he followed the route he'd memorised back in the hotel, up the narrow pavement of Great Windmill Street and on to Brewer Street.

He soon found the narrow alleyway he was looking for, and strolled past tables full of revellers braving the elements so that they could smoke as they drank. No-one gave him a second glance as he walked down the well-lit side street, looking left and right for the hidden flight of stairs that would lead up to his night of pleasure. He soon saw the sign that simply said 'Models' and walked up the narrow staircase.

He knocked on the door and it was immediately answered by a woman who looked to be in her sixties. After giving him the once-over, she stood aside to let him in. Zhabin found himself in a small hallway, and the old woman took a seat behind a rickety desk and picked up a well-thumbed copy of *Hello* magazine. Three small wooden chairs were lined up next to her, each one occupied by a call girl.

The first two were instantly dismissed. One had bright red hair, which Zhabin found distasteful, while the second was carrying too much weight for his liking. The third, though, was more to his tastes. She looked to be about thirty, and though he would have preferred someone a bit younger she ticked a lot of his boxes.

Zhabin smiled at her, and the girl got to her feet.

'Sixty quid,' the old woman said.

Zhabin pulled out a roll of notes, counted out three twenties and handed them to the aging receptionist, then gestured for the girl to follow him.

'You do it here, darling.'

Zhabin turned to the old lady. 'I'm sorry, but I am worried about hidden cameras and such. It would do my reputation no good if people learned that I was in such a place.'

'There's none of that going on here,' the woman said.

'Quite, but I prefer to do these things in familiar surroundings. My hotel is quite close by.'

The receptionist looked at the brunette Zhabin had chosen, and the younger woman shrugged her shoulders.

'Okay, but it'll be two hundred if you take her off the premises, and she has to be back in an hour.'

Zhabin still had the roll of money in his hand, and he began counting. 'How much for the whole night?'

'Five hundred,' the old woman said without hesitation.

The price wasn't a problem, but Zhabin made an appropriate grumbling fuss as he handed the woman a wad of notes.

'Have her back by nine in the morning.'

Zhabin's prize disappeared through a door and returned a minute later wearing a heavy overcoat and carrying an umbrella. He led her back downstairs and out onto the main street, where he hailed a taxi.

Fifteen minutes later, they strolled into the Egremont Hotel, where the receptionist lived up to Zhabin's expectations. He'd pictured a twenty-something with piercings and tattoos, and was right on the money.

'I called earlier,' he said, and handed over the Venezuelan passport, while his escort took a seat on an ancient leather sofa and thumbed through a leaflet.

Zhabin was surprised how quickly the registration process went, and assumed it was so that the girl could get back to watching whatever reality TV show he'd interrupted. It also explained why she hadn't bothered asking about his lack of luggage, which most guests tended to carry with them.

Armed with his room key, he gestured for the prostitute to follow and walked her up two flights of stairs. The room he entered was about right for the price. A double bed with a sorry-looking duvet, plus a writing desk and built in wardrobes. The light switch was a dimmer, and Zhabin set it to halfway.

The girl went into the toilet and locked the door, and Zhabin guessed she was administering some chemical fortitude to see her through the night ahead. It didn't matter to him, as long as she performed her duties.

By the time she emerged from the bathroom, Zhabin had stripped naked and was lying on his side, gently stroking himself. He hadn't even learned her name. No doubt, any name she gave would be false. He asked anyway.

'Liz,' she told him, unzipping her dress and letting it fall to the floor. She seemed quite impressed with his body, he noted. Not what she expected, given his elderly looks.

'Lie on your back,' Liz said, shucking off her bra and stepping out of her thong. She reached into her handbag and produced a condom. She had it on him in seconds, and as Zhabin lay back she straddled him and fed him inside her.

She writhed gently, moaning, and Zhabin wasn't sure if she was showing signs of genuine pleasure, or was just very good at her job. He was swayed towards the latter, because after just a couple of minutes, he was close to bursting.

'I want to be on top,' he said, and gracefully twisted and threw her underneath him. Liz didn't object as he moved above her, his hands next to her head.

Zhabin gazed at her face, but she had her eyes closed as she ground beneath him. As he neared his own sweet climax, he moved his fingers under the pillow and found the wooden ends of the garrotte. With each surge of his hips, he eased it towards him, sliding the thin metal wire under her head until it was in position at the back of her neck.

Zhabin worked his hips faster, until the moment of glorious release finally neared.

But the true pleasure was yet to come.

With practised dexterity, he let go of the garrotte and crossed his hands over, then grabbed it again and pulled the wire tight across the girl's larynx. As with the others, he would look her in the eye while he stole her life, heightening the sensation building in his groin.

Liz's eyes opened instantly, but instead of her hands going to her throat to relieve the pressure, they went straight to Zhabin's face.

It wasn't what he'd expected.

A thumb pressed deep into his eye socket while her other hand tore at his beard, her long fake nails gouging three lines into his face. He jerked his head backwards and increased the tension on the wire, suddenly fearful of losing control of the situation. Hands grasped for his face, but he managed to keep himself just out of reach.

Zhabin could no longer see into her eyes as she squeezed them shut, as if to increase her reach, but the thrill had already gone out of this encounter. He needed to end it quickly, but the woman was a fighter. It obviously wasn't her first violent confrontation, and she was fighting him with all she had. What was supposed to be an evening of sweet pleasure was quickly turning sour. Her body bucked underneath him, like a rodeo bull on steroids, and she managed to get a knee into his side with enough force to knock him off balance. As he fell to his side, Liz was able to reach his face, and her claws dug deep into his cheek once more. She grabbed hold of his beard and yanked, pulling half of the false hair away from his face, despite the strong adhesive he'd used.

He had to regain control of the situation, and that meant maintaining his grip and seeing the job through. The woman was beginning to weaken, having gone more than thirty seconds without a breath. Her exertions began to take their toll, and her struggling finally ceased as her hands went to her throat, trying to claw away the wire.

Zhabin watched her eyes close and felt her body go limp, but he kept the garrotte taut, just to be sure. A red line began to form where the thin wire had penetrated the skin, but he kept the pressure on for another thirty seconds.

When he finally let go, he was panting and sweating like he'd just run a marathon. Thankfully, she hadn't been able to alert anyone by crying out, so he had plenty of time to compose himself before leaving.

He crawled off the body and removed the condom, which he put in a plastic zip-lock bag, then quickly dressed, stepped into the bathroom and looked at his face. There were deep scratches on both cheeks, and his beard was hanging off on one side. He knew he wouldn't be able to stick it back on, so he got the make-up remover from his coat and spent fifteen minutes taking off the disguise. His face stung where the solvent dripped into his wounds, but there was little he could do about the pain. Instead, he was more concerned about getting back to the apartment Bessonov had lent him without anyone seeing the wounds.

When the false nose had been removed, Zhabin put the prosthetic in another plastic bag along with the false facial hair and solvent, then returned to the bedroom.

His DNA would be everywhere, he knew, including under the woman's fingernails and in the fibres of the bed sheets. That wasn't so much of a worry. He'd never been arrested in his life, so the only match they'd find on any database throughout the world would be that found near the bodies of his other victims. The police would have another name to add to the growing list of dead whores, but they'd be no closer to identifying him.

He checked that he had his wallet, then pulled on the overcoat and stood in front of the mirror. He found that if he pulled the collar up around his face, the scars were hidden, and on such a cold evening it wouldn't attract any attention.

Zhabin opened the hotel door a crack and listened for other guests, then stepped out into the deserted hallway, placing the 'Do Not Disturb' sign on the door handle. He could see the fire exit at the end of the short corridor, and was grateful to see that it wasn't alarmed. He pushed through and out into the chilly evening, then descended the metal staircase and walked calmly out of the alley, his collar high against his cheekbones.

With any luck, the body wouldn't be discovered for a couple of days, long after he'd flown home. If it were found any earlier, the disguise should keep the police occupied long enough for him to complete his mission and make his way to the airport, another German businessman on his way to the next international meeting.

Chapter 28

28 January 2016

When Ellis rolled into the office just after six in the morning, she was pleased to see three members of the team already hard at work.

Howes, Solomon and Bailey had done a sterling job of stepping up during such a difficult time, especially with so many experienced operatives out of action. Hamad Farsi's recovery was coming along nicely, but it would be a long time before he would grace the office with his presence.

'Morning, everyone,' Ellis said, heading over to Solomon's desk. 'Any leads on our shooter?'

'It's slow-going,' Solomon admitted. 'We've got over two hundred known snipers around the world, and we're trying to establish their whereabouts. So far we've crossed seventeen off the list, either dead or incarcerated, but it looks like time is not on our side.'

'If he's working for Bessonov, figure Russian or Eastern European.'

'That's where our focus is at the moment,' Solomon told her. 'Speaking of which, what news on Bessonov?'

'Still not talking,' Ellis said. 'Somehow his lawyer got wind of the arrest and went to the police station. He advised his client not to say a word.'

'Surely the evidence against him is enough to charge him, though?'

Ellis had thought so, too, but until the lab came back with a definite match on the blood samples it was a stand-off. She'd hoped to bring in the farmer and his sons to find out what links they had to Bessonov, but the police had made a gruesome discovery in the barn. The youngest Fletcher had reported his brother and father missing the day before, but it was only when a team of officers had turned up to conduct a search that their bodies were discovered. Despite intense questioning, though, the young farmer hadn't been able to offer them anything they didn't already know.

The gangster was thorough when it came to covering his tracks.

'Shame we can't beat a confession out of him,' Bailey said. 'If we could get him to give up the name of the sniper, I could go back to bed.'

'Welcome to the real world, kid.' Ellis turned to Solomon. 'Let me know the moment you find a likely match.'

'Will do. When does Andrew get back?'

'His flight arrives just after five this evening,' Ellis said. 'I'll be meeting him at Heathrow and going to the hospital with him. I'd like this resolved before then.'

She walked to her small office and unlocked the door, then booted up her computer and went to fetch a drink while it went through the security protocols.

One thought niggled her as she added powdered milk to her coffee: *Why a sniper?*

From the start, SO1 had ruled the method out as an option, much as her own team had.

Back at her desk, she brought up the file containing Milenko's itinerary. The president would be staying at Ambassador Greminov's residence during his stay, and apart from the actual signing in two days' time his only other engagement was a business banquet later that evening.

Ellis brought up Google Maps and dumped the Street View character outside the venue, then panned around looking for likely vantage points. Goosebumps crept up her arms as it struck her that on the opposite bank of the Thames stood a dozen large buildings, any of which would provide a perfect perch for a sharpshooter.

She picked up her desk phone and dialled the number for the commander of SO1.

'Oscar, Veronica Ellis. Sorry to catch you so early, but I was working the sniper angle again and think I may have spotted his opportunity.'

'If you're going to say the buildings opposite the hotel where Milenko's appearing tonight, we've got it covered.'

'Oh . . .' On reflection she should have expected it. The special-operations team hadn't lost a single dignitary over the years, so of course they would have checked out all possible threats. It still seemed strange that they could be confident the entire southern bank was a sniper-free zone. 'How will you manage to control such a large area?'

'I won't go into specifics,' the commander said, 'but we've had people on the doors of every building for the last twenty-four hours. No-one gets in unless they live there, and all guests have to be pre-registered with our men until midnight tonight. It's a pain-in-the-arse job, and I wasn't happy when they named the venue, but the hotel is co-owned by a minister and I bet they're being paid handsomely to host the dinner.'

Typical, Ellis thought. 'I'd be grateful if you could send me a list of those names.' Any new faces would be worth checking out, even if her counterpart thought he had all bases covered.

'Okay, I'll have it sent over later this morning.'

Ellis thanked him and hung up. Cross-referencing the names with known players might reveal a name they'd discounted. With time running out, they needed all the help they could get.

Ellis often wished MI5 investigations were as portrayed in the movies, where a neat sequence of clues ultimately led them to the bad guys in the nick of time, but the reality was that it was slow, painstaking work. Hundreds of man-hours spent in front of a computer, running algorithms and mining vast amounts of data were the tricks that kept the nation safe, not a single operative with a flashy car and a licence to kill.

She could have done with one now, though. Almost half of her team were hospitalised, just when she needed them most.

Richard Notley picked up the phone and dialled his office for the last time.

'I won't be in today,' he said to the manager once they'd been connected. 'I've got the flu.'

'You don't sound sick,' the voice replied.

It was exactly the kind of reply Notley had expected. He'd hated Doug Massey from the moment they'd met. Massey had been transferred in from another branch in the accounting firm and was considered a go-getter among the higher management. Among the staff, he was considered a kiss-ass and control freak, and not a day went by without Massey berating someone for slovenly work, invented or actual.

'Yeah well, I *feel* sick.'

'You do realise we've got deadlines to meet, don't you?' Massey asked.

Notley couldn't give a rat's ass about deadlines. Today was to be his last on this miserable planet, his last day away from Marian. It made him glad that Massey was being his usual self.

'Tell you what to do, Doug. Ask Helen to photocopy every one of my client sheets, then roll them up tightly and shove them up your arse.'

Notley put the phone down, the hint of a smile on his face. The perfect goodbye. Now he could concentrate on his preparations. The first order of the day was to take a shower, and he dwelled under the hot water for half an hour, letting the intense spray wash over him. He thought about Marian, as he did every day, and for the first time in weeks, a sense of calm overwhelmed him.

He would soon be with her again.

After dressing, he had a light breakfast, and then drove to the high street, where he purchased a bouquet of lilies from the florist. From there, it was a twenty-minute drive to the cemetery.

Marian's grave was situated near a fence, and to the right of it was an empty plot. He'd purchased them both after her death, so that he could be buried next to her when his time came.

That time was drawing near.

'I got you these,' Notley said, laying the flowers next to her headstone. 'Your favourites.'

He spent the next half an hour telling her about how he'd spent his time since his last visit, culminating in his phone call to the office.

'So this is it, sweet. Today's the day. Just a few more hours and that bastard will be dead and we'll be together again.'

The bastard in question was Oliver King, who held the position of health secretary in Her Majesty's Government.

Notley didn't blame the surgeon who'd operated on Marian, or the nurses who'd provided her aftercare. He didn't even blame the hospital administrators. No, Oliver King was the man solely responsible for Marian's death, thanks to his push to privatise the National Health Service. Over the last few years, the changes the government had put in place were designed to ensure the public service failed, paving the way for full privatisation and an insurance-funded healthcare system similar to that in the US.

The contract for musculoskeletal surgery had been awarded to a private company, who had then controversially subcontracted it back to the hospital, but only after ensuring a sizeable chunk of the £230 million contract was kept back as profit. That had resulted in staffing levels being cut to the bone, and when Marian had suffered internal bleeding during the night, the warning signs were not spotted.

What should have been a routine hip replacement resulted in her death, and the coroner had highlighted a catalogue of errors. The hospital trust had been held ultimately responsible, but Notley knew where the actual blame lay.

Tonight, he would have his chance to make the health secretary pay for his actions.

It hadn't taken long to discover a public engagement that King would be attending. Notley had spent a couple of hours visiting government websites and reading online health journals before discovering the business dinner with the Tagrilistani president. King had announced it as an opportunity for Britain's specialist healthcare providers to share their expertise with their new trade partners, and he would be one of three ministers attending the event.

Notley didn't care about the other two. He was just thankful that the prime minister wouldn't be in attendance, as security would have been much tighter.

He said his farewells to his wife, promising to see her soon, then drove back to his house and prepared an early lunch. At two in the afternoon, he took a bus into the heart of the city and walked down to the river. A biting wind fought him all the way, and he was exhausted by the time he reached his destination.

What he saw there made his heart slump.

More than twenty people were already gathered near the steps leading up to the hotel, and a few were holding placards adorned with Cyrillic lettering. Most of them were chatting, sharing a hot brew from a Thermos flask, while a couple chanted in Russian, their target being the four policemen standing a few yards away.

It was clearly a pro-Russian protest, and Notley could only assume these were the advance party. Many more would turn up before the dinner guests started to arrive, putting a huge dent in his ideas. Security would undoubtedly be stepped up, making it almost impossible to get close enough to his target.

The protesters were contained behind a set of crowd-control interlocking barriers, and another set had been erected on the opposite side of the entrance. Notley guessed the entire building would be cordoned off by the time the dignitaries arrived. He hadn't factored any of this into his plan, but he was a quick thinker and it wasn't long before he realised his only chance would be to get in among the protesters.

He took out his phone and surreptitiously photographed the scene, making sure to get a good shot of the placards. He then walked farther along the street before checking his camera work. He was able to clearly make out the writing, so replicating the banner shouldn't be a problem.

Notley flagged down a taxi and had it take him home, where he immediately went to his garden shed and gathered everything he would need to complete his mission.

Ellis watched the minute hand of the wall clock tick towards twelve; she was acutely aware that time was running out. The guests for the business dinner would be arriving in four hours and her team were no closer to revealing the sniper's identity than they had been yesterday.

Out on the main floor her people were still hard at work, but she felt they were fighting a losing battle as time wore inexorably on.

Elaine Solomon caught her eye as she put down her phone and pushed her chair backwards. She strode towards Ellis's office, carrying a couple of sheets of paper.

'What have you got?' Ellis asked.

'A woman was found dead at a London hotel this morning,' Solomon said, handing over one of the reports.

Ellis rubbed her temple. 'Tell me why this has been passed to us, now of all times.'

'She was killed with a garrotte,' Solomon told her. 'The Met ran the MO against the national database and came up empty, so they sent a request to Interpol. That's what came back.'

Ellis looked at the printout in her hand, and saw seven matching murders. Each had taken place in a different country, over a period of three years.

'So the killer gets around,' Ellis said. 'What does it have to do with us?'

'I called Interpol's headquarters in Lyon for more information, and they think the same man is responsible for all those deaths. They found the same DNA at each of the scenes. They also sent this.'

She gave her boss the second sheet of paper, and Ellis saw that it was a list of assassinations that had taken place over the last eight years. All had been carried out by a sniper and some of them were highlighted in yellow.

'I marked the ones that are of interest to us,' Solomon said. 'Check the dates.'

Ellis compared the two sheets. 'These women were all killed within forty-eight hours of the assassinations.'

'Exactly. Interpol thinks the sniper is behind the murders of the women, which means he could be here.'

Ellis read through the printouts again, then turned them over. 'It doesn't say who he is?'

'That's the downside,' Solomon conceded. 'We have his DNA from the murder scene, but it doesn't match any record in the world. The guy's never been arrested.'

'It's a start, though,' Ellis said, the wheels turning quickly in her head. 'Drop everything you're doing and concentrate on this lead. I want you to get flight records for the forty-eight hours after each assassination, then match them with all flights into the UK over the past seven days.'

'Someone who moves around this much is bound to have more than one identity,' Solomon pointed out.

'True, but probably not an infinite number of them. Chances are he has used one twice. If he did, go through airport CCTV and find him.'

Solomon trotted back to her desk and gave the rest of the team their new orders, while Ellis picked up her phone and dialled Gerald Small's extension. She asked him to pop into her office and he arrived thirty seconds later.

'We need to match some DNA,' she said, 'but can't afford to wait hours for the results to come back. Any ideas?'

'I think the Met has a unit that can be transported in the back of a car.'

'How quickly does it display a match?'

'It can take hours, depending on the size of the database it's searching,' Small said.

'What if we only wanted to match against a known sample?'

'In that case, a minute or so.'

We could have done with one at Bessonov's place, Ellis thought.

'Call the Met and ask if we can borrow it. If they give you any problems, put them through to me.'

As soon as Small left, Ellis placed a call to Oscar Rendell, commander of SO1, and told him what they'd learned in the last few minutes.

Solomon popped her head into the office and held up a piece of paper.

'Hold on, Oscar,' Ellis said, bidding her enter.

'A description of our killer,' Solomon said. 'The girl worked at a brothel in Soho and the manager got a good look at him, as did the receptionist at the hotel.'

Ellis thanked her and returned to her call. 'Our suspect is male, six feet tall, late fifties to early sixties, with a large, red bulbous nose and a black beard. They found his blood and skin under her nails, so there's a chance his face is wounded.'

'I'll tell my men to keep an eye out for him,' Rendell said.

'This guy has managed to stay off the radar for the best part of a decade,' Ellis said, 'so assume he knows a thing or two about disguises. We're working on finding a portable DNA device and I'd like to deploy it near those buildings.'

'Given what you've just told me, I think we can bump this up to a credible threat. I'll throw some more bodies into the mix. When will the DNA gadget arrive?'

'I'll get back to you on that. For the time being, let your men know what they're looking for. There's no telling when he'll turn up.'

'Will do.'

'And Oscar, please keep this low-key. If he sees the place swarming with armed police, he'll probably walk away. We need to catch this guy.'

Ellis hung up, and for the first time in days she felt they had the advantage. If they could apprehend the sniper, there'd be a good chance of finding a money trail to prove that Bessonov had paid for the hit. That worm still wasn't cooperating, but the more she could throw at him the better the chance of something sticking.

Her phone rang, and she snatched it up. 'Ellis.'

'The Met said we can have the DNA unit. They just need to know where to deploy it.'

Ellis gave Small the instructions, then created a summary and fired it off to the home secretary's office before locking her computer and walking to Solomon's desk.

'I need you to send SO1 a copy of the DNA found at the hotel as soon as possible. I'll be gone for some time, but if anything comes up, call me on my mobile.'

Ellis swiped her way out of the office and took the elevator down to the car park. She had a couple of hours to kill before she had to pick Harvey up from the airport, so she thought it a good time to thank Greminov for his help in getting her agent home safely.

It was a two-minute drive to the ambassador's residence, and when she turned into the street she found it blocked by civilians holding placards and chanting in Russian. She remembered that President Milenko was staying there during his trip, and these people were obviously trying to persuade him not to go ahead with the trade deal.

Fat chance, she thought, though it would be good to offer her thanks to the president, too.

She left her car parked on double yellow lines and pushed her way through the crowd. When she reached the front, she saw several armed police officers, and none of them looked relaxed.

Ellis edged out of the throng with her ID raised, and an officer approached her. After studying her credentials, he made a call over his radio, then waved her through once the reply came.

The door to the residence was already open by the time she reached it, and the same attaché showed her up to Greminov's office.

As the double doors opened she saw the ambassador sitting behind his opulent desk, with President Milenko standing at his side.

'Miss Ellis,' Greminov said, remaining in his seat. 'How fortunate that you should pay us a visit.'

Sarcasm dripped from every word, and Ellis was immediately on her guard.

'I just came to thank you – both of you – for helping to bring Andrew Harvey home. It really is greatly appreciated.'

'It was the least we could do,' Milenko said, 'given the threats you made.'

'Mr President, I apologise for the way I communicated my—'

Milenko raised a hand to silence her, and Ellis felt the presence of another person entering the room.

She turned and found herself face-to-face with John Maynard.

'Take a seat,' the home secretary said, and pointed to a leather sofa on the right-hand side of the room.

Ellis could tell the minister was pissed and did as she was told.

'You've kicked up one hell of a shitstorm,' Maynard said. 'You had strict instructions to drop the matter, but instead you send a bunch of mercenaries into a sovereign nation and give the Russians a bloody nose. Can you imagine what that has done for already strained relations? President Demidov is accusing Britain of numerous acts of war, and they've already expelled our ambassador in Moscow. Oh, and just for good measure, the forces they pulled out of Tagrilistan last week are storming back into the country in even greater numbers, and this time they're not even pretending it's an aid convoy. In short, you've moved us to the brink of World War Three.'

Ellis had expected some sort of backlash, but not this. The possibility of an escalation had always been in the back of her mind, but she hadn't envisaged the Russians making such a bold statement. Openly sending troops into Tagrilistan showed real intent, and it wasn't something the international community could readily ignore.

She could deny any knowledge of Gray's actions, but that would do him and his men a great disservice. They'd put themselves in harm's way to save Harvey, and deserved recognition rather than being fed to the wolves.

'I'm sure it's just posturing,' Ellis said. 'I believe the recent withdrawal was tactical and was only ever going to be temporary.'

'If only that were true,' Maynard said. 'They're sending in enough firepower to destroy Tagrilistan twice over, and this time they're massing fighter-bombers near the border. There are already reports of intense fighting inside the country, and President Milenko's casualties are rising rapidly by the hour. The PM wanted to give you an earful personally, but he had to convene an emergency COBRA meeting to try to deal with this crisis.'

'Then perhaps the first thing he should do is advise Demidov that we know about his plan to assassinate President Milenko this evening.'

Milenko looked at her quizzically, then turned his attention to Maynard. 'And just when did you intend to inform me of this?'

'That was the reason for my visit, Mr President,' Maynard said, taking a printout from his briefcase. 'We have unconfirmed reports that an as-yet-unidentified assassin may have been tasked with killing you. It has been suggested that Russia is behind the contract, though we have no direct proof at this moment in time.'

'It sounds very much like the threats I receive each day,' Milenko said. He looked at Ellis. 'Would I be correct in assuming you came up with this . . . information?'

'Yes, Mr President. My team—'

'Miss Ellis,' Milenko said sharply, cutting her off as he walked around the desk. 'It seems very convenient that just before you are caught red-handed sending armed forces into my country, you concoct this story to justify your actions. Unconfirmed report? Unidentified assassin? I think I've heard enough.' The president turned to Maynard. 'I trust I can leave it to you to deal with this woman?'

'Sir, this is a real threat,' Ellis said, getting to her feet.

'Enough!' Maynard said. He took out his phone and thumbed through the contacts until he found the person he needed. 'This is John Maynard. I want you to revoke all access and privileges for Veronica Ellis, effective immediately.' He turned to Ellis. 'This isn't the first time you've gone off the reservation. Consider yourself suspended, pending disciplinary action.'

Ellis was infuriated at their unwillingness to listen, but knew that screaming at them wasn't going to help her cause.

'I'll need to collect some things from my office,' she said, but the home secretary shook his head.

'Call one of your subordinates and ask them to pick them up for you. You're not to visit Thames House until this matter has been dealt with.'

So this is it, she thought, though in truth it wasn't that much of a shock. It would have been naïve to expect Tom Gray to bring Harvey home without incident, and any fallout was always going to land on her doorstep. At least Gray managed to bring Harvey home alive; she vowed silently to do all she could to deflect any blame away from Gray and his men.

Without another word, she picked up her bag and walked out of the office and down the stairs; the attaché was waiting to let her out into the street.

She fought her way back through the crowd and climbed into her car, then called Solomon.

'Maynard has suspended me,' Ellis said. 'He'll probably send over my replacement soon, but in the meantime I want you to keep working on an identity for our sniper.'

'Oh, Veronica, that's awful!'

'No, leaving Andrew stranded in Tagrilistan is awful. I'll do fine on the lecture circuit and I'll have plenty of time to write my memoirs. Before I do any of that, though, I want to stick it to Bessonov, so find out who he hired.'

'We did find a match on two of the assassinations. The same Argentinian passport was used just after each killing, but the last one was so long ago that the CCTV has been wiped. We contacted their consulate and asked for the photo of the applicant, but they have no record of it.'

Ellis cursed silently. This was one slippery fish, but she felt the net tightening. 'Okay, see if you can dig up the last time the passport was used, anywhere. We need to know what he looks like.'

It was still far too early to meet Harvey's flight, so Ellis backed out of the street and drove to the hospital.

The layout was now very familiar, and two minutes after parking her car she was walking down the corridor to the private ward Farsi and Thompson were sharing – an added security measure to protect them from Russian retaliation. She flashed her ID at the cop standing guard outside, knowing her revoked access wouldn't have trickled down this far so soon.

Inside, she found her colleagues lying in their beds. Farsi was reading a book, half of his body still encased in plaster. He looked over at Thompson, who was sleeping, and put a finger to his lips.

'She's only just dropped off,' Farsi whispered. 'She hasn't been sleeping well.'

Ellis took a seat next to his bed. 'I can imagine. She's been through a hell of a lot recently. How's she holding up?'

'It's hard to tell. She seems withdrawn, and she doesn't want to speak about what happened.'

'And how about you?' Ellis asked. 'Still having those nightmares?'

She was aware that the incident had affected him psychologically, and the latest report she'd received from the shrink suggested he still felt responsible for Harvey's abduction.

'Not recently,' Farsi said, 'but I put that down to the drugs they're pumping into me.'

'Well, I've got news that might help,' Ellis told him. It had been a couple of days since her last visit, and they had a lot of catching up to do. 'Andrew is on his way home. Gray managed to get him out.'

'Thank God! How is he?'

'You'll see soon enough,' Ellis said. 'I'll be bringing him here later this evening. He got knocked around a bit, but nothing too serious from what Gray told me.'

'If this carries on, we'll soon have our own dedicated wing in the hospital.'

Ellis managed a smile, but hoped it wouldn't come to that. There'd been more than enough violence directed towards her people in the last couple of weeks.

Her people.

She'd almost forgotten Maynard's order to suspend her.

'You'll notice a few changes when you get back to the office,' Ellis said. 'For starters, someone else will be taking over my role.'

'What? Why? Is this because you sent Gray in to rescue Andrew?'

'Not so much that, but the effect it had on the region. The Russians are royally pissed off and pouring troops into Tagrilistan. Maynard thinks we're on the brink of war.'

'Are we?' Farsi asked.

'I very much doubt it. If they succeed in killing Milenko this evening, the trade deal is off and they'll have a chance to court the next leader of Tagrilistan. If we manage to catch the sniper first, we can hopefully connect the dots back to Moscow. Not even the Chinese would stand in their corner if they knew Demidov ultimately sanctioned the hit.'

'That'll be hard to prove,' Farsi said.

'I know, which is why we need to capture that sniper. The money trail will be the easiest to follow, but we need to take him alive.'

Thompson's body jerked in her bed, as if she'd been shocked, but seconds later she was back into a deep sleep, a gentle snore emanating from her.

'I'd better go,' Ellis said. 'If she wakes up, you get to tell her the good news. Say I'll be back with Andrew sometime after seven.'

Ellis left and walked back to her car, glad that the forecast rain had held off. Traffic was already beginning to build as the rush hour kicked in, and it was a tortuous, ninety-minute drive to Heathrow Airport. During it, Ellis found herself tapping her feet and fingers nervously and realised that she wouldn't be able to relax until she saw Harvey walk out into the arrivals hall.

The gang would soon be reunited, only to be ripped from her.

Chapter 29

28 January 2016

The Boeing 747 descended through charcoal clouds and landed at Heathrow three minutes ahead of schedule.

Gray led the team off the plane and through immigration, where their temporary travel papers were scrutinised carefully. It took ten minutes to get through, and they bypassed the luggage carousels and headed straight through customs and into the arrivals area, five figures dressed in just about the worst smart-casual gear Tagrilistan had to offer. *Still*, Gray thought, *it beats bloodstained fatigues.*

'I don't know about anyone else,' Sonny said, 'but I intend to stop off at an off-licence, grab some beers, order a takeaway and disappear off the face of the planet for at least a week.'

'It's about time you had a great idea,' Smart said with a smile. 'Count me in.'

Mark Howard declined the offer, preferring to head home and check on his tropical fish, while Gray and Harvey said they expected someone to be waiting for them.

Ellis was easy to spot, her immaculate platinum hair making her stand out in the crowd. Gray approached her with his arm extended, expecting a handshake. He wasn't prepared for her to throw her arms around him and squeeze him tight.

'Bless you, Tom. Thanks for bringing Andrew home.'

The hug was over before he could reply, and she moved on to Harvey, giving him the same treatment. As their bodies parted, Harvey scanned the large hall, a confused look on his face.

'Sarah didn't come with you?' he asked.

Ellis remained silent for a moment, and Gray knew bad news was imminent.

'Sarah's in the hospital. She went after Bessonov when we thought the mission to rescue you had failed. She got hurt pretty badly.'

Gray felt a flash of anger building, but Harvey beat him to it.

'If you tell me he's still walking the streets, I'm gonna kill him.'

'He's been arrested,' Ellis said. 'The police are close to charging him with Sarah's abduction, but we want the sniper to really turn the screw. And we think he'll strike tonight.' She took Harvey's elbow gently. 'Come along.'

As she led them out of the airport and to the car park, she condensed the last few days of activity into a couple of minutes.

'Is there anything we can do to help?' Smart asked.

'We've got it covered,' Ellis said. 'Besides, you guys have done enough already.'

'In that case, we'll share a taxi into town,' Smart said. 'Tom, call me when you're done.'

Gray gave each of the trio his best man-hug and thanked them for their help. 'I'm officially declaring us too old for this shit,' he said before they left.

Ellis and Harvey also offered their gratitude, and the party split up.

'Let's get you to the hospital,' Ellis said to Harvey. 'I haven't had a chance to tell Sarah you're safe. I went to see her a couple of hours ago, but she was sleeping.'

'Then let her sleep,' Harvey said. 'I want to see this guy taken down.'

'I'll take you to where we think the sniper will strike from, but I'm not sure they'll let us anywhere near the place,' Ellis said. 'My decision to send Tom and his team into Tagrilistan inflamed the region, and Maynard suspended me.'

'That's bullshit,' Gray said. 'Maynard and the PM should be kicked out of government for leaving Andrew to rot over there.'

'We all know your feelings on the powers that be,' Ellis said, 'but that's not going to happen. If someone is going to take the fall, it won't be those at the top.'

'Sounds like you're not going to fight this,' Harvey noted.

'What's the point? I'm guilty as charged. The only defence I could possibly offer is that Tom took it upon himself to launch the rescue attempt, but I'm not going to stab him in the back. It was my call, and I'd make it again.'

Had it been any other civil servant, Gray knew the outcome would have been very different, but Ellis was a woman of her word.

'If the sniper is taken down, won't that count in your favour?' he asked. 'I'm sure Milenko would be grateful, and he might put in a good word with Maynard.'

'Possibly,' Ellis said, 'but I'm not banking on it. I just want Bessonov to pay for what he's done, and catching this guy will go a long way towards that.'

'Where is this going to take place?' Harvey asked.

'There are three new residential projects on the south bank of the river, and they all offer a decent view of the Orion Hotel. That's where Milenko will be entertained this evening.'

Traffic was still relatively heavy as they drove back into the city, and Harvey pressed for news on Thompson's condition. As Ellis told him all about Thompson's ordeal, Gray couldn't help thinking it was going to be a long time, if ever, before she made a full recovery. He knew a few fellow soldiers who had gone through a lot less and had caved in on themselves, while others went back to work within a few weeks. There was simply no telling how it would affect her in the long term, but for her sake – and for Harvey's – he hoped she would be able to put it behind her one day.

'Sounds like she went through a hell of a lot,' he said to Harvey. 'You both have. You're going to need to be strong for her.'

Gray hoped putting the onus on Harvey would help his friend to forget his own torment. The worst thing that could happen would be for the couple to wallow in their collective misery.

'What do you know about the sniper?' Gray asked, changing the subject before Harvey had time to dwell on his words.

Ellis shared the information the police had given them as she made a right turn and pulled into a car park next to a red-brick giant. The building was a ten-storey residential block, one of three that overlooked the Thames. The other two looked similar, though the one in the middle had a penthouse that made it slightly taller.

'Where's the police presence?' Gray asked. A ten-metre-wide walkway ran past the buildings, separating them from a sprawling office complex. He could see a few people leaving work and others using it as a cut-through, but no-one appeared to be there in an official capacity.

'I told them to keep a low profile. We don't want to scare this guy off. I'd imagine they're inside the buildings, checking people as they enter.'

A woman toting three carrier bags walked into the nearest building, closely followed by a man fitting the vague description of the subject. A minute later, a man wearing a black leather jacket emerged and walked towards the car park. He glanced in at Gray as he passed, then carried on to a silver estate car. The driver got out and walked round the back, popping the trunk, and Leather Jacket handed him a small glass tube. Gray couldn't see what they were doing as the car was parked the wrong way, but it looked suspicious.

'Any idea what's going on there?' he asked.

'That'll be the portable DNA unit,' Ellis said. 'Anyone close to a fit will have their mouth swabbed and checked against our known sample.'

Two minutes later, Leather Jacket walked casually back to the building, his manner suggesting he hadn't identified an international hit man.

Gray's watch told him it was almost a quarter to seven, and he hoped the stake-out wouldn't last too long. He'd booked himself onto the last flight back to Florida, where his daughter awaited him. Having repaid his debt to Harvey, he just wanted to get back to Melissa and put this whole episode behind him.

Ivan Zhabin leaned against the corner of the office building, his fedora pulled down tight and his collar turned up to combat the cold. His hands went to his face, making sure the beard was still firmly in place. He hadn't wanted to wear it again, but the scrapes on his cheeks were still fresh and swollen, and though he'd done his best to disguise them using make-up, they still looked hideous on close inspection.

His main concern was getting out of the country after the hit. None of his legitimate passports showed him sporting facial hair, and he wouldn't welcome any extra scrutiny. The alternative was to stay in London for a few more days until the marks had receded, but that had its own dangers. It wouldn't take long for the police to find the girl and start making enquiries. By not waiting to take the shot in Whitehall as initially planned, he was already a day ahead of schedule, but the sooner he left the country the better.

Zhabin was due to meet with the estate agent in fifteen minutes, and continued to scan the area for signs of anyone who appeared to be acting out of the ordinary. All he'd seen for the last ten minutes had been office workers leaving and residents returning home. No-one appeared to be loitering in the shadows or talking into their jacket collars. In fact, the whole place looked very much as it had the day before.

Zhabin still wasn't prepared to let his guard down.

He grabbed the handle of his wheeled suitcase and walked down the wide pavement. He faced straight ahead, but behind the tinted glasses his eyes were darting everywhere, looking for signs of trouble in doorways and the alleys between the buildings.

He saw nothing to give him any cause for concern.

Which struck him as odd.

When planning a hit, he always started out by looking at it from the perspective of the local security services. What would they do to protect the mark? The Metropolitan Police Service was one of the most respected in the world, and given what was happening on the other side of the river, he would have expected at least a couple of patrol cars in the area.

Perhaps they didn't consider Milenko important enough, or had simply discounted a threat of this nature. He'd done his research and it showed no confirmed sniper kills in England in the last few decades, so perhaps it wasn't something the British threw their resources at.

He reached the end of the walkway, where a car park was filling up quickly as residents returned home for the evening. The majority of the vehicles were empty, but he saw three people sitting in a saloon, a woman behind the wheel. Light rain had settled on the windscreen, which made it difficult to make them out.

Police? Security services?

There was no way he could tell, but they didn't appear to be paying him much attention. All three heads were pointing towards the apartment buildings, so they may have just been waiting for a fourth before heading out for a meal.

Zhabin continued to the corner of the office complex and turned left, then left again at the main road. Four minutes later, he was back where he'd started, and when he glanced down the walkway he saw that only one thing had changed.

Outside the middle building, standing beneath the bronze nameplate that proclaimed it Ashcroft House, a pretty blonde woman holding a clipboard was stamping her feet to fight off the cold.

The estate agent.

He walked towards her, again checking for signs of danger, but as with earlier he only saw people going about their normal business. The woman saw him approaching and held the clipboard to her chest so that he could see the company logo.

'Mr Baume?' She smiled. 'I'm Erica.'

Zhabin extended his hand. 'Sorry to drag you out on such a miserable evening,' he said, 'but I have a flight in three hours and would like to see this place before I return to Germany. If I like it, we can start the ball rolling tomorrow.'

The woman's smile broadened at the prospect of a quick sale. 'Then let's take a look, shall we?'

Erica led him towards the entrance, just as another couple were heading inside. She held the door open for them, then ushered Zhabin in out of the cold. He wheeled his luggage into the foyer as Erica began her pitch.

'The apartment is on the market for four hundred thousand, but there might be a little wiggle room in there. The owner is leaving the country and wants to complete as soon as possible.'

Zhabin was barely listening. His focus was on the surroundings, always plotting an alternative exit. To the left were a three-seater couch and a coffee table, and Erica was following the signs for the ground-floor elevator.

As they turned a corner, Zhabin's pulse quickened.

A man wearing jeans and an open suit jacket was holding a clipboard and asked the couple in front for their ID before consulting a list of names. Off to his side, a second man wearing a leather jacket was taking a keen interest in Zhabin. The bulges in their coats could only mean one thing.

'Oh, sorry, I forgot to mention. There's some kind of security thing going on today,' Erica said. 'I found out earlier when I showed another client an apartment in the next block. Don't worry – I called ahead about our appointment, so we should be on their list. I'm sure they won't keep us long.'

Zhabin managed a smile, but inside his heart was pounding. He gripped the silenced pistol in his overcoat pocket as the one in the leather jacket ambled over and showed him a police ID.

'What's in the suitcase, sir?'

'My clothes,' Zhabin said. 'After I view this apartment I have to catch a plane back to Germany.'

Leather Jacket nodded. 'Mind if I take a look?'

The couple in front were waved through and pressed a button to summon the elevator.

'Sure, no problem.'

Zhabin wheeled the case over to a table and placed it on top, then unzipped it and lifted the lid. He took a couple of steps backwards to let the cop get a closer look.

'We'll also have to take a DNA swab,' the cop said as he started removing items from the suitcase. 'Just a sample of saliva. It won't hurt at all.'

At the mention of DNA, a chill went through Zhabin. The only thing linking him to his murders was his genetic make-up, and while many countries had a copy, they'd never had anyone to link it to.

That was all about to change.

A bell announced the arrival of the elevator, and the couple walked in and hit the button for their floor. Zhabin watched them from the corner of his eye, his main focus on the man going through his belongings. He watched as shirts and trousers were removed, followed by the toiletry bag, and Zhabin knew it wouldn't be long before he found the false bottom containing the dismantled rifle. That, along with a DNA match, would be enough to put him away for several lifetimes.

Zhabin had considered this scenario many times: what to do if faced with the choice of pushing a bad position or slipping away. The right thing to do would be to shoot them all and run. Get the next plane out of the country and chalk this one down to bad luck. If he did that, though, he could kiss his reputation goodbye. No-one was going to hire a killer who backed down at the first hint of trouble, no matter how good a shot he was.

Ultimately, he'd decided that reputations could be salvaged, and it would be hard to do that if he were incarcerated or dead.

As the elevator doors closed, Zhabin drew the gun and shouted, 'Hey!' at the cop, who looked up at him in surprise.

With the man's chest exposed, Zhabin put a bullet through his heart. Before his body had time to fall to the floor, Zhabin turned and pushed Erica out of the way so that he could get the other one in his sights. The target was reaching inside his jacket but never stood a chance.

Erica froze, mouth gaping in shock. Her eyes slowly went from the downed cop to Zhabin, who had the barrel pointing at her forehead.

'Do as I say and you can walk away from this.'

He stepped to the elevator and hit the button, then told Erica to grab one of the dead cops and drag him to the doors.

The woman looked horrified at the suggestion, but as soon as the gun was thrust in her face again, she found the courage. She wasn't the biggest female he'd come across, but was deceptively strong. She completed her task just as Zhabin pulled the other cop over and laid him next to his partner. As he'd expected, the chest shots with the low-velocity rounds had lodged internally, so there were no exit wounds or mess to leave behind.

As he waited for the elevator to arrive, he threw his clothes back into the case and zipped it up, all the while keeping a close eye on Erica.

The elevator doors opened with a *ping!*, and Zhabin told Erica to pull the bodies inside. Again, he had to use his gun to convince her to do as she was told. Once she'd completed the task, he reached in and hit the button for the top floor. Erica stood at the back of the car, shaking, tears running down her face.

Zhabin was aware that there were CCTV cameras operating in the lobby, meaning any description Erica gave wouldn't aid the police in their search for the murderer, but there was a chance that she might hit the button to stop at a lower floor and raise the alarm, and he needed time to clear the area.

'Sorry,' Zhabin said as the doors began closing. He raised the pistol and squeezed the trigger, then stepped back as the three bodies disappeared from sight and began the climb to the penthouse suite.

Anyone finding the bodies would immediately call the police, but it would take them precious minutes to review the cameras to see what had happened and identify a suspect. By that time, he would be well clear of the area. His immediate goal was simple: get back to the apartment Bessonov had provided him with and lay low for a couple of days until the swelling on his face receded. He could then ditch the disguise and make his way out of the country.

He watched the numbers above the elevator doors slowly climb, then wheeled the suitcase towards the exit. As he pulled the door open, a woman ran inside, rain dripping from her hair. She offered a quick thank-you, then walked around the corner to the elevators.

Zhabin stepped out into the cold night and saw that the earlier drizzle had turned into a downpour. He made sure his collar was still turned up and headed for the taxi rank, where a queue had already formed. He saw eight people ahead of him in the line and half a dozen cars waiting patiently to take them to their destinations. Zhabin hoped some of them were travelling together, otherwise he would be forced to wait for more cars to arrive, and with every passing second grew the chance of someone discovering his handiwork.

He was relieved to see the first four people in the queue get into the same cab, and risked a glance back at the building as it neared his turn.

'That guy matches your description pretty well,' Gray said, indicating the man in the black overcoat and fedora pulling a suitcase along behind him as he left the middle building.

'He certainly does,' Ellis said, 'but they must have cleared him.'

'I don't think so,' Gray said. 'I watched him meet a woman outside a few minutes ago, and I was expecting someone to come out to check his DNA.'

'Maybe they did and you missed it,' Harvey said.

'No way. He pinged my radar when I first saw him, and I was just waiting to see how the guy reacted after he did the test.'

Ellis turned to look at Gray in the back seat. 'How sure are you?'

'One hundred per cent.'

'Then I'll check it out. Keep an eye on him while I'm gone.'

Ellis climbed out from behind the wheel and ran to the second building, using her jacket to protect herself from the rain. When she disappeared inside, Gray turned his attention to the suspect, who was nearing the front of the taxi queue.

'If he gets in a cab, we'll lose him,' Gray said. 'I'm gonna stall him.'

Before Harvey could object, Gray opened the rear door and removed his wallet from his pocket, then jogged over to the suspect, who had his hand on the door of a taxi.

'Excuse me!' Gray shouted.

The man looked round at him, and Gray saw something in his eyes. Not quite panic, but he could sense the man was on edge. He held up his wallet. 'I think you dropped this.'

He watched the man pat himself down, then shake his head. 'Not mine,' he said, as he opened the cab door. He put his suitcase inside, giving Gray time to cover the ground between them.

'Say, don't I know you?' Gray asked, and clamped his hand on the guy's arm.

The man spun, this time with anger in his eyes.

'I don't think so.'

'Sure I do. You're Professor Higson, from Oxford University. You were my chemistry tutor.'

Gray felt powerful fingers dig into the pressure points in his wrist, and he was forced to release his grip.

'You're mistaken.'

Gray had run out of ways to keep the man occupied, but a shout from behind him told him he'd done enough.

'Tom!' Ellis shouted. 'It's him!'

The sniper's eyes went wide, then constricted as his knee came up, trying to make contact with Gray's groin. Gray managed to arch his back and avoid the blow, but received a punch to the side of his head that rattled his teeth. By the time he'd shaken it off, the man was running.

Gray chased after him and saw the sniper run into heavy traffic, narrowly avoiding a collision with a speeding bus. Gray waited for a gap and sprinted after him, horns blaring as he made the same mad dash to the tree-lined pavement on the other side of the road.

The sniper lost his hat as he ran past a row of shops, his overcoat flapping in his wake like a superhero's cape. People scattered as the figure hurtled towards them. Gray was having a hard time keeping up. Despite running at least three times a week, he was built for endurance, not speed.

The sniper was thirty yards ahead of him. Gray saw him glance backwards a couple of times, and just before he reached the next junction he stopped and turned.

When the sniper's arm came up, Gray knew what was coming. He threw himself behind a tree just as a bullet thumped into it. He waited a second and stuck his head out, and saw the sniper disappearing around the corner.

Gray set off again, stopping at the junction and poking his head around the corner to check for his target.

Nothing.

The street was almost empty, few souls braving the cold, wet night. A bus was pulling away, and through the rear window Gray saw a black-clad figure climbing to the upper deck. He set off in pursuit, but the vehicle sped effortlessly away from him, heading towards a set of traffic lights. Gray prayed for them to turn red and slow the bus's progress as his legs pumped frantically, but the lights remained green and it took a right turn, disappearing round the corner.

Gray continued after it, knowing the sniper could get off at any stop and melt into the night.

The lights eventually changed, and as traffic drew to a halt he took the opportunity to cross the road and round the corner, where he saw the sniper's conveyance waiting at a bus stop. It was more than a hundred yards away, a sprint of roughly twenty seconds. Gray went for it.

Traffic was lighter here, and he managed to get across the road safely, then put everything he had into covering the ground.

Fifty yards out, he saw the flashing ambers turn off. The driver indicated to pull out. Gray started waving his arms as he ran, hoping to get the bus driver's attention, but when he got to within twenty yards the vehicle took off once more.

Gray stopped, his hands on his knees as he tried to catch his breath. He knew it was pointless to continue, so he pulled his phone from his pocket to look up Ellis's number. As he did so, a car screeched to a stop next to him.

'Tom, get in!'

Gray threw himself into the saloon and Ellis gunned the engine.

'He's on the number seven bus,' Gray gasped, 'and he's armed.'

Ellis tossed her phone to Harvey in the back seat. 'Call it in, get as many units here as you can.'

While Harvey made the call, Gray told Ellis to reduce her speed. 'We don't want to let him know we're on his tail,' he said hoarsely, still winded. 'Just stay behind him until the police arrive.'

Ellis settled in two cars behind the bus.

'What did you see back there?' Gray asked.

'He killed three people,' Ellis said. 'Two police officers and the woman he was with. I arrived just as the elevator opened.'

'Then let's hope we can stop him before anyone else gets hurt.'

'The police are on their way in unmarked cars,' Harvey said from the rear seat. 'I told them to wait for him to get off the bus before they make their move, otherwise it could turn into a hostage situation.'

Up ahead, the bus indicated to pull over at another stop, and Ellis stopped a dozen yards behind it. Gray opened the window and stuck his head out to see who was getting off.

'He's still on board,' he said as the bus pulled back into traffic.

Ellis followed, keeping her distance until it stopped once more outside a shopping centre.

'That's him!' Gray said, flinging open the car door.

The sniper was scanning the area and saw Gray climb out; instantly he broke into a run, pushing past late-night shoppers and into the shopping centre.

Gray heard Ellis shouting for him to stop, but he wasn't about to let the man out of his sights. Ellis could call in their location, but he wanted to make sure the sniper didn't sneak out a side entrance and disappear.

He reached the entrance to the shopping centre and saw his foe bounding up an escalator, pushing past a mother and her two young children and almost knocking the eldest one over the side. Gray followed, skirting round the family and arriving at the top of the moving stairs just as a bullet flew past his head.

The sniper turned and ran again, disappearing into a gap between two shops. Gray approached cautiously, sticking his head round the corner for a split second before pulling it back, wary of the man's weapon. He saw a fire exit slowly closing, and rushed towards it. He held the door slightly ajar and heard feet pounding on the stairs, and he stepped inside to determine if they were going up or down. They sounded like they were heading back towards the ground floor, the suspect clearly looking for a way out of the building.

He took out his phone and called Ellis's number, updating her on the situation as he took the stairs two at a time. When he reached the bottom a chill hit him as the cold night air blew in through a set of double doors. Gray ran through them and out into the loading area, which was deserted except for a shadowy figure splashing through the puddles and out of the exit gate.

Gray looked around for a weapon and found a thick cardboard tube that was as sturdy as a metal pole, then set off after his quarry.

'He's heading down Dixon Street towards Lancashire Road,' Gray told Ellis as he sped down the rain-lashed street.

'Ostanovit' sdelku! Ostanovit' sdelku!'

Richard Notley had no idea what they were chanting, but he'd managed to get to the front of the throng and was pressed up against the security barriers, jiggling his home-made placard along with the rest of the protestors.

As he'd expected, some of them had tried to engage him in conversation, but he'd made a few hand signs and pointed to his ears, indicating that he was deaf. That had been received with a few shrugs and pats on the back, and he was accepted as one of the crowd.

Since then it had been a tense hour, watching the security being stepped up as the time for the dignitaries to arrive approached. Initially, there had been just four policemen watching the crowd, but that number had been joined by six suited security men, and though Notley was unable to determine if they were armed, he had to assume they were.

Half a dozen business leaders had already arrived, with three more limousines queued up to disgorge their passengers. The security detail had gone from passive to alert since the first of the guests had walked up the stairs to the hotel, and Notley was concerned that he wouldn't have a chance to get close enough to his target to manage an effective strike.

The nearest guard was about three yards to Notley's left, and when he turned away, Notley lowered his placard so that it covered his waist, then dug into his pocket and eased out the small bolt cutters he'd brought along. His earlier reconnaissance of the scene had shown that the security gates were fastened together with plastic ties, and he'd managed to position himself right in front of one of the joins. The two barriers were connected at the top and bottom, and Notley bent down and quickly snipped the lower one. When he stood up again, no-one seemed to have taken any notice of his actions, but his pulse still raced along.

Another vehicle pulled up at the bottom of the stairs. The hotel doorman performed his duty and revealed an elderly man and woman, who climbed out before the limo gracefully made way for the next in the queue. Notley had no idea what car his target was going to be travelling in, so it was a case of waiting until he recognised the health secretary, Oliver King.

When he saw him, he would only have seconds to strike.

He didn't have long to wait.

The next car stopped in the customary spot and when the door was opened, King emerged and smiled at the gallery of press photographers gathered near the top of the stairs. He took a couple of steps, and then Notley's plan began to fall apart.

He used the bolt cutters to snip the last remaining tie holding the barriers together just as the entire security team seemed to tense up and begin scanning the crowd. One set of eyes seemed to rest on him, and he began to panic, imagining that somehow they'd discovered his plan at the last minute.

The health secretary was forced back into his car by two security agents and the driver told to go.

This can't be happening!

Notley kicked the barrier aside and ran towards the nearest agent, who thrust an arm inside his jacket. Notley knew he must be going for a gun, and he threw the placard towards him. As the agent put a hand out to prevent it from hitting his head, Notley ran past and rammed him with his shoulder, knocking the man off his feet.

King's car was just a couple of yards away; time slowed as Notley's fingers danced over the buttons of the phone in his pocket with practised ease. One to wake it up, one to select the contacts list, one to highlight the top entry, and the last one to make the call.

He was running only a yard from the car when the device secured around his abdomen received the signal, level with the rear door. He could see King's face, a mask of confusion, and Notley felt a pang of sadness at not being able to confront the man face-to-face, to explain his actions, but the time for regret was long gone.

As the bomb around his waist exploded, Notley's last thought was an image of Marian's face.

She was smiling.

Zhabin began to feel the pressure as he emerged from the side street onto a busier road.

He'd no idea who was following him, but was certain it wasn't the police or security services. They would have approached with weapons drawn rather than concoct a feeble story about recognising him.

He'd have time to figure that out later. For now, getting out of the area was the only thing on his mind. He glanced back and saw that the man was still behind him, and this time he was carrying something. He was also on the phone, and Zhabin guessed he was calling in his position.

Traffic was too heavy to try to commandeer a car, but the perfect conveyance was fast approaching: a motorcycle courier. Zhabin raised his pistol when the bike was ten yards away and squeezed the trigger. The bike slewed to the left and the rider was thrown off, landing in a heap on the pavement. A few people immediately ran over to tend to the injured rider, giving Zhabin the opportunity to mount the vehicle and roar away.

He would clear the immediate area and dump the bike, then call Dimitri to pick him up and take him back to the apartment, where he could hide out for a couple of days. Dimitri could arrange a new disguise, and Zhabin had a contact in Argentina who could provide him with a new passport. All he needed to do was to change his appearance, email a photograph of his new likeness to Buenos Aires and the document would be couriered over within a few days. As Bessonov was the one that had brought him to England, it was in both of their interests that he get out of the country as soon as possible.

But that only worked if he could escape this part of town, and his pursuer was still chasing him, barely ten yards away now as Zhabin righted the motorcycle.

He raised his pistol, aimed at the man's chest, and fired. But balancing the bike had made him send the round wide. The slide of the handgun locked open, indicating an empty magazine.

No time to reload. He dropped the weapon and gunned the bike. The stranger made one last effort to stop him by throwing what looked like a stick at him, but it bounced short and off target.

Zhabin popped the clutch.

Time to go.

Gray saw the sniper take down the biker and climb onto his machine. If he didn't stop the man now, the authorities might arrive too late. The police were no doubt on their way, but because of

Harvey's request for a silent approach, there was no telling if they were ten seconds out or ten minutes.

Gray sprinted for all he was worth and was gaining ground fast, but not quick enough. All he could do was throw his makeshift weapon and hope to hit the rider, but before he could bring his arm back he found himself staring down the barrel of the sniper's pistol. He was caught out in the open, with nothing to hide behind and nowhere to run. The shooter was within spitting distance and unlikely to miss.

Gray braced for the impact and saw the man's arm pull left as the gun fired, the bullet somehow flying wide. The sniper looked at his empty weapon for a split second and let it drop.

Now.

He threw the tube as hard as he could, but it slipped out of his wet hand at the last second, and instead of flying towards the sniper's head he saw it bounce near the front of the machine as the bike sped forward.

It turned out to be a better throw than he ever could have hoped for.

The tube skidded into the front wheel and became lodged between the spokes, and when it came up against the front forks, the wheel stopped dead. The rest of the bike, however, carried on, and the sniper was thrown over the handlebars, doing a somersault before smashing face first into the back of a stationary bus.

Gray was on him in seconds and found the man unconscious but breathing, blood flowing freely from his nose. Gray put him in the recovery position before calling Ellis with his location.

She arrived less than a minute later, with the first of the armed police cars close behind.

'Is he dead?' Ellis asked.

'He'll live. I called an ambulance just after I got off the phone with you.'

The incident had brought traffic to a stop, and the police officers administered first aid while they waited for the paramedics to turn up.

One of the officers asked Gray for a statement, and he accepted a seat in the back of a police car while recounting the events from his sighting of the sniper at the taxi rank.

'Veronica Ellis will be able to fill you in on the rest of it,' Gray said when he'd finished with his account. He got out of the car and walked over to Ellis, who was standing a few feet from the still unconscious sniper, rain soaking her through.

'You need to get yourself home and dry off,' he said.

Ellis shook her head. 'I'm not letting this one out of my sight.'

Gray looked around and saw at least twenty officers on the scene.

'I think the police have got this covered,' he said, stealing a glance at his watch and seeing that he had about three hours before he had to check in for his flight to Florida. He took Ellis's arm and led her back to the car, then got in behind the wheel. 'I'll drop Andrew off at the hospital.' To Harvey he said, 'I'm sure you'll want some time alone with Sarah. Sorry I won't be able to pop in and see her, but please give her my regards.'

Harvey nodded, his smile thanking Gray for his understanding.

'After that –' he turned to Ellis – 'I'll drop you home and get a taxi.'

'Where are you staying tonight? With Sonny and Len?'

Gray managed a smile of his own. 'I'm going home to see my girl.'

Chapter 30

3 February 2016

Veronica Ellis turned into Marsham Street and was fortunate enough to find a parking space right outside the Home Office building. Her sadness at attending her official termination meeting was tempered by the thought that she would never have to visit this ugly building ever again.

The late winter morning had blessed her with an almost clear sky, though the temperature was still closer to zero than she would have liked.

After passing through layers of security, she was escorted to John Maynard's office and told to take a seat in the waiting room. Ellis knew it would be at least five minutes before she was seen, a favourite trick of the home secretary. Why he insisted on keeping people waiting was beyond her, but she suspected it had something to do with the size of his penis.

She was still smiling inwardly at the thought when the door to the office opened and John Maynard gestured for her to enter.

Ellis couldn't help sneaking a glance at his crotch as she walked past him.

She wasn't surprised to see that the home secretary wasn't alone, but she'd expected the head of HR and perhaps a lawyer or two, not Alexander Parrish.

'Take a seat, Veronica.' Parrish smiled at her from behind the home secretary's desk.

'Thank you, Prime Minister.'

Maynard stood off to Ellis's right, hands in his pockets and hatred plastered all over his face.

'Quite a couple of weeks we've had,' Parrish said, leaning back in the chair. 'From the reports I've read, it seems a lot of the credit has to go to you and your department.'

'My team did an outstanding job under very challenging circumstances,' Ellis agreed. 'I'm just glad the trade deal was able to go ahead as planned.'

'Indeed. President Milenko and I had a very long chat afterwards, and he wanted me to convey his gratitude.'

'It's what my team do,' Ellis said, before correcting herself: 'I mean, it's what *they* do.'

Parrish sat upright and, after glancing at Maynard, he clasped his hands in front of him on the secretary's desk. 'That's what I brought you here to discuss,' he said. 'Thanks to your tenacity, we were able to establish the link between Zhabin, Bessonov and Moscow. I've spoken to Demidov and spelled out what we know about his involvement. While he flat-out denies it, he's agreed to pull his troops back from Tagrilistan to enable peace talks to continue.'

Ellis tilted her head in acknowledgement, betraying no hint of a smile.

'When I spoke with President Milenko,' the PM continued, 'in addition to conveying his gratitude, he also told me that, although he may disagree with your methods, your actions saved his life and have brought about the hope of a peaceful resolution to the conflict in Tagrilistan.'

Ellis remained impassive, figuring there was more to come.

'In addition,' Parrish continued, 'he thinks it would be counterproductive of me to relieve you of your post. He thinks your people skills could do with a little polishing, but believes you are the right person for the job. Given the fact that the incidents last week have generated a lot of headlines worldwide, I also think we need you to continue the good work.'

You mean, tossing me aside would be bad PR, Ellis thought, but held her tongue. If she really were to be reinstated on the spot, then it wouldn't do to antagonise her paymasters any more than she had already done.

'This doesn't mean you're completely off the hook,' Maynard said, joining the conversation. 'You blatantly disregarded orders, and that will stay on your record. I'm just waiting for you to screw up one more time and I'll be all over you like stink on shit.'

'Eloquently put,' Parrish said, turning serious. 'But I have to echo John's sentiments. We can't have you playing the Girl Scout any more. You'll be under enormous scrutiny, and if you stray from protocols one more time, I'll be forced to take action.'

'Understood, Prime Minister,' Ellis said. 'You mentioned the link to Moscow. I've been out of the loop for a few days . . .'

'Zhabin broke,' Maynard said. 'We told him we were in the process of extraditing him to Venezuela for one of the assassinations, and he'd obviously heard about prison conditions there. In exchange for a British prison cell, he gave us his bank accounts and we tracked the money back to Demidov.'

That was indeed good news, but Demidov wasn't the Russian who concerned her. 'What about Bessonov? Please tell me you managed to pin something on him.'

'Forensics found enough blood matches in the basement to link him to at least a dozen murders over the last couple of years,' Maynard said. 'We also matched Thompson's blood and his DNA on the bloodstained suit, so he'll be going down for that, too. His reign is over.'

Ellis wanted to consider it a victory, but given the hell Harvey, Thomson and Farsi had been through, it would be a hollow one at best.

'I'd better get back to the office,' she said. 'I have a feeling there's a lot to catch up on.'

Ellis rose and shook the PM's hand, and – despite her loathing for him – Maynard's, too.

'Oliver King also asked me to thank you,' Parrish said. 'Without your timely intervention, he would have been caught out in the open and I'd be looking for a new health secretary.'

'Thank God for reinforced cars, eh?' Ellis smiled. 'How long before I can get my access back?'

'Your security card is waiting on reception at Thames House,' Maynard said. 'All other privileges have already been restored.'

Ellis smiled at the home secretary, knowing it was killing him to give her a second chance.

'Thanks, John. I look forward to working with you again.'

With the lie delivered, Veronica Ellis left for the short drive back to her office.

Chapter 31

12 February 2016

Ellis steered the rented Chevrolet off the freeway and into the suburbs, the windows open as the Florida sun beat down from an azure sky. The satnav told her to make a left turn at the junction, and she obeyed the electronic instructions until she found herself outside Tom Gray's house.

It looked much as it had a few weeks earlier, though the grass was a little longer. The most striking difference was the real-estate sign on the front lawn.

Ellis climbed out, and Harvey and Thompson got out of the rear seats.

'Nice place he's got,' Harvey noted, as they walked towards the front door. His gait had returned almost to normal, but Sarah still walked tentatively, the result of the skin grafts she'd been undergoing to heal the cuts on her legs.

'Are you sure he'll be pleased to see us?' Thompson asked.

'I don't see why not,' Ellis said. After her last visit, she knew what kind of reaction to expect if they just turned up on his doorstep, so this time she'd called ahead. 'We're bringing him good news, and we're not here to separate him from his daughter again.'

She knocked on the door, and Gray opened it, looking genuinely happy to see them.

'Come in.' He smiled and led them through to the kitchen. 'So what brings you over here? Your call said it wasn't work-related. I hope that's true.'

'I just wanted to thank you personally for all you did,' Thompson said as Gray put on a fresh pot of coffee. 'Andrew wouldn't be here if it wasn't for you.'

She threw her arms around Gray and hugged him tight.

'I had a lot of help from some good people,' Gray said, once she'd let go. 'How are you holding up? I hear you went through a lot.'

'I'm good,' Thompson assured him. 'The scars are healing nicely.' She held up her hands and showed off her fake fingernails.

Harvey went over to Melissa, who was sitting at the dining table drawing a picture. 'Remember me, darling?'

Melissa looked nervous, shifting her gaze towards her father, so Harvey backed away.

'She's still a little shy around some men,' Gray explained, lifting his daughter up. 'Hopefully that will change once she starts nursery.'

Ellis sipped the coffee Gray had placed in front of her. 'I noticed the "For Sale" sign outside. You going somewhere?'

'Yeah, I found a place in San Giovanni in Fiore near Ken and Mina. Melissa thinks of them as Grandma and Grandpa, and I thought it best if she had more family around her. They have quite a large English community over there, and it's the perfect opportunity for Melissa to learn a second language. They say the younger they start the easier it is.' Gray shrugged. 'We really should have gone there in the first place, but I always liked the idea of living in America.'

'That's a fair point,' Thompson said. 'You can feel isolated without friends and family around you.'

'The reason I'm here,' Ellis said, 'is to pass on some good news. Andrew told me you had an agreement to replace McGregor's helicopter if you broke it.'

'I did,' Gray admitted. 'That's the other reason for selling up. We don't need a place this big, and after I buy a house in Italy I'll use what's left to square things with Mac.'

'Well, the good news is that he got his chopper back, all in working order.'

'He did? How?'

'A gift from President Milenko,' said Harvey with a smile.

Gray looked confused. 'I thought you said he was the main reason Veronica lost her job?' He turned to Ellis.

'He was,' Ellis said, 'but when he found out that it was your actions that stopped the sniper, he wanted to repay you.'

'But it wasn't me,' Gray said. 'You told me that something had gone pear-shaped in the apartment block and the sniper was trying to get away. Even if I hadn't stopped him, he wouldn't have been able to complete his mission.'

'You know that,' Harvey said, 'and we know that, but Milenko must have got a . . . slightly different account. He also had Veronica reinstated.'

Gray turned to Ellis. 'You got your job back? Congratulations!'

'It was a combination of Milenko and the PM,' Ellis said. 'While you were chasing Zhabin – that's the sniper's name, by the way – an attempt was made on the health secretary's life. It was pure coincidence that the call came in just as Oliver King was getting out of his car. The security team heard about the threat and forced him back inside, which saved his life. A bomb was detonated outside the car, but the reinforced chassis barely suffered a scratch. Our actions saved both Milenko and King, and I guess the PM would have found it hard to justify sacking me.'

'I saw that on the news,' Gray said. 'Did anyone claim responsibility? They were calling it a terrorist attack.'

'Far from it. His name was Richard Notley, an accountant from London. His suicide note blamed King for his wife's death in hospital a few years ago.'

'There was no mention of a suicide note,' Gray said.

'And there never will be. If it ever got out that NHS privatisation was the reason for the attack, the Left would have a field day. Not something the PM wants to have to deal with right now.'

'So how long are you guys staying?' Gray asked. 'I've got plenty of spare rooms but no beds in them.'

'Just overnight,' Ellis said. 'We're booked into the Radisson.'

Gray saw Melissa taking an interest in Thompson, and decided to make the most of it.

'Do you want to go outside and play with these lovely ladies?' he asked his daughter.

Melissa smiled, and he handed her over, then opened the French windows that led onto the expansive rear garden.

'Careful, she'll wear you out,' he warned them.

With the women out of the way, Gray asked about Hamad Farsi.

'He's doing well. He's recovering at home and should be back to work in a few weeks. As will Doc Butterworth. I told Ellis how he'd done a good job patching me up over there, and she managed to arrange a flight home last week. I went to see him, to offer my thanks.'

Gray nodded. 'I knew about Doc. Len told me he'd made it home. But that's great news about Hamad. Give him my regards.' Gray took a sip of his coffee. 'So how are you and Sarah really holding up?'

'I won't pretend it's been easy,' Harvey said. 'Sarah wakes up sweating most nights, and once or twice she's woken me with her screams. She insists everything's fine, but throughout the day there are signs that she's still traumatised. She jumps when the postman arrives, and when we went for a walk in the park a few days ago, her eyes were everywhere and I could feel her shaking.'

'What about professional help?' Gray asked.

'Five have arranged counselling sessions for both of us. The woman we're seeing is supposed to be one of the best in her field. It's early days yet, but I'm hopeful she'll help Sarah break through this.'

'And you?'

'I'm good,' Harvey said. 'According to the shrink, I have high resilience factors. I guess that comes from growing up on a rough estate as a teenager. Sarah's different, though. She had what she calls a sheltered background, and all this violence was completely new to her. It's not something you can screen out at the application stage, unless you're looking for a field-based assignment. Sarah was in it for the career progression, and the ability to withstand extreme torture wasn't something that came up in the job interview.'

'She seems happy enough now,' Gray noted, watching the women play with Melissa in the garden.

'I think the change in location is helping,' Harvey said. 'When we drive through London she's constantly on edge, especially if we have to go within a mile of Bessonov's place. Once the plane took off, the change in her was remarkable. It's as if she literally left all of her troubles behind.'

'Well, you're welcome to stay as long as you like,' Gray told him. 'I can get a double bed for one of the spare rooms. I'm sure she'll love the sunshine. Speaking of which . . .'

Gray went to the fridge and brought out a plate of steaks, burgers and chicken breasts, along with a bag of vegetables. 'I thought we'd have a barbecue tonight.'

'Sounds great,' Harvey said.

'Like I said, you're welcome to stay longer . . .'

'We would, but I'm afraid we have to head back tomorrow. We have a three-week break in Aruba planned for the end of the month, but first I need to prep the team about a new threat coming out of the Middle East.'

'Oh? Anything I should be concerned about?'

'I shouldn't think so. An ISIS splinter group. Up until now they've had a rigid structure, so why this new unit was created is worrying us. It's been suggested they may be about to bring the fight to us.'

'I suppose that was inevitable,' Gray said. 'Any idea when?'

'Not yet, but Six have a man in their ranks and he's keeping us updated. We're confident we can stop them when they make their move.'

Gray carried the food out to the garden and got a fire going under the grill before preparing a side salad. Sarah was given the job of buttering the bread, while Harvey's task was to thread chicken cubes, onion and peppers onto skewers.

'Anything I can do?' Ellis asked.

'Yeah,' Gray said with a sly grin. 'Andrew told me about your ISIS problem. If you need any help – anything at all – do *not* call me.'

If you enjoyed this story and want to know when Alan McDermott will release his next book, just send an email to alanmac@ntlworld.com with Next Book in the subject line.

About the Author

Photo: © Darlene McDermott, 2013

Alan McDermott is a husband and a father to beautiful twin girls, and currently lives in the south of England.

Born in West Germany to Scottish parents, Alan spent his early years moving from town to town as his father was posted to different army units around the United Kingdom. Alan has had a number of jobs since leaving school, including working on a cruise ship in Hong Kong and Singapore, where he met his wife, and as a software developer creating clinical applications for the National Health Service. Alan gave up his day job in December 2014 to become a full-time author.

Alan's writing career began in 2011 with the action thriller *Gray Justice*, his first full-length novel. *Gray Salvation* is the sixth title in his Tom Gray series.

21704948R00182

Printed in Great Britain
by Amazon